PRAISE FOR *MURMURATION*

"Mr. Balman has written what I consider one of the Great American Novels of the 21st Century. In *Murmuration*, the second novel in the Seventh Flag trilogy, he has turned on its head the traditional notions of heroism, patriotism, loyalty and gender. Balman weaves three decades of experience with conflict and extremism into a heartbreaking tale of diaspora and displacement that has defined the saga of so many migrants to the United States. As one who has made that journey, I urge all my countrymen and women—whether Somali or American—to read *Murmuration*."

—**Mohamed Abdirizak**, Foreign Minister of Somalia

"The book we should all be reading right now! *Murmuration* is a work of absorbing historical detail but also a multi layered story of love, honor, loss and the plague of radicalism. Sid Balman Jr. carries us from West Texas, into the battle-ground of Mogadishu and refugee camps in Kenya to suburban Minnesota giving us a deeper understanding of our global struggle with radicalism. Nothing is ever what it seems."

—**Donatella Lorch**, award-winning war correspondent for the *New York Times, Newsweek* and NBC News

"When a young Somali immigrant is confronted by hatred, it's no surprise that he will rebel against the society that rejects him. *Murmuration* is a fast-paced thriller that captures the horror of the Somali refugee crisis and brings that horror home to America. It is a story of fear, revenge, compassion, and, ultimately redemption. Sid Balman, Jr. writes about the global threat of ISIS and white supremacy with the confidence and authority of someone who has witnessed it firsthand. This novel is a compelling glimpse into a dangerous world."

—**Clifford Garstang**, author of *W̶h̶a̶t̶ ̶t̶h̶e̶ ̶Z̶h̶a̶n̶g̶ ̶B̶o̶y̶s̶ ̶K̶n̶o̶w̶* and *T̶*

"Drawing on his personal experience in conflict, Mr. Balman immerses the reader in the purgatory of an African refugee camp, the snap of a passing bullet, the horror of a deadly crocodile strike, and the satisfaction of a sniper's kill shot. He chronicles the turmoil in the head of a young Somali lured by unexpected sexual access, the calls to violence from an Imam preaching nihilism, and the torments inflicted by white nationalists inside American prisons. More than a good read, the novel presents the back story to today's headlines."

—**James Bishop**, US Ambassador to Somalia (Ret.)

PRAISE FOR *SEVENTH FLAG*

"*Seventh Flag* tells a tough-as-Texas multigenerational story. A soul-searching read that should make people think twice about what our conscience and families might ask of us in the end. Balman expertly guides readers through the paths that people take to become evil, and the horrific choices that must be made to fight loved ones who have tread that path. A must-read . . . a fun white-knuckle ride that has honest tension and high stakes."

—**Jef Rouner**, *Houston Chronicle*

"To me, what made this book stand out was the core belief that "we are all Americans" together in this battle against extremism, racial bigotry, and hate, in whatever form it may take."

—*Readers' Favorite* 5-Star Review

"At precisely the moment when our diverse and multi-ethnic nation needs a spiritual lift, Sid Balman gives us a portrait of the complex racial and generational relations that define who we really are as Americans. You can smell the creosote of the desert and taste the huevos rancheros in this tale of West Texas. A splendid account of what being American is all about. A rich portrait useful to us all."

—**Mike McCurry**, former White House Press Secretary

"*Seventh Flag* is a thriller with action that heightens in the second half of the book, which opens after the events of 9/11. The narrative has the quality of reportage, rife with anecdotes and historical asides, and deals with such hot-button issues as religion, patriotism, and sexuality. Balman dives into political parties, the dark corners of the Internet, and the rise of hate groups and terrorist cells."

—**Jennifer Levin**, Santa Fe New Mexican

"Think you know what shapes Texas? Sid Balman's tale of a *Seventh Flag* over Texas will rattle what you think. This saga of a generational partnership "as unlikely as the idea of a United States" is rooted in a true event before the Civil War that led to Texas, of all places, being home to more Muslim-Americans than any other state."

—**Mark Stein**, *New York Times* best-selling author of *How the States Got Their Shapes*

"Sid Balman's story comes alive through sympathetic characters and descriptions of places so nuanced I imagined I could almost feel again the scratchy grey wool of the West Point uniform. Anyone paying attention to the global struggle with radicalism will come away with a much keener understanding of the humans who fall prey, the context that claims them and the necessity to tackle this challenge with more finesse than we currently muster."

—**Kimberly C. Field**, Brigadier General USA (ret)

"*Seventh Flag* is a book about pluralism. It's also a book about the tensions increasingly found in pluralistic societies, and about the plague of violent radicalism, including white supremacy and ISIS that sweeps across the novel's world and two families over four generations."

—**Emma Sarappo**, Washington City Paper

MURMURATION

MURMURATION

A NOVEL

SID BALMAN JR.

BOOK 2 IN THE SEVENTH FLAG TRILOGY

SPARKPRESS

Published by SparkPress, a BookSparks imprint,
A division of SparkPoint Studio, LLC
Phoenix, Arizona, USA, 85007
www.gosparkpress.com

Published 2021
Printed in the United States of America
Print ISBN: 978-1-68463-091-2
E-ISBN: 978-1-68463-092-9
Library of Congress Control Number: 2021902737

Cover illustration by Yvette Contois, 2020
Interior design by Tabitha Lahr

For Barbara:
Suffering Is Measured by What We Lose.

Let everything happen to you
Beauty and terror
Just keep going
No feeling is final

—Rainer Maria Rilke

PROLOGUE

Charlie Christmas knew he was the least likely cowboy in West Texas, unless he counted his dark alter ego, his former self, the Somali refugee Sayiid Awale.

There were plenty of African American ranch hands, but none any blacker than Charlie Christmas, skin the color of coal oil and teeth as white as the polished elephant-ivory dice he won throwing craps in the Kenyan refugee camp where he spent two years with what was left of his family after they fled the carnage in Somalia following the aborted American-led humanitarian invasion. And none with friends like Ademar Zarkan, a fourth-generation Texan, one of the first Muslim women to have graduated from West Point and a sniper who struggles to reconcile her roles as an assassin and a mother; Stone, an Army captain and lapsed Jew who brought them together amid a war and famine in East Africa the likes of which the world has rarely seen; or Buck, the fearless mixed-breed Army K-9 and best friend to the refugee boy who would come to define their life's work.

Charlie Christmas was certain of something else. There wasn't another cowboy in West Texas, or anywhere else for that matter, who had stumbled into the American dream like him. Although some of the time it seemed more like a nightmare—the war in the early 1990s, the ravening pirates, the tragic trek across the Somali savanna to Kenya, the hellish limbo of the refugee camps, and the white supremacists who hounded them from Indian country in the Badlands of South Dakota to their new home in Minnesota.

Through it all he could count on the Zarkans and the Laws—iconic families that had carved an agricultural empire eighty miles east of El Paso near the tiny West Texas town of Dell City, financed in large part by a Texas Supreme Court decision that redefined lucrative water rights in the American West. He shared Islam with the Zarkans, all four generations of them, and was certain their ancestors had somehow crossed paths in the mid-1800s when America was importing dromedaries from the Middle East and Africa for the US Army Camel Corps. But he shared something just as deep with the Laws, particularly Ademar and Jack, the patriarch, who didn't give a shit about religion and whose partnership with the Zarkans dated back to the 1950s when Ademar's great-grandfather saved Jack's ass during a brawl at a Juarez cantina. Jack Laws had saved Charlie's ass too, and his family, so many years ago in Kenya. Charlie Christmas never forgot, nor did Sayiid Awale.

Nearing seventy, and with almost a quarter century of life in the United States, Charlie Christmas felt like an American, even amid the chaos of the nation in 2021—or perhaps because of that chaos and how the hot rush of the danger that rides with it can seem like an old friend. The truth of it was that he felt *American* the day an Army sergeant in Mogadishu, who hired him as a translator, discovered he was born December 25, 1952, christened him Charlie Christmas and assigned him to Second Lieutenant Ademar Zarkan. The relationship that began that day would shape their entire lives. But his given identity and name, Sayiid Awale, never entirely left him. Life was like that for Charlie Christmas, as it is for many immigrants who cross the burning bridge—two people living in the same body, one an undertow that pulls them relentlessly back and the other a wave that pushes them inexorably forward. The Yin and Yang of the immigrant. Charlie Christmas talked to himself frequently, and those who knew him chalked it off as some kind of tic. But it wasn't a tic at all. It was a running dialogue between the forgotten and the forgetful, between the Somali and the American, between Sayiid Awale and Charlie Christmas.

PART
ONE

CHAPTER 1

Tragedy and irony are codependent. Neither can articulate its fullest expression without the other.

William Shakespeare knew it when he imagined Lady Macbeth, Romeo and Juliet, Othello. So did Charlie Christmas and White House Chief of Staff James Baker, who, at almost the same moment thousands of miles apart, picked up a newspaper, and with a sharp, simultaneous inhale, gasped at a photograph that would alter the course of history for both of them, for thousands of troops, and for almost three million Somalis. The celebration for the fall of the iron curtain was an all-nighter, and the triumphant Western powers had decided after one too many tequila shots that the oxymoronic concept of a humanitarian invasion was a thing.

The photographer, American Kevin Carter, received a Pulitzer for it, and took his own life four months later. Carter wrote in his farewell note, "I am haunted by the vivid memories of killings and corpses and anger and pain." The macabre dance of tragedy and irony was not lost on Carter as he captured the image on his Nikon. What could be more tragic than a starving child as a hulking vulture hopped nonchalantly toward her, his next meal? What could be more ironic than the unwritten photojournalist's rule not to intervene in a story, even if it meant stopping a predator from tearing the innards out of a helpless, immobile toddler? Carter snapped the photo. It was his job, and he did it well—well enough as a young freelancer to win journalism's highest award. But afterward, by all accounts absent much existential debate with himself or his comrades, Carter dropped such journalistic pretense like the shovelful of bullshit that it is to help the child reach the feeding station.

The greater irony—the mocking, belly-laughing irony given the gravity of the consequences—was that he took the photograph in Sudan, 1,200 miles from Somalia. Drought and famine were sucking lives out of both nations like the demon Surgat, the mythological custodian of the keys to Hell, but the growing appetite for American military intervention was focused on Somalia. Sudan was a different story, particularly since an obscure Saudi extremist named Osama bin Laden had moved into a three-story pink-and-beige stucco house on Al-Mashtal Street in Khartoum, the capital. But James Baker, whom President George H. W. Bush had moved from the State Department to head his staff at the White House during the waning days of his presidency, wasn't going to let such a minor detail get in his way. And he didn't clarify when an aide placed the photograph, clipped from the New York Times, on the table in front of Bush during a White House meeting in the secure Situation Room, which included acting Secretary of State Lawrence Eagleburger, Chairman of the Joint Chiefs of Staff General Colin Powell, and National Security Advisor Brent Scowcroft.

In a world without the Soviet Union, without Moscow's jackboot on the neck of so many potential despots and geno-cides, from Belgrade to Algiers, only the United States had the power and determination to stamp out regional crises like the one in Somalia. Further, Bush was flush from his whirl-wind triumph building a diverse global coalition to reverse

Iraqi President Saddam Hussein's invasion of oil-rich Kuwait, and executing an almost flawless military operation that took only five weeks of combat. In one stroke, he saved Kuwait and shook off the decades-old stigma of America's failure in Vietnam. The United States was at a zenith of its power not experienced since the defeat of Hitler, and the room full of national security officials were confident they could save thousands of starving children by swatting away the tin-pot warlords in Somalia like a pesky fly at a summer picnic. Baker knew a photograph like the one of the child and the vulture would hold great sway over a family man like Bush, and he had worked out the stagecraft of the meeting with Eagleburger, his former deputy at Foggy Bottom. Revealing the location of the photograph was not on anyone's sheet of talking points.

"This is a tragedy of massive proportions," Eagleburger, an asthmatic and heavy smoker, wheezed, "and, underline this, one that we can do something about. We must act."

Less than a week later, Bush dispatched Eagleburger to United Nations headquarters in New York to inform Secretary General Boutros Boutros-Ghali that the United States was prepared to intervene in Somalia.

Charlie Christmas wasn't yet Charlie Christmas that day in Mogadishu. He was Sayiid Awale, sipping watered-down Nescafé in the Sheraton Hotel, an espresso machine salesman from a middle-class family in a failed nation where fancy coffee was a distant memory. He had no idea the photograph would spur an invasion by the last Guardians of the Galaxy, the United States, with guided missiles that could chase bad guys down city streets like mechanical bloodhounds and soldiers that seemed as invincible as that half-man half-robot policeman in his favorite movie, Robocop. "*Wallahi!*" he exclaimed under his breath, a common Somali expression for *I swear to God*, as he read an editorial in a local newspaper about the irony of how a misrepresented photograph of a starving Sudanese child could lead to an American military intervention in Somalia.

Charlie Christmas liked the Americans, even more than the Italians, Somalia's colonial power for sixty years until 1942. But he was forever grateful to them for embedding espresso and pasta into the Somali diet. *It's always about the food with the Italians*, he muttered to himself. *They can't govern for shit, but they sure know how to eat.* Somalis can have a wicked sense of humor, particularly when it comes to irony, and the realization of another foreign invasion would have seemed all the more ironic if he had known that within months Italian forces would engage in combat for the first time since World War II in the aptly named Checkpoint Pasta Battle outside a spaghetti factory in the heart of Mogadishu. *Wallahi!*

Jim Bishop, the US ambassador in Somalia, was Christmas's favorite American of all time for hiring him as a part-time translator and embodying the essence of what Christmas felt made America resilient, powerful, and enduring. Understated. Humble. Powerful. Bishop didn't look anything like that musclebound Robocop Christmas so admired—just the opposite. Bishop may have seemed like an *aw-shucks* Midwesterner, small frame that barely filled a medium-sized windbreaker and a baseball cap pushed up over his forehead, but he was made of steel. He relished that misinterpretation, which had given him an edge in so many ways throughout his life—crouched on a wrestling mat in front of an incautious high school opponent or during tense negotiations with African strongmen in hot spots like Niger, Liberia, and now, Somalia.

Bishop's bravery and steadfast leadership during his last days in Mogadishu left an impression on Sayiid Awale that defined the American that Charlie Christmas would become.

Less than a year into Bishop's ambassadorship, Somalia had descended into chaos. The national government imploded after the ouster of longtime dictator Mohamed Siad Barre, clan warfare spread across the country, and a drought choked the life out of the starving nation. Andrew Natsios, the head of the US Agency for International Development, said at the time that it was the "most acute humanitarian tragedy in the world today." Operation Provide Relief, the United Nation's flaccid effort to provide food, had become some kind of sick joke. It wasn't enough to turn the tide on the famine, and most of it was hijacked by the warlords, who sold it at prices beyond the desperate reach of those who needed it. Christmas felt as if he was watching something profoundly obscene, like children herded into a gas chamber at Auschwitz or a Black man hanged from a tree in Mississippi, when he watched the NGOs from groups like International Medical Corps and CARE offload bags of rice and other essential goods into the greedy hands of doped-up, heavily armed militiamen rather than to starving children.

That was the situation in which Bishop took the rudder at the US Embassy, and within a year he was overseeing the evacuation of all diplomatic personnel. It was a day Bishop would never forget, nor would Charlie Christmas. While the last American personnel boarded five US CH-53 helicopters at dawn for evacuation to ships just off the coast in the Indian Ocean, Bishop faced a situation right out of a State Department crisis management exercise. A local police commander, grenade in one hand and radio transmitter in the other, stood outside Gate One at the embassy, threatening to order Somali gunmen to fire on the helicopters if they attempted to take off with the evacuees. US Navy Seals in full battle gear kept the police commander in their sights while Bishop talked him down. Sayiid, before his rebirth as Charlie Christmas, helped with translation during the tense negotiation, and at one point was convinced the police commander would pull the pin from the grenade. He would always remember that moment—the sun rising out of the ocean, the crackle of small-arms fire in the distance, and a lone American diplomat the only bar between him and eternity.

Christmas's loneliness and isolation were profound as the helicopters took off with the last Americans in Somalia, leaving him in the dusty backwash of their rotors and the detritus of what remained in the embassy buildings—cans of tuna fish, shredded documents, half-empty bottles of Jack Daniel's, and televisions still tuned to Christiane Amanpour on CNN.

Bishop and other American officials had hinted at the military invasion to come, and the possibility of asylum in the United States for Somalis like Christmas who had worked for them. Months later, sitting in the Sheraton choking down drip coffee that made him long for a strong Italian espresso and staring at the photograph of the starving child crawling to the UN feeding station, Christmas realized that it might actually happen.

Wallahi!

CHAPTER 2

Sometimes the universe opens up to us, provides a door through which we can choose to pass, a bet we can choose to place, an unknown risk we can choose to take for an ambiguous opportunity the enormity of which can only be fully appreciated in hindsight—like adopting a stray puppy, a flash of gold in a prospector's pan, or a chance meeting in Manhattan at Broadway and Forty-Sixth with a woman who steals your heart. Operation Restore Hope, the muscular US-led invasion of Somalia, opened that door for an unemployed Somali espresso machine salesman and a Syrian-American Muslim girl from the high desert of West Texas on her first deployment after graduation from West Point. Neither Charlie Christmas, sipping coffee and reading the newspaper in the Mogadishu Sheraton, nor Ademar Zarkan, tossing her cap into the air at Michie Stadium along with almost a thousand fellow West Point graduates, could have known how gravity, or fate, or karma, was pulling them together into a journey that would define the lives of so many people and alter the destiny of nations. The universe opened up to them when they met on the tarmac of the Mogadishu airport during the kind of summer heat in Somalia that drives even camels under the shade of an acacia tree.

It had been a long road to that day for Ademar Zarkan, not just the four years of what some might consider torture and brainwashing at West Point, but the twenty-two years prior to that in the West Texas town of Dell City, population four hundred, not a particularly diverse, progressive, or tolerant corner of the world. But West Texas produces a certain type of woman, one who has a way with a petticoat and a 30.30, and Ademar was surrounded by them. There was her great-grandmother and matriarch of the Zarkan family, Sana; her grandmother, Bernia; and Mother Almira. And on the Laws' side there was Marcelina, matriarch and mastermind behind the farming empire they built in the high desert after World War II; Bitsy, who lost her life in the World Trade Center on 9/11; Eulalia, who survived a brutal rape in Juarez to found a wildly popular country-rock fusion band; and Lola Mae, high school cheerleader and mother to the only man Ademar ever loved.

The planets for the Zarkans and the Laws began to align almost one hundred years earlier in the White House, where President Franklin Pierce and Secretary of War Jefferson Davis hatched a plan to start the US Army Camel Corps. Camels, which could carry heavy loads for days without water and subsist on indigenous vegetation, made so much sense to Pierce and Davis, who planned to integrate them into the US Cavalry stationed in the desert Southwest. And they did just that, shipping thousands of dromedaries and hundreds of Arab-Muslim handlers from the Middle East to the Texas port of Indianola, where they embarked for bases in West Texas, New Mexico, and Arizona. Ademar's great-great-great-grandfather, Mustafa Zarkan, was on one of those ships and remained behind after the experiment failed several years later, due to the camel's ornery disposition, the Cavalry's opposition to change, and the Civil War. Zarkan eventually made his way to Texas as part of a vanguard that grew into the largest Muslim population in the United States. Ademar's grandfather, Ali, drifted to Dell City after World War II, a broken man and a fallen Muslim who'd lost his way amid the gore and trauma of jungle warfare against the Japanese in the Western Pacific. But a chance meeting in a Juarez cantina, where he waded into a bloody knife fight to rescue Jack Laws from the switchblades of three drunk *vaqueros*, landed Ali a job and spawned a relationship that spanned three generations.

Almost all of them were gathered in Michie Stadium at West Point for Ademar's graduation, most importantly the only man she ever loved, Crockett Laws II—or Deuce, as they called him—and her older brother, Tamerlane Zarkan II, nicknamed T2. Deuce, T2, and Ademar had grown up thick as thieves in Dell City amid the iconic rural traditions of Texas—farming, ranching, hunting, rodeo, and football, especially football, which earned Deuce, the gunslinging quarterback, a slot at West Point, and T2, a linebacker built like a brick shithouse, a scholarship to the University of Texas at El Paso. Ademar was every bit as athletic and tough as either of them, and football was the first activity in which societal norms encroached on their relationship. T2 had to restrain Ademar from swinging at Deuce when he suggested she try out for cheerleader, like his Mom Lola Mae had done twenty years earlier. Not only did Ademar feel patronized, the last thing Deuce intended with his innocent suggestion, but the idea of a Muslim girl dancing around in a short skirt and skimpy tank top offended her on almost every level. Ademar practiced kicking in secret all summer before football tryouts, and earned a spot on Coach T's squad as the first woman to play for the Dell City Cougars. Her football experience, along with a perfect grade point average and three consecutive Texas high school barrel racing titles, made her a near-perfect candidate for West Point, and she became part of the *long gray line* one year after Deuce.

Ademar was a tomboy, but her exotic, natural beauty—punctuated by eyes the color of polished turquoise and wavy hair as black as raw Brazilian tourmaline—began to emerge in her early teens under faded jeans, an untucked denim yoke shirt, and a straw cowboy hat. Often, the strongest unions start as friendships, absent the angst and awkwardness of new relationships before they reach equilibrium. And they tend to endure long after the enmity of familiarity drive them into the uneasy ceasefire of bitter compromise that frequently settles over a romance that's outlived its shelf life. A feeling inside Deuce, so different from the mutated bromance he felt within their trio, began to form toward Ademar, but he was conflicted over how to act on it without threatening their friendship or violating Muslim tradition. Women have a mystical intuition around issues of love and sex, and Ademar understood exactly what was happening between her and Deuce, welcoming it as a progression along the continuum toward the life she imagined with him. She acted on those instincts during the moment in the elevator alone with Deuce in El Paso's Providence Hospital after her brother Anil's hand was torn off by a chili picker, which would have killed him if Deuce hadn't reached into the machinery to save his life. A tear rolled down Deuce's cheek as he told Ademar about his guilt at not acting earlier to prevent the accident altogether. Ademar felt the oft-conflicted instincts residing in a woman, particularly a seventeen-year-old woman, that begin as nurturing and end as intimacy. The exact moment when Ademar took Deuce's face in her hands and kissed him, they both knew their friendship had evolved into something else.

The dynamics of the trio with T2 remained unchanged as the friendship between Deuce and Ademar morphed into intimacy, and in some ways grew stronger as they all began to realize that their union would be the perfect expression of the bond between the Laws and the Zarkans. An object in motion stays in motion. But Ademar and Deuce took their time, relishing the inertia drawing them toward the ultimate act of teenage romance. After that first time, Ademar and Deuce lay naked and entwined under a blanket, spent and breathless in the back of a pickup truck at the base of the soaring Guadalupe Mountains outside Dell City. The eyes of a half-dozen deer bedded down for the night shimmered under the light of a full moon. Ademar whispered in Deuce's ear, so close she could feel his heart. "A gift," she said. "Only for you."

Ademar's thoughts drifted so many places as she went through the grand graduation ceremony at West Point, and, as they often did at odd times, to that night with Deuce back in Dell City. Their eyes met in the audience at Michie Stadium, where Deuce had graduated the previous year, and the smile they shared, the smile they always shared, held the secret of that first time.

Ademar, who had learned to shoot through the open sights of a 30.30 during deer hunts outside Dell City with Deuce and T2, was an expert markswoman and captained the West Point rifle team. She had chosen to serve in the military police after graduation, figuring that would be the only loophole through which a female soldier might see combat. That's why Ademar was selected for convoy security in Somalia as her first assignment, and that's the twist of fate that brought her together with Charlie Christmas.

CHAPTER 3

The three most important days in Charlie Christmas's life were the birth of his son Amiir, his assignment as a translator to Second Lieutenant Ademar Zarkan, and the loss of his virginity to Pia and Hanna during a backpacking excursion in Alaska when he was eighteen. As an adult, he wore a slim gold chain around his neck with small totems for each of those days—a gold letter *S* for his son, a 7.62 mm shell casing from Ademar's M24 sniper rifle, and a tiny wood carving of a snow-white willow ptarmigan, the state bird of Alaska.

The Awales were a prominent family in the northeast region of Somalia known as Puntland, and Charlie's father, Mohamed, was a leader in the ruling Darood Clan and a senior official in the national Department of Education. As a measure of presumed stature, his father named him Sayiid—loosely translated as *lord, master*, or *great warrior*—and sent him to the Hamar boarding school in Mogadishu.

Sayiid was always tall for his age, lanky with the lean muscles of a soccer player and an easy smile that exuded the kind of humble confidence that drew people to him, especially people of the opposite sex. He was a wanderlust and a dreamer whose favorite book was *Call of the Wild*, Jack London's epic tale of a sled dog and gold prospector in the Klondike region of Alaska during the early 1900s. Sayiid decided that if he ever had a dog to call his own, he would name it Buck, after the half–St. Bernard, half–Scotch Collie in London's novel. Sayiid's favorite subjects in school were geography and English, which he figured would prepare him for the adventure he intended to have in Alaska after he graduated from Hamar. Sayiid's aunt Beydaan had migrated years ago to Logan, Utah, and, unbeknownst to his father, she had helped him gain admission to nearby Utah State University. Sayiid went over it again and again in his head, the pitch he planned for his dad, and launched into it in their home library after Saturday prayers.

"Aabanimo," said Sayiid, using the most formal, most respectful Somali term for father, as he sat on the couch next to the worn brown leather chair reserved exclusively for the head of the household. "I have good news; at least I think it's good news. And a plan for what I want to do after graduation."

Mohamed Awale knew his son well and loved him, perhaps more than he should when it came to indulging rather than educating, and he had been prepared by his sister for this conversation. "I think I know what's coming, Sayiid; your auntie Beydaan filled me in. Utah State?"

"*Ku sharfan*," Sayiid responded, a Somali phrase for *thank you* that implied pride and respect. "Auntie Beydaan helped me find a job at a factory there, and a group house with some other students. But I'll need some . . ."

"Money," said his father, cutting him off. "I want you to go, son. I'll help. I'll miss you; your mother will miss you, but it's your time. The world is so much bigger than Somalia, than Africa. Much to learn in the West, in America. But don't forget . . . don't ever forget who you are."

"*Ku sharfan! Ku sharfan.*"

Sayiid's father was not much for affection, but he enthusiastically returned his son's embrace, knowing full well that a man, where there had once been a boy, would return from

America. His father was surprised at how close he was to shedding a tear—the tear of a parent anywhere who feels both pain and love in the pride and remorse of a child leaving for the uncertain, perilous journey into adulthood. He removed the thin gold chain from around his neck, a chain with a tiny Somali flag and a silver Islamic crescent, that Sayiid's father never removed, and placed it on his son. Over his lifetime, Sayiid would add four more totems to that chain—a letter, a shell casing, a small wooden bird, and a bone from the wing of an eagle.

Sayiid could barely make ends meet his first year of college, even with the $200 monthly allowance from his father and three night shifts a week assembling NordicTrack exercise equipment at the Icon Health factory for $7 an hour, enough money in a month to feed a small Somali village. His flatmates, Chet from the California Central Valley and Brian from Kentucky, spent most of their time outside class worshiping at the altar of a four-foot bong, playing Nintendo, and inducing coeds back to their place. Sayiid didn't mind. Like many students, he suspended his religion for college. And, besides, he looked forward to having his morning coffee in the kitchen, pretending to read the Logan Herald Journal while admiring the parade of panties and T-shirts between the bathroom and his friends' bedrooms. Up to that point, Sayiid had only seen Somali women, with their statuesque frames and voluminous backsides, and fantasized over the Rubenesque nymphets in Baroque Peter Paul Rubens *Three Graces*, whose fleshy thighs invited intimate exploration in the imagination of a fourteen-year-old Sayiid, who had torn that page from an art history book in the Hamar library. He realized there was a lot more on the menu after a few months of admiring these American girls shuffling across his living room, with their sleepy eyes, flawless backsides, and perky nipples peeking out of skimpy tank tops. But he was still among the sexually uninitiated, still wrestling with how to rationalize a one-night stand under Qur'anic law, and emerged from freshman year with his cherry still intact.

Finances were another aspect of his roommates' life that he couldn't figure out—how Chet and Brian, both from families of modest means, could afford their lifestyle without jobs or scholarships.

"Dude," Sayiid asked them one evening in the American slang he perfected so quickly, "how do you two do it? Selling weed, or what?"

"Hells no," replied Chet, the hipper and more articulate of the two. "Feast your eyes on this." And he pulled out a scrapbook of photographs from his and Brian's summer in Alaska.

Utah had introduced Sayiid to snow, but what really blew his mind was the photograph of an enormous moose emerging like some prehistoric creature from the Tanana River with a snow-capped Mount Deborah in the distance.

"And? What's that got to do with money?"

"Look at the last two pages, bro."

Chet had fashioned a collage of photographs from the North Pacific Seafoods' salmon processing facility in Kasilof, where he and Brian had worked the previous summer. While there were plenty of older folks gutting and filleting fish, Sayiid noticed quite a few attractive young women along the conveyor belt, and one photograph of Brian pretending to French-kiss a decapitated salmon.

"Fifteen dollars an hour, plus overtime," Chet said. "Seven days a week for as long as you can take it, plus housing and as much pussy as you can handle. We lasted eight weeks, pocketed ten large each, then headed to Denali for a week of camping before school started."

"I'd be down for that," Sayiid said.

Five months later and $8,500 wealthier, but still a virgin, Sayiid was on a bus headed to Denali National Park for an annual bluegrass festival. Chet had told him to bring a tent since the festival was in an open meadow with no accommodations, but to save money he opted for some plastic sheeting in which he could wrap himself if it rained. The weather was perfect the first few days, and he struck up an easy friendship with those camped near him as they spent their time like gypsies serenaded by the likes of Arlo Guthrie, Joan Baez, Doc Watson, Nickel Creek, Alison Kraus, and the Soggy Bottom Boys. The sweet smell of marijuana mixed with campfire smoke hung in the air, and an hour didn't go by without someone passing a joint. Sayiid figured he could rationalize the occasional Husky IPA under Islamic law, but drugs, even a harmless toke, might cross the line of blasphemy in the eyes of his Imam in Mogadishu. More importantly, it would disappoint his father.

Something about Hanna and Pia changed his mind. The two German women, both in their late twenties, had camped next to Sayiid on the first afternoon, and within a few days they had forged the kind of bond one only makes on the road, where identities are fluid and truth is elusive. They were the type of Germans drawn to esoteric ideas and obscure philosophies, as long as discussion did not brush against the brittle, thinly concealed angst from the war and the genocide that many of them feel they should carry like a cross.

The three of them heard the splatter of rain on a cast-iron skillet near the fire before they felt it, their final night in Denali a potential rainout. Hanna motioned toward Sayiid's plastic sheeting, smiled, looked over her shoulder at their tent, then smiled again—a different kind of smile that implied something other than humor. Hanna put her hand on Sayiid's thigh and passed the joint.

"This is my first time," he said, beginning to feel the creeping euphoria, so different from the acceleration of emotion after a few beers. He laughed, and they all laughed with him for what seemed like a long time, but actually it was not more than a few seconds.

"My first time was with an old boyfriend in Berlin," Pia said. "It was the first time for something else too."

"And mine was with you, Pia, two years ago, also in Berlin at your flat," Hanna replied. "Remember? And it was our first time for something else as well."

The two women exchanged a knowing glance and reached around Sayiid to embrace. The musk of femininity and patchouli engulfed him, embedding a memory in his olfaction that would titillate him for the rest of his life. They each placed their chin on either side of Sayiid's shoulders, and Pia whispered in his ear, "Come with us."

That scent effused from the inside of the small tent and grew in intensity with each piece of clothing they removed, until they were all without clothes and seemed to be floating in it. Sayiid could not really tell where one of them began and the other ended during those hours of languid, sometimes desperate sensuality. The aroma of that night inside the small tent stayed with him forever, the eternal perfume of his awakening into manhood. It remained on him for several days afterward, and on a T-shirt of his that Hanna had worn the next morning, which Sayiid never, ever washed.

Years later, the more dangerous his life became, the more he thought about that night with Hanna and Pia—even now, or especially now, almost two decades later, waking up to the sound of distant gunfire in his Mogadishu flat with his wife, Ebla, and their son, little Sayiid, who they nicknamed Amiir, *prince* in Somali. He held Ebla in great esteem and had grown close to her over the years, but their marriage was arranged, and the day they met felt more like duty than romance to both of them. Their relationship endured, with warmth, respect, and a deep love for their son. But it lacked passion, and Sayiid could not conjure excitement for his wife or climax without imagining the scent of Pia and Hanna. Perhaps it was Ebla's ceremonial circumcision as a young girl that kept her from feeling the full orgasm she had read about in Western magazines like *Cosmopolitan*. Ebla felt silly faking it on behalf of what she imagined was Sayiid's fragile male ego, and over the years the frequency thinned to almost nothing.

That morning in the summer of 1993, Ebla opened her legs in bed as a kind of good-luck offering for Sayiid before an important meeting with an American military officer at the Mogadishu airport to discuss some translation work.

"I'm late," he said, kissing her knee and gently slapping her ample backside.

"Okay, Mister American Translator," she replied with a histrionic frown. "You may regret it."

Ebla was right. Sayiid would regret that moment for the rest of his days, but nowhere near as much as Charlie Christmas.

Sayiid made his way carefully through Mogadishu, avoiding the hot zones and roadblocks erected by the militiamen loyal to the most powerful warlord in Somalia, General Mohamed Farrah Aidid, an esteemed military leader and politician who had led the coup that ruptured the East African nation into warring fiefdoms. Aidid defied United Nations' peacekeeping efforts, sanctioned an attack that killed twenty-four Pakistani peacekeepers, and held a very loose rein over the militiamen roaming Mogadishu in their "technicals," improvised pickup trucks equipped with armor and heavy weapons mounted in the bed. They reminded Sayiid of something out of Robocop, or his second favorite movie, Mel Gibson's post-apocalyptic thriller Mad Max. He felt relatively safe in the morning from Aidid's fighters, who, in their Ray Ban Wayfarers, New York Yankees' baseball caps, gold chains, and black canvas high-tops, could have been extras in a *GQ* photo shoot, absent the automatic weapons slung over their shoulders and the bandoliers of grenades strapped across their broad, muscular chests.

But Sayiid knew all bets were off by early afternoon, when they jammed their cheeks full of Khat leaves, a strong stimulant that unleashed their dark, predatory instincts.

Operation Restore Hope, the US-led military intervention in Somalia, was all about policing the militias, ensuring the delivery of relief supplies, and ending the famine—through negotiations if possible or through the fiery barrels of the airborne cannons aboard an AC-130 if necessary. Sayiid was not much of a patriot, but war was bad for business, and he felt helping the Americans would be the best long-term bet for him and his family. In the meantime, translating for the troops paid well and allowed him to put food on the table with as little risk as possible. At least that's what Sayiid thought as he filled out the paperwork for the job at the makeshift US base next to the airport tarmac.

"Name," the Army sergeant asked.

"Sayiid Awale."

"What?"

"Sayiid Awale."

"Said what?"

"S A Y I I D . . . A W A L E," he said, spelling it out.

"Uh-huh, date of birth."

"December 25, 1952."

"Okay, what was that name again? Never mind. For purposes of your work with us, we'll call you Charlie Christmas. Good with that?"

"I suppose so," Sayiid replied, then to himself, *Charlie Christmas; I like it.*

After the formalities of application were done, a woman wearing a sand-colored, sweat-drenched T-shirt, fatigues, and desert combat boots thrust her hand out to shake with Charlie Christmas.

"Second Lieutenant Ademar Zarkan, *As-Salaam-Alaikum*," she said, *peace be upon you* in Arabic, the standard Muslim greeting.

"*Wa-Alaikum-Salaam*," he responded with the traditional rejoinder, trying to hide his shock at being assigned to a female soldier, a Muslim female soldier no less. "I'm Sayiid Awale, but the sergeant says that won't work, too hard for you Americans. He said to use Charlie Christmas, since I was born on Christmas day. Let's just go with that."

"Charlie Christmas; cool. Pleased to meet you, Charlie Christmas."

If there had been any camels on the tarmac, the heat would have driven them under a nearby acacia grove, and their hands stuck together from sweat and sand as if they had been glued. It never would have happened if Kevin Carter hadn't taken the photograph of the starving girl and the vulture, if President Bush hadn't been moved enough by it to invade Somalia, if Charlie Christmas hadn't gone to Alaska and didn't speak perfect English, and if Ademar hadn't attended West Point or captained the rifle team. Synchronicity borne on the wings of fate, by the karma of a Somali espresso machine salesman and a Muslim girl from West Texas. That handshake was just a moment in a lifetime of moments they would share that didn't mean much in isolation. But stacked one upon the other, those moments reached beyond inconsequence, traveling at light speed through a fold in the universe that could propel their lives to undiscovered galaxies or pull them into the black hole of despair.

CHAPTER 4

The Somali pirate leaned close enough that the unfortunate Filipino hostage in chains smelled the chieftain's last meal of seafood stew, and his rancid sweat. The hostage spent a lifetime toiling in the boiler rooms of massive cargo ships and was no stranger to the smells of hard work in cramped quarters with other men. But nothing could have prepared him for the alien prancing around the cave—a cross between Fred Astaire and Manananggal, the mythical Filipino witch that lives off the flesh and blood of men.

"You may call me *Ibliis*. It means devil," the pirate hissed in an effeminate whisper tinged with a faux British accent.

"Time is up," Ibliis said, with an ostentatious pirouette away from the hostage toward his motley crew gathered in an isolated cave outside the coastal pirate enclave of Hobyo. "Your country doesn't give a shit; your company doesn't give a shit. Unfortunately for you, no money. What you do in the next five minutes will mean life or death. Your choice."

Ibliis was a large, tightly muscled Black man, no older than thirty, with a gold ring in his left ear. The Somali looked as if he stepped out of the Johnny Depp classic *Pirates of the Caribbean*, which had been released that year and he had watched dozens of times. Ibliis was so enamored with Depp's persona that he affected the costume of a swashbuckling seventeenth-century pirate—billowing pantaloons, a black vest over a loose white cotton chemise, black bandana over three strands of shoulder-length dreadlocks, skull-and-crossbones thumb ring, 666 tattooed under his left eye, a razor-sharp cutlass hanging from his belt, and a pearl-handle Colt Python .357 Magnum tucked in his waistband.

"Your choice," Ibliis repeated, drawing the cutlass, spinning back toward the hostage, opening the pantaloons to reveal his tumescence, and quoting his favorite Al Pacino line from the movie *Scarface*. "Say hello to my little friend."

The Filipino hostage didn't blink, didn't tremble, didn't beg for mercy, and certainly didn't introduce himself to Ibliis's little friend. He cleared his chest, coughed, and spit a large green glob in the pirate's face. "Fuck off, bastard."

Ibliis leaned back and roared with laughter that echoed through the cave. "This one is brave," he said, dancing back around to face his mates and winking the eye just above the tattoo that symbolizes the Antichrist. Ibliis raised up on his toes like a matador preparing for *el momento de verdad*, the moment of truth, and, before anyone in the room could take a breath, spun back to the hostage and took off his head with one clean, precise stroke of the cutlass. Eyes wide open in terror as if he had literally seen the devil just before the blade passed through his neck, the hostage's head rolled to the ground while his body froze in place. Ibliis straddled the stump of the man's trunk and pissed into the spurting cavity of blood and bone.

The lawlessness in the high seas off the Somali coast had grown out of an effort by indigenous fisherman to protect the troves of snapper, anchovy, and grouper that foreign firms started poaching after the Navy disbanded following the 1990 coup. What began as a peaceful campaign quickly evolved into kidnapping for ransom, and violence. In any nation that suddenly falls into a crisis of governance—whether it be Somalia or the United States—sociopaths like Ibliis emerge under a cloak of nationalism. Pirates off the coast of Somalia complicated the US-led peacekeeping mission, hijacking relief shipments and taking hostages, in some cases Americans or Europeans working for nongovernmental organizations. The military policing mission envisioned by Pentagon planners in 1992 had mushroomed less than two years later into a regional war requiring significant naval assets.

Charlie Christmas knocked on the screen door of the makeshift barracks constructed at the Mogadishu airport where Ademar bunked. "Ranger, we've got a briefing."

Charlie Christmas and Second Lieutenant Ademar Zarkan had found a good working relationship and an easy rapport in the three months since she first arrived. He was her translator, and they were together almost all the time as they rode shotgun to provide security for food deliveries. While neither of them were devout Muslims, their faith gave them a context for trust that both of them found elusive with other soldiers. He had noticed her Ranger tab, signifying completion of grueling Army special operations training, and started calling her Ranger since she used his nickname.

"Captain Stone wants us in the briefing room, like, five minutes ago," Christmas said.

"Here I am, Charlie," she said, stepping out of the barracks in a T-shirt, fatigues, and an El Paso Chihuahuas baseball cap turned brim backward.

"What's with that dog on your hat, Ranger?"

"Minor league baseball team near where I live in Texas, their mascot."

"I like dogs," he said. "You ever read that book by Jack London, *Call of the Wild*? There's a dog in there named Buck, righteous hound, cool dog. If I ever get a dog, I'll name it Buck."

"Yeah, I read it. But that kind of dog would fry in this heat. What's Captain Stone want? Another escort mission?"

"Your army, Ranger. We'll find out soon enough," Christmas said, opening the door to the briefing room and stepping back to hold it open for Zarkan. "Rangers first."

The lights dimmed, and a picture of Ibliis in all his ostentatious glory flashed on the screen. Charlie, who had seen *Pirates of the Caribbean* a few times and had endeared himself to Ademar and the other troops with his dry, ironic humor, could not suppress a laugh. "Johnny Depp's first mate! I saw that movie."

"No joke, Christmas," Captain Prometheus Stone said. "Public enemy number one. Intel says he decapitated a Filipino hostage last week, and now he's holding two Americans working for the United Nations that were on a ship he hijacked. Let all the others go."

"What's he want?" Ademar asked.

"Money," Charlie said. "What else?"

"That's right," Stone said. "Ten million dollars tomorrow, or they're toast. Our job is to rescue them. And your job, Zarkan, is to kill him."

Ibliis was clever but had no idea about the real capabilities of the American military. His brazen disregard for the deadly reach of modern weapons stunned the strike force stepping out of a Seahawk helicopter on to the deck of the USS *Cushing*, a Navy destroyer tasked with protecting the shipping lanes off the two-thousand-mile Somali coastline, as far north as the Gulf of Aden and as far south as the Seychelles. Twenty-four hours before Stone's briefing, Ibliis and his crew seemed to explode out of the setting sun in three commercial powerboats to surround the 1,200-foot cargo ship thirty miles off the coast. Ibliis leaned on one knee in the bow of his boat, Jolly Roger whipping in the wind, laughing as the crew on the cargo ship attempted to fend them off with a water cannon. He drew the pearl-handled .357 from his belt and fired two shots directly into the hull of the ship, which didn't pierce the thick steel but made enough of a racket to grab the captain's attention.

"Fifteen men on a dead man's chest. Yo-ho-ho and a bottle of rum," Ibliis roared like some caricature of a pirate from Robert Louis Stevenson's *Treasure Island*, as his crew brandished automatic weapons and grenade launchers. "This is not a drill, Cap'n. Drop your anchor. We're coming aboard . . . or we're fucking blowing this tin can to the sky." Ibliis, last of the twelve men to clamber on board, drew his cutlass with a flourish and leaped to the deck, hands outstretched and bowing deeply, as if he were acknowledging a cheering audience during a curtain call after a theatrical production. "The Americans stay. Bring them to me in the captain's bridge. Everybody else on my ship."

He didn't waste any time toying with the two Americans, a man and a woman working for the United Nations, knowing full well that it wouldn't take much time for the Navy to arrive and negotiations to begin. The USS *Cushing* pulled within two hundred yards of the cargo ship in three hours, as the sun set and darkness descended on the high-seas standoff. Ibliis had timed it that way so he could negotiate what he was sure would be a king's ransom in the dark, without the threat of military snipers. He knew nothing of thermal sights with night-vision capabilities, a profound miscalculation on his part, and at that exact moment Second Lieutenant Zarkan had him in the crosshairs of the thermal sight on her M24.

Ademar could hear through her earpiece the tense negotiations via telephone between an American officer on the *Cushing* and Ibliis. Charlie was translating in real time any side comments between Ibliis and his crew, and also carrying on a running dialogue in his head with Sayiid Awale, his former self.

"Look at yourself," Sayiid said to him. "Charlie Christmas, the American stooge."

"*Aamus!*" he snapped under his breath to his meddlesome alter ego, the Somali version of *shut up*. "Somalia is in the state it's in because of assholes like Captain Hook over there. Damn right I'm helping them, and making bank doing it."

A slight storm began to blow in as the negotiations between Ibliis and the Americans continued for hours, nothing serious but enough to rock the ship and complicate Ademar's potential two-hundred-yard shot.

"Cap," Ademar said through her mouthpiece to the commanding officer in charge. "This is getting more difficult by the minute, with this storm."

"Hold tight, LT," he replied. "That's why you get the big bucks."

"Fucking-A," she muttered out of the side of her mouth so only Charlie could hear.

"You ever kill, Ranger?" Charlie questioned.

"No," she replied bluntly, "unless you include half a dozen deer, bunch of jackrabbits, and more rattlesnakes than I can count."

"First blood," Christmas said.

"First blood," she repeated.

The extended negotiations had given four Navy Seals, frogmen and trained assassins, enough time to reach the cargo ship underwater and climb aboard from each side and the stern. Without a sound, creeping around the ship wearing nothing but wetsuits and armed with only eight-inch MK commando knives, they cut the throats of all but Ibliis and two of his mates in the bridge with the hostages.

"Nine down, Cap," one of the frogmen whispered in the mike to the commanding officer. "All accounted for and in position at the bridge."

"Hold," the commanding officer said, "until the sniper takes out that pirate fucker, then you take the other two."

"Roger that."

"You have the ball, Zarkan," the captain said. "Take it when you got it."

The inscription on a stained-glass window in the West Point chapel, a passage from Revelation in the Bible, flashed into Ademar's mind. *Quis ut Deus; Who is like God.* She blinked a drop of sweat out of her eye, careful not to hold her breath as she waited for a lull in the waves to take the headshot. *"Allahu Akbar,"* she whispered. *God is great.*

Charlie touched her lightly on the shoulder. *"Allahu Akbar,* Ranger. *La Ilaha ilAllah.* There is no God but God."

Ademar's M24 was silenced to minimize any noise when she pulled the trigger. She aimed for the 666 tattoo under Ibliis's left eye, and the tracer bullet bolted through the darkness just above the waves like a phosphorescent angel of death. The window on the bridge shattered, and blood splattered on the opposite side a millisecond later. Following the fight through her scope, Ademar saw the three frogmen in black neoprene wetsuits hurtle into the bridge a few seconds after that and kill the other two pirates. From that distance, the Seals looked as if they were punching the pirates in the chest, but Ademar knew that commando knives were in those fists, and a razor-sharp eight-inch blade at the end of every blow. Something else caught Ademar's eye, and she could have sworn she saw a person leap out of the broken window into the ocean.

The hostages were safe, but the Navy recovered the corpses of only eleven pirates. Even if Ibliis had escaped, he could not have lasted long with a chunk of his head missing and a thirty-mile swim to the shore.

"Shark bait," Captain Stone concluded in the after-action briefing the following day. "First blood, Zarkan. Popped your cherry."

"They killed eleven of us," Charlie heard his shadow, Sayiid Awale, whisper in his head.

"Aamus," he replied.

CHAPTER 5

Sept. 11, 1993

Dear Deuce,

You've been deployed, so you know how hard it is to find time to write. But that doesn't mean I don't think about you, T2, and everyone else. I miss you, my horse Ziyada, and that goofy hound, Blue—everything, really. But these aren't feelings I didn't expect.

What I didn't expect is how it felt to kill. Not like firing a grenade into a tank kind of killing. But up close and personal killing; staring someone straight in the eye and pulling the trigger killing. They didn't teach us that at West Point. Sure, they taught us plenty about history, engineering, military tradition, tactics, honor, patriotism, and all that. But they don't—well, I suppose they can't—teach us about killing and death, at least not in a way that fills this hole I have in my soul right now. Islam has nothing for me either. I'm empty, as a soldier and as a woman—struggling to balance that part of me that gives life and that part of me that takes it.

It can be confusing here, the fog of war and all, to tell the good guys from the bad. But the guy I killed was bad, real bad—some kind of wannabe pirate who was kidnapping for ransom and cutting off their heads if it wasn't paid. Probably doing a lot worse before he killed them. I can't go into all the details in a letter. Security and all. I'll fill you in when we see each other. But he was on a ship holding two Americans hostage, and I was on another one two hundred yards away. I could see every detail through my scope, and the weird part was that he had 666 tattooed under one of his eyes, the symbol for the Antichrist. Spooky!! I shot him right through the middle 6, and some Seals rescued all the hostages, also killed eleven other pirates. Remember how you had a hard time shaking that image of Anil's face with his hand caught in the chili picker? I know how you felt. I can't seem to shake that bastard's face just before I shot him, the 666. He looked right at me just before I pulled the trigger, like he knew I was there. The Antichrist.

It got me to thinking about that letter Abuela Marcie wrote your dad during the spring of his first year at West Point, when he was questioning all the rah-rah BS and his faith. I understand now what he meant by asking her if taking a life was an act of hubris, as if one would be confusing himself with God because he could do it. I'm not sure why, but I wrote down her response to him, kept it all these years, and brought it with me to Somalia. I felt less confused after reading it. In case you don't remember, here's what she wrote.

'*Dear Crockett,*

There is only one God, but he has many names—Tam calls him Allah. None of us should ever confuse ourselves with God just because we can kill. There are many references to a "just war" in the scriptures, like this passage in the New Testament, Romans 13:4: "For he is God's servant for your good. But if you do wrong, be afraid, for he does not bear the sword in vain. For he is the servant of God, an avenger who carries out God's wrath on the wrongdoer." A time may come when you will kill. Do so only with the greatest of remorse, and only if you're sure it's for a just cause. You will know the difference.'

There's a translator assigned to me here, a Somali named Charlie Christmas; yeah, Charlie Christmas! Well, that's not actually his name, but that's what we call him because his real name was too complicated and he was born on Christmas day. Good guy. He's someone I can talk to about these things, since I certainly can't tell my CO. You know the Army would have me on some kind of watch list for mental cases if I did. He's Muslim and sees things like I do.

Well, that's all I have to report for now. Don't know when I'll see you again, but I'm sure looking forward to it.

Love, Addie

CHAPTER 6

A number of minor legends have grown out of Dell City lore, mostly Texas Rangers like Bob Coffey or businessmen like Jack Laws who helped carve it out of the unforgiving high desert. But two names stand as tall as the majestic Guadalupe Mountains skirting the eastern edge of Dell City for bringing it the first and only Texas State six-man football championship—Tamerlane Zarkan and Crockett Laws. Crockett put on a dazzling offensive display in leading the Cougars to a thrilling last-second victory over the Jayton Jayhawks at the Alamadome in San Antonio. But it was the heroics of Ademar's father, Tamerlane Zarkan, that defined one of those moments of grit and luck that seem embedded in so many Texas legends. Shunning Doc Alvarado's advice to leave the game with an open fracture to his wrist, forty-seven seconds remaining, and three points behind, Tamerlane batted down a pass and, on his back, miraculously intercepted the ball with his one good hand. Andrew Solomons, editor of the *Hudspeth County Herald*, called it simply *The Catch* in his story the next day. And from that point forward, that term, *The Catch*, became synonymous with a stroke of good luck, a monumental feat, or a job well done. It was *The Catch* when Jack Laws prevailed in a high-profile, multimillion-dollar water-rights case in the Texas Supreme Court, and it was *The Catch* when Eulalia Laws won a Grammy with her band, the Karma Cowgirls.

In that same vein, Ademar's two-hundred-yard kill in the dark of night from the deck of a pitching US Navy destroyer became known as *The Shot*. There was no shortage of grizzled combat legends among the Seals and Green Berets deployed to the provisional American military base at the Mogadishu airport. Word of Ademar's marksmanship spread through all of them like wildfire, and she couldn't walk ten feet without someone giving her the Army's congratulatory *hoo-ah* for *The Shot*. The story took on grandiose exaggerations among Somalis in the streets and cafés of Mogadishu, where there was no love lost for Ibliis. And they relished the irony of a woman, an American Muslim woman, taking the seemingly indestructible pirate's life with a single bullet. Unbeknownst to Ademar, Charlie Christmas had retrieved the M24 shell casing that housed the famous 7.62 mm bullet, and it found a home dangling next to the letter *S*, the tiny wooden ptarmigan, the Somali flag, and the Islamic crescent on the necklace that his father had given him before the trip to Alaska.

Charlie had a certain *je ne sais quoi*, the indefinable special something that drew people to him and engendered trust. Americans of all ranks looked to him as their fixer, an important source of intelligence on matters as inconsequential as the best black market to purchase pasta or as critical as the timing of the next shipment of Khat from Kenya. Charlie was not surprised when Captain Prometheus "Pro" Stone pulled him aside one morning in the canteen for a frank assessment of Ademar's mental state after the shooting.

"Hell of a shot; still can't believe it," the captain said.

"You know those Texans, Cap'n Pro," Christmas replied. "Born to it, like a baby to its mother's tit."

"Bullshit, Christmas. What are the odds? Two hundred yards on the high seas at night. That was the hand of God, or Allah, or whatever."

"You know what we say, Cap'n . . . God is Great."

"Does she seem okay to you, Christmas?" the captain asked. "First kill and all. Could be fucking her up a little . . . would be natural."

"I don't know, Cap'n?" he replied. "Ask her."

Ademar was a few tables away, lost in her coffee, and Stone motioned her over. Ademar had a sense for what might be coming, but one thing she'd learned about Stone in their few months together was to expect the unexpected. What came next, even from the enigmatic warrior-philosopher, surprised even her.

"What's up, Cap?" asked Ademar, throwing one leg over the bench and placing her coffee cup on the table like a gambler intent on not revealing her tell at a high-stakes Texas hold 'em game in Vegas.

"Charlie and I were just admiring your shooting," said Stone, keeping his cards as close to the vest as Ademar. "Just wanted to be sure you're okay, first kill and all."

"I'm fine," she responded quickly, a little too quickly.

"Good to hear," Stone said. "Snatching a life; no small thing."

"I said I'm fine, Cap. Let's not make this a woman thing."

"It's not like that, Ademar," said Stone, the only time he had ever used her first name. "But since you brought it up, why are you a sniper? Don't get me wrong; I'm all-in for someone doing whatever job they can do regardless of anatomy, color, or God. But seems like the last job a woman would choose. Why did you?"

"Because I'm a good shot," she said. "Because it was the only way for me to break into combat."

"What else?" asked Charlie.

"You really want to know? Well, I've been pondering that question myself since killing Ibliis. I chose to be a sniper for the same reason I chose to be a kicker on my high school football team. Sure, it pissed me off that a woman couldn't play football, couldn't serve in combat, couldn't join the club just because of anatomy, but that wasn't really it. I chose to be a sniper because it's safe. Not like safe from danger, but safe as in having my own space, a place that doesn't require some secret handshake or some other silly male-bonding ritual. A place where only I call the shots, literally and figuratively; where I'm the game-changer on the field. Growing up in rural West Texas—not exactly Cambridge or Berkeley, if you get my drift—I devoured every book I could lay my hands on. My mom thought I was a lesbian when she read my copy of *A Room of One's Own* by Virginia Woolf, feminist writer in England in the 1920s."

"I read that book," Stone said. "Wrote a paper on it at Cornell."

"Then you have some idea of what I'm talking about, Cap. That room she wrote about was literal—a place to write fiction. But it was also a metaphor for a place a woman could claim as hers and hers alone, a quiet sanctuary where she could do whatever she wanted, think whatever she wanted, write whatever she wanted. A place where she called her own shots.

"That's why I'm a sniper; that's my room," she said, standing up and walking out of the canteen.

Ademar's words left them both speechless, as if the light had been turned on in a darkened room where they had thought the shadows on the wall reflected reality.

"It's like that cave in Plato's Republic," said Charlie, who had taken a philosophy course at Utah State, and was sure that Stone, with his Ivy League education, would know what he was talking about. "The guys chained to the wall of a cave with a fire behind them. All they can see are the shadows of what's going on between them and the fire, and they think that's reality."

"Read that one too," Stone said. "Learned more about you two in the last thirty minutes than in the last three months.

"The first woman I ever knew, really knew, was my mother. And she taught me never to underestimate a person. Guess I forgot that a little about Ademar, and you. Here I thought Ademar might just need a few days with her fiancé, Lieutenant Laws. Could be I've lost my perspective, forgotten the gray area, or that it even exists."

"Don't be too hard on yourself," Charlie said. "We all miss something."

"Keep a secret, Christmas? There's a little surprise coming her way might help with that."

"Lock and key, Cap'n," Christmas said, drawing his thumb and forefinger across his lips as if zippering them closed.

American cargo planes swarmed into the Mogadishu airport like geese heading south for the winter, lines and lines of C-141s, C-135s, C-130s, and C-5s descending every few minutes to disgorge troops, war materiel, and relief supplies to fuel the engine of what was becoming a complex humanitarian mission amid an escalating combat operation. Charlie, Ademar, and Stone had gathered on the tarmac to greet some VIPs in from the Pentagon to kick the tires on behalf of the newly elected president, Bill Clinton, who would take office in a few months. Seemed everyone had heard about *The Shot*, and the VIPs had specifically requested to meet Ademar for a photo op on the tarmac to publicize a tiny victory and to highlight the value of women in the military at a time when they were considering opening up more combat billets to them. And it certainly wouldn't hurt the Clinton Administration's agenda in the Middle East to elevate a Muslim soldier.

The day was way too hot for anything more than a T-shirt, but Ademar and the captain stood by the runway in full-dress uniforms waiting for the VIPs to disembark from the modified Gulfstream V. Charlie, of course, did not have a uniform, but he had dug a white button-down shirt from his bag and pressed it into something resembling appropriate wear for meeting an American military VIP. One by one the VIPs walked down the ladder from the sleek Gulfstream, shaking hands with Ademar, Charlie, and Captain Stone, then gathered before the media for a few photographs.

"It's my distinct honor to meet Second Lieutenant Ademar Zarkan," the Army general said. "She represents the best of what this man's, excuse me, America's military has to offer.

"Lieutenant Zarkan's skill and courage with her sniper rifle the other night removed a significant threat to our mission, and to the Somali people. Brings to mind another American woman who made a name for herself with a rifle in the mid-1800s, Annie Oakley, known as *Little Miss Sure Shot* when she traveled with Buffalo Bill's Wild West Show. On April 5, 1898, Oakley wrote President William McKinley a letter, and I'm quoting here, 'offering the government the services of a company of fifty lady sharpshooters who could provide their own arms and ammunition should the US go to war with Spain.' The president turned her down, but I'm glad to say we've learned a few things since then about the value of women like Oakley, or Lieutenant Zarkan, in the military.

"I'd also like to commend her translator, Sayiid Awale, who we affectionately call Charlie Christmas since he was born on Christmas day. He was with her the other night on that dangerous mission, and their partnership represents what our two nations can do together to help Somalia regain its footing. Thank you."

Charlie's smile dimmed at the mention of his real name, and, predictably, his alter ego had something cynical to whisper in his ear. "Charlie Christmas, America's token nigger."

A C5 cargo plane had accompanied the Gulfstream on

the flight from US European Command in Stuttgart, and the pilot had positioned it behind the podium during the general's comments. The rear cargo door came down once the general stopped speaking, and the captain nudged Charlie Christmas.

"What?" Charlie said, as he and Ademar turned toward the C5.

"Wait for it," the captain said under his breath so only Charlie could hear.

Several pallets of supplies rolled off the plane, and behind them, with a dog on a leash, strode Second Lieutenant Crockett Laws II and Staff Sergeant Tamerlane Zarkan II— Deuce and T2.

Stone stepped to the mike, making sure to wring out the full drama of a rare feel-good story for the media to balance coverage of the US-led mission in Somalia that far too often included the word *faltering*. "That's Lieutenant Zarkan's brother and her best friend from Texas. Both Army, hoo-ah! They've been temporarily deployed here to bring the vanguard of our four-legged troops to help with convoy security."

The image of Ademar hugging Deuce and T2 while Charlie knelt next to them with an arm around the dog appeared in almost every American newspaper the following day. For a moment, everyone had exactly what they wanted, especially Charlie, who finally possessed the dog he'd coveted since reading Jack London's *Call of the Wild*. From then on, there was no question who owned that dog, a four-year-old cross between a yellow lab and a Belgian Malinois, one ear straight up like a Belgian and the other flopped over like a lab.

"I'm calling him Buck," Charlie said, peeking under the dog's back legs to confirm it was a him.

Deuce was one year ahead of Ademar at West Point, where intimacy between cadets is forbidden, and they had learned how to temper their affection, how to translate it into a secret language where everything could be said with the casual brush of knees under a library table or the touch of fingers passing a pepper mill in the cafeteria. They probably could have bent the rules at a forward-deployed base in a war zone, not a particularly romantic setting, but Ademar and Deuce maintained their old West Point practices, as much out of affection for each other as nostalgia for the game they had made of it years earlier. After lunch, where they sat legs touching at a picnic-style table in an airplane hangar that had been converted into a cafeteria, the captain told them about another surprise.

"Y'all gonna like this," he said. "A good old-fashioned pig hunt, just like those javelinas you have in Texas or we have in Arizona, only bigger. 'Sted of horses we're riding choppers."

The Blackhawk is the Army's workhorse helicopter, a utility aircraft that can transport up to a dozen troops, carry five tons of gear, or—equipped with rockets, missiles, and gun pods—provide close-air support to soldiers on the ground. The load on that day was Ademar, Deuce, T2, the captain, Charlie, and Buck.

"And check this out," the captain said as he pulled a lever action 30.30 out of a scabbard. "Just like we hunted deer and pigs with back in Arizona, and I'll bet you did out there in West Texas too. I always deploy with it. Brings me luck."

"Damn straight," Deuce said. "Ranch rifle. Just like the one my *abuelo*, my granddaddy, gave me on my eighteenth birthday. Open sights too. Got my first deer with it."

Somalia is next door to Kenya and has most of the same animals—elephants, giraffes, antelopes, and the like—but the captain's hunting party was looking for a bush pig they could wrap in banana leaves and cook under the sand on the beach at the Mogadishu airport. They planned to serve it luau-style—minus the pina coladas, of course—and with all the fixings they could muster given the limitations of a war zone. It didn't take long for the helicopter pilot to zero-in on a half-dozen pigs at a watering hole, and he landed the Blackhawk far enough away, about two hundred yards and behind a small hill, not to spook them. They dismounted, and he handed the 30.30 to Charlie, who had been practicing secretly with the captain and had become something of a sharpshooter himself. Ademar certainly was not in the mood to kill anything, even a pig, after her encounter with Ibliis, and the rest of them had all killed plenty enough to happily cede the honors to Charlie.

"Charlie Christmas, at your service," he said, handing Buck's leash to Ademar to restrain the dog from rushing the pigs, and working the lever with one hand to chamber a round and cock the hammer like he saw John Wayne do in *True Grit* just before he rushed on horseback at "lucky" Ned Pepper and those two other outlaws. Within thirty seconds Charlie had crawled to the top of the hill and dispatched a boar that must have weighed 250 pounds.

"One shot," he said, flashing that dazzling white smile back at his companions. "Not *The Shot*, but not too shabby."

The quiet moments in a war always seem quieter; the small indulgences more indulgent; the rare intimacies more intimate. The four of them, five counting Buck, and dozens of off-duty troops lay splayed out on the beach next to the azure Indian Ocean, like bloated, motionless lions after feasting on pulled pork *African-style*, as Charlie called it. The VIPs had brought for a reward a few cases of Lone Star longnecks, frosted bottlecaps poking out of the ice in an ammo can, and each soldier was permitted one. "Rules are meant to be broken," Ademar said to Charlie when she handed him a beer, referring to the Muslim prohibition on alcohol, and on pork. The ocean extinguished the sun as it settled below the water, a silent explosion of blue, yellow, and purple. Barefoot and digging their war-weary feet into the warm sand for just a few hours was a gift from whichever deity they worshipped. They could have been any four friends by a campfire after a day of surfing at North Jetty in Humboldt, except for the occasional distant crackle of automatic weapons fire. Captain Stone felt mellow and propped himself up on one elbow, his drained longneck falling against Buck's nose with a gentle thump. Prometheus Stone was a warrior, a romantic, and an intellectual—a Jew of Greek descent and a hard-hitting strong safety on the Cornell football team, whose father, a third-generation reform rabbi, never forgave for enlisting in the Army instead of entering the rabbinate.

"War is hell," he said, which brought a sardonic chuckle from all of them, and a tail wag from Buck.

"I was on temporary duty in Bosnia a few months ago, same kind of mission, trying to help the civilians in Sarajevo endure that shit-show. There was an apartment building on the Muslim side of sniper alley, the no-go zone on the main street where the trolley used to run. Bosnian-Serb snipers on every roof; bodies everywhere, too dangerous to get them. People hunkered behind anything they could find for protection, waiting for what seemed like a safe moment to sprint across the street. There had been a report of a booby trap in one of those apartments, and we went in to clear it.

"Weirdest thing; on our way down the stairs we heard a television. No electricity; couldn't figure. Knocked on the door, and there was a family, like any family anywhere—mom, dad, two kids goofing in their PJs, eating cornflakes and watching the Flintstones on TV. Normal, except the dad had connected a bike to a small generator and was pedaling it like crazy for electricity so the kids could watch. Kind of broke my heart.

"Like sitting here with you kind of breaks it. I'm wondering how much breaking a heart can take."

Charlie got it, could feel it, but Sayiid Awale could not and whispered in his ear. "Eating pork; drinking beer. *Kafir.* Unclean, undeserving!" The harsh words jolted Charlie, pulled

him back into his shoes, and reminded him of his father's part-
ing words before the trip to Alaska—*Remember who you are.*

Ademar, Deuce, and T2 were the only ones left on the
beach after a few hours. T2, intuitive and gracious as always,
despite wanting to spend every minute of the forty-eight hours
in Somalia with his sister, picked up his empty longneck and
headed back to the barracks.

Ademar hadn't felt like a woman in months and exhaled
in relief as she rested her head on Deuce's shoulder. Deuce
cupped her head in his hands and traced the outline of her ear,
down her cheek and across her throat, brushing her nipple on
the way down. They stayed like that for what seemed like a
long time, staring into the ocean, absorbing every inch of a
memory that might have to last a lifetime.

"Look," Ademar said, pointing to the ocean, where a
bloom of bioluminescent jellyfish floated across the waves like
pendant lights in the wind. "They're dancing, for us."

"Reminds me of Rancho Seco, that night after the party.
Your gift," Deuce said. "And the moonlight in the deers' eyes."

"I remember," she said, and pulled a blanket over them
with just their heads peeking out so they could watch the
glowing sea creatures on the waves and move their bodies to
the same cosmic rhythm.

That night was nothing like their first night, and nothing
like any time between then and the beach in Mogadishu. They
were older and more familiar with the intimate details of each
other's desires. But it seemed different to both of them that
night on the African beach, well beyond the natural curation
of their sensuality. The innocent, tentative explorations of
their youth yielded to the immediacy, desperation, and sorrow
of a last supper and left them both in tears.

CHAPTER 7

Charlie Christmas knelt at dawn by the sea for morning prayer, the first of five that observant Muslims perform daily, as the call for worship from mosque loudspeakers levitated over the broken city of Mogadishu. Salah was his eternal spiritual bond to the two million inhabitants of Mogadishu, most of them kneeling on small prayer mats that morning like Charlie, and with almost two billion Muslims throughout the world. At these moments, five times a day, Charlie felt he was one with Sayiid Awale, and that his nemesis was not some schizophrenic manifestation of his disassociating identity. Along with his new persona came the nightmares that would jolt Charlie awake, and, in a cold sweat under the inky darkness of a city without light, he swore Sayiid sat at the foot of his bed like a harbinger of eternal damnation. Charlie realized October 3, 1993, might be his last day on earth, and while reciting the same prayers he had recited for most of forty years, he wondered if his moment of death would unite the two conflicting and conflicted souls. With the looming battle only hours away, Charlie added the prayer for divine protection from the dangers of enemies. "O Allah, we ask You to restrain them by their necks, and we seek refuge in You from their evil."

After completing her prayers a few hundred yards up the beach, Ademar reflected on the upcoming mission in the heart of Mogadishu, the belly of the beast. Growing up in West Texas, she was not particularly observant, as much out of apathy as avoiding the inconvenience of praying in the corrals, barns, classrooms, and sports fields where she spent most of her time. That all changed at West Point, not because she became more devout, but because of the way it reminded her peers that a Muslim, and a woman, had every right to be where they all were at that time. Ademar was not a crusading Muslim or feminist, but lived those values in the way she conducted herself every day, by showing not telling. Prayers that morning did not comfort Ademar as much as the words from the Bible about a "just war" in the letter to Deuce's father from Abuela Marcie during his first year at West Point. Certainly, saving thousands of children from starvation was a righteous cause, but the mission in Somalia had become something else, and she was about to find out what that something else was.

Like many young American men in the turbulent 1960s, President Clinton objected to the Vietnam war and was not required to serve due to a high draft number. Clinton was still a reluctant warrior when he inherited the mess from the breakup of the former Soviet Union—loose nukes and simmering powder kegs like the Balkans and Chechnya. Three generations of US policy had prevailed in the Cold War, but the West was not prepared for what came slithering out of the cauldron the USSR had been stirring for decades. The Balkans were incinerating in the flames of genocide, Rwanda was not far behind, Haitians fled by the thousands in hopes of reaching the nearby coast of Florida, the Middle East threatened to explode at any moment, and thousands of American troops were fighting a war in East Africa that had never officially begun and had no clear exit strategy. The institutions that had functioned so well as bulwarks against anarchy and global destruction during the Cold War—NATO and the United Nations—could not evolve quickly enough to control the flames of global disorder. President Clinton was the most powerful person in the world, and he decided to double-down in Somalia. The worthy humanitarian mission launched on a whim by a lame-duck president was now Operation Gothic Serpent, a series of risky special operations strikes aimed at capturing Mohamed Farrah Aidid and prying open his grip on a starving nation. On that October morning, Second Lieutenant Ademar Zarkan and Charlie Christmas were the tip of the spear Clinton hoped to thrust into the heart of the Somali warlords.

Clinton wanted out of Somalia and tasked General William F. Garrison and the Pentagon brain trust with devising a strategy for unifying the feuding factions while continuing the massive relief operation. The plan was to remove the warlord Aidid from the field of play and to convene the other clan leaders at a peace conference to broker a deal that would lead to elections while guaranteeing safe passage for relief supplies. Garrison, overall commander for Gothic Serpent, had briefed Stone and his other senior officers the previous night, and the captain sketched out the mission the following morning for the initial strike force, which included 160 troops, 19 helicopters, support aircraft, and 12 armored vehicles. The soldiers would make their way to the Olympic Hotel near the Bakaara Market, the heart of Aidid's stronghold, and snatch the Somali strongman along with his closest advisors.

"Saddle up," Stone barked. "It's what you do right now that makes a difference."

Convoy security on an overseas relief mission in a warzone was about as close as a female soldier could come to combat in the US military, but participating in this strike would take it to a level that no amount of ambiguity could hide. Stone pulled Ademar, who had not even bothered to bring her combat gear to the briefing, and Charlie aside afterward to give them the direct order into combat.

"Don't say it, Zarkan," Stone said. "We both know the regs. You're the best sniper we've got, and I want you in a chopper in case it goes to shit."

"I'm good with it, Cap," she said.

"You too, Christmas. We may need you. And if it really goes in the crapper, you may need this," the captain said, smiling and handing him the 30.30 he killed the bush pig with a few weeks earlier.

"Are you sure, Cap'n?" Charlie asked.

"Affirmative, Christmas."

Ademar, Charlie, and two other snipers in a Blackhawk helicopter rode over the convoy of armored personnel carriers and Humvees as they headed into Mogadishu on the road from the airport. Somali boys on the ground seemed to wave at them as the helicopters passed overhead, but Charlie knew better. He leaned close to Ademar so she could hear him over the chuffing of the helicopter blades. "Trying to catch a signal on their phones," he said. "Warn those boys in town we're coming."

The convoy seemed to have maintained some element of surprise, reaching the Olympic Hotel with minimal kinetic engagement. They snatched a dozen or so of Aidid's lieutenants, but not the head man himself. Ademar's and Charlie's Blackhawk hovered overhead while ground forces pushed their captives, hands zip-tied behind their backs, into several APCs. Their Blackhawk pilot flashed a thumbs-up and turned the helicopter for a return trip to the base with the convoy and its captives. But Charlie knew his countrymen, and he knew the Americans were in for a fight. Charlie fed his hand through one of the door straps and leaned way out so he could see most of the road back to the base, his necklace horizontal in the powerful rotor downwash. He tapped Ademar on the shoulder, and she grabbed another strap to see where Charlie was pointing. Like ants swarming over a picnic blanket for pastry crumbs, forces loyal to Aidid barricaded every intersection along the escape route with skeletons of old cars, oil drums, whatever they could find, and burned tires to obscure the vision of snipers overhead.

Than all hell broke loose.

"RPG!" one of the other snipers yelled, alerting the pilot and everyone on board that a rocket-propelled grenade was hurtling toward their chopper. The pilot stomped on the foot pedals controlling the pitch of the Blackhawk, narrowly avoiding the missile but throwing Ademar feet first out the door. She dangled in space with only the hand strap keeping her from falling to her death or, gravely injured, into the hands of Aidid's men. She bounced like a rag doll against the side of the chopper. Without hesitation, Charlie dangled his legs out of the helicopter so he could scooch his ass out of the cockpit and stand on the landing skid, which would give him enough leverage to push Ademar back inside. The sharp ping of metal striking metal confused Charlie, but he figured it out quickly as sunlight pierced the jagged bullet holes suddenly opening in the side of the Blackhawk. Charlie felt an intense burning in his left calf as he wrapped his arms around Ademar's waist and dove back into the helicopter. Safely inside, both of them saw the growing puddle of blood under Charlie's leg, and pulled up his pants to assess the damage.

"It's nothing," Charlie said as Ademar wrapped gauze from the onboard medical kit around what was a minor wound and tied it just above to stanch the bleeding.

"Through and through," Ademar said, staring into Charlie's eyes and mouthing *thank you* before returning to a prone shooting position in front of the door. The co-pilot looked back at them, then to the pilot. "Skinny caught one in the leg, but we're good to go."

Charlie heard the co-pilot refer to him as a *skinny*, a demeaning term many of the soldiers used for Somalis because of their wiry physiques, and so did Sayiid Awale. "You hear what Captain America just said?" he whispered in Charlie's ear. "After you took a bullet rescuing one of his. What's next? Shooting some of us with that toy rifle?"

Charlie had no time to think or respond, helicopters taking heavy fire and foot soldiers calling for close-air support to help fight their way through the blocked streets of the Bakaara Market.

"HQ giving the green light to engage," the pilot shouted to Ademar and the other snipers lying in the chopper door, eyes affixed on their scopes and M24 barrels probing the air like a praying mantis stretching for its prey.

"Engage with who, what?" Ademar shouted back, unable to distinguish civilians from armed militiamen in civilian clothes.

"Anything with a gun that's fucking with us, Zarkan! Didn't teach that at West Point? You need an instruction manual?"

Charlie, kneeling just behind and over her left shoulder, pointed to the Somali gunner manning a .50 caliber machine gun mounted in the bed of a converted pickup truck, a *technical*, as he wheeled around to fire a burst toward American soldiers clustered around an APC. In a millisecond, before Ademar could process what the Somali gunman was doing or whether she should fire, a 7.62 caliber bullet from the sniper next to her struck him square in the face. For a moment, the gunner's body didn't realize what had happened to his head. Ademar's fellow sniper exhaled and chambered another round. "Roland the headless Thompson gunner," he said under his breath, referring to Warren Zevon's song about a mythical Norwegian mercenary in Africa. "Talking about the man." The Somali gunner slumped to the bed of the pickup truck, as if his spine had been yanked out of his body. Where the dead militiaman had been standing, a comrade popped up like a maniacal black jack-in-the-box, and Ademar took him out—center mass through the heart. Five more Somalis tried to man the .50 caliber and five more died, until a soldier on the ground ended it with an RPG that transformed the technical and its occupants into smoke and body parts.

Ademar's heart raced. She had killed three men in less than five minutes, but that was only the beginning. Over the next twenty-four hours the operation would unravel into a grotesque orgy of death and gore worthy of Hieronymus Bosch, the fifteenth-century Dutch painter famous for his macabre, nightmarish depictions of Hell. Eighteen Americans and more than one thousand Somalis died that night, and Aidid had taken hostage Chief Warrant Officer Michael Durant after his Blackhawk was shot down in the middle of Bakaara Market. What began as an offensive operation to snatch Aidid morphed into a search-and-rescue mission in the middle of the night against an entire city.

Ademar lost count of how many Somalis she shot that night, but not Charlie Christmas.

Their Blackhawk landed in a park near the market just before dawn to evacuate two wounded soldiers. "Cover me," Ademar told Charlie as she hopped out of the chopper to help them climb aboard.

"What?" he said.

Ademar simply pointed to the 30.30 still in the leather scabbard and braced against the side of the helicopter. Such an odd, conflicted moment for Charlie, proud and embarrassed at the same time—proud to have been asked and embarrassed that he would even consider taking up arms against his countrymen on behalf of a foreign occupying force.

"In for a penny, in for a pound, asshole," his alter ego, Sayiid Awale, whispered in his ear.

"It's not like that," he muttered forcefully and loud enough that the co-pilot looked at him as if Charlie might be losing his marbles.

Charlie unsheathed the loaded weapon like a sword and braced it against the side of the helicopter door, scanning the dark alleys around the park for any possible threats as Ademar assisted the two wounded soldiers. Cocking the lever to chamber a bullet in the very gun he had seen in so many American westerns, Charlie felt like an anachronism amid the power and precision of the most advanced weaponry in the world—as if he'd brought his grandfather's rusty old pocket knife to a gunfight. But he didn't have much time to dwell on it. Charlie sensed something dangerous before he saw it, a Somali boy, who couldn't have been much older than his own son, stepping into the otherworldly blue fluorescence of the corona from a sparking electric fire at the base of a light pole. Charlie turned toward the boy, struggling to raise an unwieldy RPG launcher in the way that frustrated teenage boys do when they aren't quite as strong or as tough as they think. Charlie could have sworn he heard the boy yell *Kadi*, a Somali oath that literally means *piss*, and would have laughed at the comical scene if it hadn't been so threatening. Within a matter of seconds, the gravity of the moment settled in. Charlie had to choose sides, really choose sides, forever and with no turning back.

"Don't do it," Charlie yelled at the boy. "Don't!"

"You don't," Sayiid Awale hissed in Charlie's ear.

Charlie yelled again, "*Jooji*," *stop* in Somali, as the boy pointed the weapon at the helicopter and screamed "*Allahu Akbar*" in the cracking prepubescent voice of a thirteen-year-old.

"Can you kill the boy?" Sayiid Awale hissed again.

Charlie Christmas didn't answer. He pulled the trigger on the 30.30 and dropped the boy with one shot.

"Traitor," Sayiid Awale hissed.

CHAPTER 8

President Clinton and his top national security aides watched in stunned silence. Nothing could have prepared the former Arkansas governor for the footage of Somalis dragging two dead US soldiers through the streets of Bakaara Market, stomping their naked bodies, slapping their faces with leather sandals, and burning American flags. Eighteen months into his presidency and three days after the debacle in Mogadishu, Clinton and his advisors decided they had done everything possible to right the foundering Somali ship of state. Although the East African nation was nowhere close to normal, and by many measures still isn't today, much of the nation was peaceful, the famine had been blunted, and the regional powers had agreed to shoulder the burden of peacekeeping. Clinton had a knack for extending his finger into the political wind and predicting which way it would blow. Many people, particularly in the Muslim world, saw it as Clinton flashing them his middle finger. They chastised him for turning away from a crisis in Black Africa and leaning into the festering white genocide of Bosnia-Herzegovina, just a few hundred miles from Venice and the first real challenge to the post–Cold War order inherited by the West. But the American presidency is often about choosing the least bad option, and

Clinton knew that even the best outcome in Somalia would not be deemed worthy of the blood and treasure it would cost. Somalia smelled like Vietnam, and he was no Richard Nixon.

"I want to bring our troops home from Somalia," Clinton, a few days after Bakaara Market, told the nation in an address from the Oval Office announcing the withdrawal. "It is not our job to rebuild Somalia's society or even to create a political process . . . The Somalis must do that for themselves."

Charlie Christmas, wounded leg propped up on a chair; Ademar Zarkan; and Captain Stone watched Clinton on a live feed in the mess hall. Stone was under no illusions about the chance for any meaningful progress in Somalia, other than sticking the proverbial finger in the dike of a biblical famine. But after twenty years in the military, and more than his share of misconceived strategies that had him tilting at windmills rather than prosecuting sound strategies, holding off the vultures and kicking a few bad guys' asses was enough. Ademar couldn't really believe her ears, couldn't process all that death on her shoulders for nothing. And Charlie felt like a fraud, a Black puppet with a permanent smile, dancing and jumping at the end of a marionettist's string stretching all the way back to Washington. This was familiar territory for Captain Stone, who had worked with local fixers like Charlie his entire military career.

"I'm fucked; my family's fucked," Charlie said. "Dead meat. Aidid and his militia have a long memory, and they'll be coming for us sooner or later."

"You're only a virgin once, Christmas," Stone said.

"Can't we do anything, Cap?" asked Ademar, realizing her woes were nothing compared to Charlie's.

"Probably not," he said. "But there is precedence for translators getting political asylum in the US if they're in danger, particularly if they take a bullet defending one of us."

"Political what?" Charlie asked.

"Asylum, Christmas, means you hit the jackpot—a one-way ticket with your family to the good ol' USA."

Charlie was an optimist, unrealistically so sometimes, and wanted to feel hopeful. But Sayiid Awale knew better.

"Don't hold your breath," Charlie's shadow snickered in his ear.

CHAPTER 9

Stone knew he was the least likely nomad in Somalia, although Ademar was a close second in her old straw cowboy hat with the rattlesnake rattle dangling from the band. They led the motliest of crews—a caravan of American soldiers, refugees, and a dog slumping five hundred miles on camels through the Somali savanna to a cluster of United Nations' refugee camps just over the border in Kenya. Ademar and Stone had convinced their commander to let them escort Charlie; his son, Amiir; his wife, Ebla; and his niece Samina to a safe haven in Kenya until their application for political asylum in the United States came through. Charlie had become something of a celebrity in Mogadishu, a hero to many for his role in the operation against Ibliis, and fans equated his life-saving gunshot in the Battle of Bakaara Market with *The Shot* Ademar made on the high seas. But the feelings of affection for him were far from universal, and to say he had a target on his back would be an understatement of mythical proportion. The American consular affairs officer in Mogadishu agreed when she processed his application for asylum in the United States. "It's a good bet," she said, "but not a sure one."

Thousands of Somalis had taken to the road since the famine and the US-led military intervention, most of them in an agonizing, dangerous five-hundred-mile trek along the coast with all their possessions on their backs or on homemade travois dragged in the dust behind them. A classic Hobson's choice faced them—potentially years of waiting with hundreds of thousands of their countrymen in overcrowded UN refugee camps near the town of Dadaab in eastern Kenya, or the continuing nightmare of life and death in Somalia. After much consultation and planning, Ademar and Stone opted against the standard route down the coast in favor of a slightly longer journey on dromedaries from the town of Buur Hakaba, a few hundred miles west of Mogadishu. Even though the two of them would be in mufti, anyone could see from their equipment and their ethnicity that they were clearly something other than Somali refugees. The alternate route was more remote, but safer and easier for the military to track them should they run into trouble. They were lightly armed, Stone with a standard-issue Beretta M9 pistol and M4 carbine, Ademar with her sidearm and M24 sniper rifle, and Charlie with the captain's 30.30 in a leather scabbard slung by a strap over the camel's hump. Buck, the Belgian Malinois and yellow lab mix who accompanied Charlie everywhere, trotted alongside him with a bright yellow tennis ball in his mouth, as content as if he were heading to the ocean for a romp in the waves.

Buck was a clever, affectionate dog, particularly around kids. But with two words—*green light*—he would transform instantly into the no-nonsense 110-pound working canine so highly trained in personnel security and ordnance detection. Other than protecting and sniffing out bombs, Buck's greatest joy was retrieving a football Ademar brought for the journey and gave to Amiir. Ademar had been the kicker for the Dell City Cougars, the first girl in Texas history to boot a field goal—thirty-eight yards in the rain, no less, to beat the Marfa Shorthorns in overtime. And she figured Amiir's kicking skills would make him a welcome addition to any American high school football squad once his family landed in the States. Endlessly, Amiir, under Ademar's watchful eye, would place the ball on a tee, then take three steps straight back and two steps to the left, holding his arm up just like the pros do in a game to prime teammates for the suicidal charge down the field as soon as the ball takes flight. Buck would wait patiently for the moment of impact, with just the very tip of his tail swishing from side to side in the dust. He leaped futilely at the ball with all his guileless canine heart as it left Amiir's foot, making a mad dash for the airborne pigskin and returning it gently to the boy for another go. Stone was into it too, spending hours during the trip endowing Amiir with the finer points of shedding blockers and tackling that he deployed with such deadly efficiency during a football career at Cornell in which he was twice selected as an all-Ivy strong safety. They called Stone the *Yom Kippur Clipper* for the speed and ferocity he mustered when tackling an unwary opponent, and for the second-round knockout of an opponent during the annual intramural boxing matches at Cornell his freshman year.

At dawn on April 2, the Army airlifted them all in a Blackhawk to Buur Hakaba, where they purchased five camels for riding and two for transporting essentials during the three-week journey. They went light on food and water, counting on bagging an antelope to supplement the Army MREs, *meals ready to eat*, or, as Charlie's eight-year-old son Amiir joked, *meals ready to barf.* And this time of year, water would probably not be a problem, although plenty of refugees had died on the trek to Kenya from dehydration or disease.

Certain traditions are ingrained into the son of a rabbi, and a few days into the trek Stone had not forgotten Passover as he ruminated on the parallels between their journey and the central narrative of the Jews' flight from slavery under the Pharaoh in Egypt.

"Biblical, ain't it?" Stone said to nobody in particular.

"What's that mean?" asked Amiir, who liked nothing more than listening to Stone wax poetic on one thing or another that struck his fancy.

"Way up there in Egypt, thousands of years ago, there was this guy Pharaoh. Kept my people, the Jews, in slavery to build his pyramids."

"What's a Jew?" Amiir asked.

"It's a religion, like Islam," Stone answered. "As a matter of fact, us Jews and you Muslims are brothers going way back."

"Mom," said Amiir, twisting around to look at Ebla on the camel next to him with three-year-old Samina in her arms. "Mom! Brothers; Captain Pro and I. Oh yeah!"

"Anyway, kid," Stone said, "Moses was our main man, and he wanted Pharaoh to let his people go to Israel. God helped him by throwing disasters on the Egyptians—bugs, disease, and stuff like that—until Pharaoh agreed. But at the last minute, Pharaoh changed his mind, and his soldiers chased us to the banks of the mighty Red Sea. God parted the sea, kind of a miracle, so the Jews could cross. But once they crossed and the Egyptian army was in the middle, he let the water go. Drowned a bunch of Egyptian soldiers."

"We have to cross the Jubba River," Amiir said.

"Bingo, kid," Stone said. "But we'll be doing it the old-fashioned way—on rafts."

"Are you a Jew?" Amiir asked Ademar, whom he referred to as the *lady soldier*. He was certain that she had powers like Wonder Woman or other female super heroes from his comic books.

"I'm a Muslim like you, Amiir," she said.

"But you're American," said Amiir, not entirely clear about the distinction between nationality and religion.

"Can be both," she said. "As a matter of fact, Texas, my home, has more Muslims than any other state in America."

"How?" asked Amiir, always another question away from the latest answer.

"Almost one hundred and fifty years ago, our president started the US Army Camel Corps. Bought thousands of camels from Somalia, from other countries too, and shipped them to the United States with hundreds of camel handlers, Muslims. He figured the camels would be good for our Army in the desert. Didn't quite work out. They're ornery, they don't get along with horses, Cavalry didn't like them, and then there was a civil war. Army sold the camels to circuses, prospectors, but the Muslims stayed in Texas, Arizona, and New Mexico. And you know what?"

"What?" said Amiir, leaning toward Ademar with one arm around the camel's hump to keep him from falling off.

"My great-great-great-grandfather was one of those camel handlers," Ademar said. "That's how my family made it to Texas."

Charlie, Stone, and Ademar tried to keep a grim situation light for Ebla, Amiir, Samina, and Awil, a jack-of-all-trades camel handler who they hired for the journey. Born in a remote Somali village some fifty years ago, Awil managed the testy dromedaries as if they were his children, doling out carrots and sticks as required to keep them heading south. Allah has given every person a gift, Awil would say, and his gift was the ability to whistle through two broken front teeth with a magical array of pitches and volumes. Awil was a whistling man. He had a whistle for every occasion—one through his top teeth to shoo the camels, another through his bottom teeth to alert someone in the distance, yet another through two fingers to sound an alarm, and another that oscillated through the side of his mouth to convey relief. But his best work came at night around the fire, when he would whistle almost any tune one of the others could name. Amiir and his two-year-old cousin, Samina, adored Awil, and he provided endless entertainment to distract them from the hardships of a five-hundred-mile camel trek through what reminded Ademar of her home on the high desert in West Texas.

They would cross the Jubba River near the halfway mark in their journey, and the closer they came to it, the more Awil withdrew. His whistling dwindled to almost nothing, except to entertain Buck and the kids at night in a call-and-response game with the Ethiopian wolves that sometimes ranged far south of the Bale Mountains along the border with Somalia. Ademar, Stone, and Charlie pulled Awil aside the night before the river crossing in an attempt to figure out what was bothering him.

"Don't like water," Awil said. "Can't swim good."

"But you'll be on a raft with the camels," Charlie said.

"Camel don't like water," Awil said. "Like me, bad swimmer."

"Suck it up, man," said Charlie, ribbing him in the way that Somali men sometimes do to each other, but he regretted the teasing the moment the words came out of his mouth. He knew full well that everything could not be swept away with a joke, an American trait that annoyed him to no end. And there was no mistaking the real terror in Awil's eyes. "Will be okay, Awil. *Inshalla*," if Allah wills it.

Charlie sensed scorn from his other, from Sayiid Awale. But it never came, for once, and the silence of it made him feel that much guiltier.

The crisp morning light and a cup of strong Ethiopian coffee seemed to lift Awil's spirits for the crossing later that day, but his mood darkened the moment they crested a hill and looked down on the Jubba River snaking through the savanna. It grew progressively darker as they loaded the camels on three rickety rafts constructed of eight heavy tree trunks lashed together with weathered hemp rope and plywood nailed on top to form a crude platform. Ademar, Charlie, Ebla, and the kids went first across the one-hundred-yard expanse of river, with their raft anchored to a cable stretched overhead from one bank to the other and hauled across by men tugging on a rope. The Jubba runs fast and big in the early spring, due mainly to rains in the Bale Mountains, and the raft lurched so suddenly to one side in the middle that Ebla and her niece nearly fell overboard. Once across safely, they watched as Stone, Awil, and the camels began their passage.

All three rafts lurched at the same midpoint in the river, but something other than turbulence had the camels chuffing and stomping. Ademar and Charlie could not quite make out the source of their anxiety, or why Awil slapped the water with an oar. Ademar peered down the barrel of her rifle for a closer view, looked up, then back through the scope—water churning, camels yanking wildly against their ropes, Awil slapping at the water, Stone hanging on the other side like a funambulist blown from his high-wire, as the raft rose from the water. Awil pitched forward, hands windmilling backward in a desperate effort to stay on board. The raft kept rising, Stone dangling by both hands off the side as a counterbalance, then it splashed upright in a cascade of foam. The waters began to calm, and Awil, smiling, flashed a thumbs-up to Ademar. Before his hand dropped back to his side, a ten-foot crocodile, gaping jaws bristling with razor-sharp teeth the size of railroad spikes, burst from the water like a breaching whale and engulfed the entire upper half of Awil's body. The beast flopped back into the murky river, spinning and churning the water with Awil's spindly legs flopping like a deflated skydancer from its jaws. Ademar shouldered her rifle within seconds. The granularity of the advanced German scope gave her a front-row seat to the carnage, but not a shot she could be sure wouldn't strike Awil. Stone viewed the world in biblical terms, and a giant lizard emerging from the deep came as no surprise given the plagues that had beset them so far. Prehistoric threats demand atavistic measures. In an instant, Stone unsheathed his commando knife and launched himself into the churning red froth. The crocodile shot out of the deep, jaws clamped around Awil's torso and Stone riding him like a bucking bronco from Hell—one arm locked over its head the other one punching the eight-inch blade of the commando knife like a piston deep into the beast until the water calmed. The captain rolled off the dead crocodile and yanked on Awil to free him, but two legs sheared off mid-thigh were all he came away with. The whistles of the gentle camel handler silenced for eternity.

Burying Awil according to Islamic tradition was the least they could do for him, and Charlie led them through the closest approximation they could manage given the circumstances. He dug a grave while Amiir poked around the edge of the river for a rock that would serve as a marker in the barren savanna. Stone waded into the water to retrieve Awil's body parts floating unceremoniously like so much faded, lifeless driftwood. Under Muslim tradition, women don't participate in the interment rituals for a man, but nobody objected when Ebla heated water for the *ghusl*, ritual bathing of a corpse to purify the deceased's soul. She gently washed Awil and wrapped him in the *kafan*, a simple cotton shroud. Everyone helped lower Awil into the grave, with his head facing toward the holy city of Mecca in Saudi Arabia. Sunlight rushed below the horizon as if their God could not end that tragic day soon enough, and they all gathered around the grave—Muslim and Jew paying their last respects to a man who lived a simple life of quiet dignity.

"*Allahu Akbar*," said Charlie, raising both hands to his earlobes in strict adherence with the *Janazah* burial ritual and placing his right hand over the left. "I seek refuge in Allah from the accursed devil. In the name of Allah, the Entirely Merciful, the Especially Merciful. All praise is due to Allah, Lord of the worlds, the Entirely Merciful, the Especially Merciful, Sovereign of the Day of Recompense. It is You we worship and

You we ask for help. Guide us to the straight path—the path of those upon who You have bestowed favor, not of those who have evoked Your anger or those who are astray."

In unison, they all said *"Allahu Akbar."*

Charlie continued, "O Allah, let your Peace come upon Muhammad and the family of Muhammad as you have brought peace to Ibrahim and his family. Truly, You are Praiseworthy and Glorious. Allah, bless Muhammad and the family of Muhammad, as you have blessed Ibrahim and his family. Truly, You are Praiseworthy and Glorious."

"Allahu Akbar."

"O Allah, forgive our living and our dead, those present and those absent, our young and our old, our males and our females. O Allah, whom among us You keep alive, then let such a life be upon Islam, and who among us You take unto Yourself, then let such a death be upon faith. O Allah, do not deprive us of his reward and do not let us stray after him."

"Allahu Akbar."

Charlie ended the simple service with the *Tasleem*, the concluding words of all Muslim prayer, reciting it facing to the right, then to the left. *"Assalaamu alaykum wa rahmat-Allah,"* peace and blessings of God be unto you.

When it was over, each of then retreated to their memories of Awil. Amiir stood alone in the dark by the river's edge as Ademar, Stone, Charlie, Ebla, and Samina stared into the fire. They all smiled, a sad smile, when Amiir began to whistle.

Charlie awoke first the next morning, scanning a ridge in the distance with the powerful military binoculars to take his mind off the horror show from the previous day. He drew in a sharp, short breath as if he had seen a ghost, and handed the binoculars to Ademar.

"You won't believe it, Ranger," Charlie said.

Like an apparition, less than a mile away, a man dressed like a seventeenth-century pirate stood beside the mast of a small wooden boat being pulled across the plain on rubber tires by four men at the other end of a rope.

"Ibliis!" she gasped.

Charlie's *other* chuckled in his ear. "The opera's not over till the fat lady sings, Charlie Christmas."

CHAPTER 10

Samina stopped eating and drinking. At night, curled so tightly into Ebla that her aunt could barely breathe, the two-year-old girl shook and whimpered with nightmares of a legless, blood-soaked Awil clawing around her like a crab with crocodiles in pursuit. Children process trauma in unusual ways, reverting to old habits that bring them comfort, and Samina often latched on to Ebla's breast for the calming salve of a mother's milk, even though there was no milk to be had. Ebla didn't mind the charade of breastfeeding, which brought her a few peaceful moments during what were mostly sleepless nights, and the chapped nipples after so many years reminded her of happier days in Mogadishu nursing little Amiir through the night while Charlie slept next to her. Ademar listened to the suckling and imagined a life back in Dell City raising children with Deuce. As if Ebla read her mind, she asked Ademar to hold Samina for a few minutes so she could relieve herself. Ebla passed the troubled, deeply malnourished girl to Ademar, gently, like a delicate porcelain doll. Some women—frequently those from larger families where the day-to-day indignities of childrearing are endured openly, happily—possess something tribal in their DNA that helps them adapt to all children and their needs. Ademar could not breastfeed Samina when the child tugged impatiently at her shirt, but the maternal imperative to nurture, to nourish, to cradle the girl in her bosom felt as natural as cradling a sniper rifle into her shoulder. It was odd, Ademar thought, that two such contradictory instincts could reside so comfortably in her, and she wondered whether all women possessed an innate power to nurture a life and to end one. Nuzzling close into Ademar's breasts seemed to placate the child, even without suckling or milk, and Ademar felt connected by a spiritual thread to every mother in the Zarkan family tree. She tenderly wiped a few sweaty locks of hair from the little girl's forehead.

"You have child?" asked Ebla, taking Samina back into her arms and settling into the sleeping bag with her.

"No," Ademar answered, "but I hope to one day."

Ebla laughed in the way that women do when they share the small intimacies of their secret society. "Even the lady warrior will have child. Creator and destroyer."

"Creator and destroyer?" questioned Ademar, propped on one elbow with her finger still in Samina's tiny, clenched hand.

"I have offended you?" asked Ebla.

"No," Ademar said. "But I don't understand."

"I am not a modern woman," Ebla said. "Women in Somalia create, build, hold world together. Our men tear down; we rebuild, not destroy.

"You are modern woman, lady warrior; woman and man; child in one hand, gun in the other; creator and destroyer."

"I look at it this way," said Ademar, clearly not the first time she had pondered the question. "I'm a Muslim, like you, but there's a deity in the Hindu religion that represents what you just described, how I see myself. Ardhanarishvara is half-male and half-female; the name means the *Lord who is half woman*—equally Shakti, their female God, and Shiva, their male God. These two forces can't be separated; they live in all of us and are the root of all creation. Do you understand?"

"Yes," Ebla said.

"Whichever God is watching," said Ebla, cradling the malnourished, dehydrated child in her arms, "I don't think will save little girl."

Samina was dead the next morning.

Ebla, who knew so many that had lost children to malnutrition or dehydration, recognized the signs that Samina's death was near. She had resigned herself to it more than a week ago when Samina stopped eating and drinking water. *So unnecessary*, she thought, but accepted it without question as Allah's will. Ademar's heart broke, as much for Samina's death as for the sight of the pitiful, cloth-swaddled body lowered into the grave in the middle of nowhere for an eternity of loneliness.

"She not lonely," said Ebla, feeling what Ademar was thinking with the sixth sense unique to women. "Only body, not soul. Child become star in death, star in sky. Tonight, all nights, Samina smiles down on us. Many friends around her. Many Somali child die."

Ademar had visited the Israeli Holocaust museum in Jerusalem, Yad Veshem, on a high school trip, and what Ebla said reminded her of the memorial there to the 1.5 million children murdered by the Nazis. The cavern for the memorial was so silent, with a single candle reflected in hundreds of mirrors giving the impression of a million stars, a million dead children. *Yes*, Ademar thought to herself, *Samina will have many friends around her.*

The death of Awil and Samina within ten days of each other shook each of them to their core, drove home what it means to be a refugee on the run—a stateless, vulnerable ghost in limbo between a troubled past and an uncertain future. At the end of the journey, if they even made it, Charlie, Ebla, and Amiir faced months or years in a squalid refugee camp waiting for a faceless bureaucrat in Washington to approve their asylum application, and a consular official in Kenya to stamp their visa. But they had to make it to Kenya first, and that would be a tall order with Ibliis on the hunt.

"We're no more than three days from Kenya," Stone said. "We're not sure he's after us, and we're on fucking camels, for shit's sake. Never catch us in that rig. And if Ibliis tried, well, he knows Zarkan could double tap him from a half mile away."

"You don't know these guys, Cap," Charlie said. "Don't underestimate him. Sure, he could be another refugee, but . . ."

"Not likely," Ademar said. "More like he's showing us only what he wants us to see. Could be fifty of his men on technicals somewhere out there."

"That's right, Ranger," Charlie said. "You can be sure he knows all about you. And he's not the forgiving type."

"Gotta thread the needle here," Stone said. "Can't take any chances with Ebla and Amiir. We keep moving, stay alert, shoot first."

The American commander in Mogadishu was able to keep close tabs on them through an electronic beacon in their gear, and they could call for help if the shit really hit the fan. But the mission was not exactly official, and neither Stone nor Ademar wanted to draw any more attention to it than necessary, particularly after the black eye in Bakaara Market and the slow-motion withdrawal of troops altogether. Just over the Lagh Dera River and a few days from the Kenyan border, they received a message from headquarters in Mogadishu alerting them to a violent dust storm sweeping down from the Ethiopian highlands. Charlie had suspected that might be the case when he woke to find their camp inundated by locusts, which often precede a major weather event.

"This really is getting fucking biblical," Stone said. "Water, locusts, and now a sandstorm. What's next?"

"The angel of death," said Ademar, citing the last chapter of the Passover story and tilting her head north to the general location where they had last seen Ibliis.

"The sand and wind should offer some cover," Charlie said.

"True that," Stone replied. "But you can forget about choppers. No cavalry riding in for the rescue. We're on our own."

What began as a few harmless locusts crunching underfoot grew by midmorning to a menacing, pulsating cloud on the horizon. They were engulfed by noon, barely able to see a camel in front of them or hear their comrades over the deafening buzz. The locusts found their way into every fold or opening, despite the group's efforts to insulate themselves with whatever they could find. They drove the camels mad flying into their noses, ears, and eyes, and the caravan was forced to hunker down behind a rock outcrop to wait it out. A two-inch locust weighs just a few grams, but it's transformed into a blinding dart under the force of a 120-mile-an-hour wind. Mayhem ensued when the sandstorm finally hit, and all they could do was stay face-down on their stomachs until it passed. At one point, Charlie thought he might be hallucinating when he saw Amiir tumbling away in the wind with Ebla, Ademar, and Stone in hot pursuit. But it was clearly no hallucination after the storm subsided and Charlie lifted his head, shaking off what must have been a pound of sand to find that he was absolutely alone. At least Charlie thought he was absolutely alone, until he saw a serpentine ripple in the sand, which he thought was a snake but turned out to be the end of Buck's tail wagging just a little bit. Both of them had come through relatively unscathed, although the tip of Buck's ear, the one that stuck straight up like a Belgian Malinois, had been torn off in the storm. Other than the camels, that was it—no Ebla, no Stone, no Ademar. Worst of all, no Amiir.

Charlie had seen his son carried away with the others chasing after him, but not by what he thought was the wind. Amiir had been around a corner in the rocky outcrop, tucked tightly into it and slightly out of Charlie's sight, when a figure emerged suddenly from the cloud of blowing locusts to snatch Amiir and scurry away like a black widow receding into its web. Short of divine intervention, Charlie knew Ibliis was the only possible explanation, and the hair stood up on the back of his neck imagining what that psychopath might do to his family and friends. Ibliis was an addicted sadist, even when he held no enmity toward his victim, like the Filipino hostage he beheaded. But the Somali pirate only had to look in a mirror or touch what used to be a jaw, cheekbone, and eye socket to kindle the hatred that consumed him for Ademar, Charlie, and Stone, the embodiments of every imagined indignity Ibliis suffered in life. He was a case study in violent radical-ization—disrespected, disenfranchised, invaded, bullied, and maimed by the Americans and by his own countryman. The plunder of piracy meant nothing to him anymore. There was only the burning red fire of hatred and revenge. That's what fueled him as he treaded water six long hours waiting for rescue after half his face was blown off by a 7.62 mm bullet, and that's why he tracked the refugee caravan for three long weeks, waiting for the sweet taste of revenge.

"Fifteen men on a dead man's chest. Yo-ho-ho and a bottle of rum," Ibliis roared in delight with Ademar, Ebla, Amiir, and Stone tied up and on their knees in the sand.

"Hey, Captain Hook," Stone said. "You really think you'll get away with this?"

"Shut up, Captain Jewboy," Ibliis snarled at Stone, whip-ping him across the bridge of his nose with the barrel of the pearl-handled Colt Python. "Surprised I know your name, Captain Stone? And you too, Lieutenant Zarkan. We have spies just like you, just like that cockroach Sayiid Awale.

Charlie Christmas! What a joke!" He took a step forward and leaned over so his mutilated face was within inches of Amiir. "The biggest joke of all . . . I have that bastard's son and wife. Yes, Ebla I know who you are, and before this day is over every one of us will defile you while your son watches. Then we will do him and the Americans. My men are very curious about the taste of American cunt."

Ibliis had counted on the wind erasing every trace of their path in the sand, making them impossible to track. But Charlie had an ace in the hole, a trump card that just might enable him to turn the tables on the pirate. Charlie held the football close to Buck's nose, and the highly trained dog seemed to understand exactly what was required of him, and the urgency in doing it. Buck put his nose to the sand and bolted off, Charlie loping behind him on a camel with the 30.30 cradled across his lap. Charlie knew Ibliis, like a heroin addict rushing home to fix with a new bag of dope, would not have the patience to wait for gratification. And even though the pirates were a few hours ahead, he figured they'd catch up soon enough. Charlie was less certain about a rescue strategy, and fretted miserably at the thought of what might be left to rescue.

"Untie the Somali bitch," Ibliis, dropping his fancy pantaloons, commanded one of his crew. "I'll go first."

"Don't look, Amiir," Ademar whispered, and Ibliis backhanded her with his massive fist, then grabbed the boy's chin.

"You'll watch me fuck your mother, boy, and you'll remember, at least as long as you live," Ibliis snickered. "Then you'll find out how it feels to be fucked in the arse."

He turned toward his crew, laughing and snorting through the skeletal mess that was his face. "Isn't this a delightful outing, boys?"

Ebla felt death creeping to her, closer with every second, and turned to Amiir.

"Do not fear, Amiir. We will meet Allah soon. Pray with me," she said, and recited the Muslim prayer for times of fear and anxiety.

"Allah suffices me. There is no God but God. On Him do I rely, and He is the Lord of the great throne."

Ibliis dropped to his knees, mocked Ebla's prayers, and moved closer to her.

"Don't you fucking touch her," Stone shouted.

"Is that the US Army I hear pissing in the wind?" Ibliis taunted.

"You know we're all worth a lot more alive than dead," Ademar said, and Ibliis stopped for a moment to consider the possibilities.

"Maybe you and Captain America," he said. "But not these two."

Ebla continued to pray. A single shaft of sunlight broke through the clouds, illuminating her face and forming what looked like a halo around her. She opened her eyes wide, but not in fear.

"Allah is calling me, Amiir," she whispered. "He will come for you."

Ibliis sneered and grabbed her tunic, ripping it down to her waist to expose the breasts that only a few days earlier had given such comfort to Samina.

Ebla took one last breath before her heart stopped, and she fell over dead.

Charlie and Buck were close enough to see the pirates and their captives through the binoculars, and they charged. The setting sun behind them and blowing sand made it hard for the pirates to tell exactly what was coming. But the pirates were spooked deeply by what they thought could only have been the hand of God that snatched Ebla. Panic overtook them when they saw the howling spectres of revenge, horsemen of the Apocalypse, wraiths straight from Hell, coming for them through shimmering waves of heat. Charlie pulled the 30.30 from the scabbard, cocked the lever with one hand, clenched the camel's reins in his teeth, shouldered the rifle, and shot one of the pirates in the chest. Buck surged ahead, barking, lips pulled back over a demonic snarl, closing the distance between him and the pirates by two yards with every stride. In one seamless motion, Charlie slapped the camel hard on the flank with the rifle, cocked it, and dropped another pirate with a .30 caliber slug into his stomach. Ademar's dog tags had fallen in the sand next to her when the pirates threw her to the ground, and she had furtively used them to saw through the worn hemp rope that bound her hands. In a cool rage, under the cover of mayhem, Ademar reverted to her hand-to-hand combat training at West Point and crushed the other pirate's windpipe with a single violent thrust into his throat.

Only Ibliis remained, still on his knees next to Ebla's corpse just as Charlie and Buck reached him. Ibliis jumped up, not bothering to pull up his pants, and wrapped Amiir in a headlock with the pistol flush against the boy's head. The only sound was Buck's low, menacing growl.

"Don't you call this a Mexican standoff in your country?" Ibliis asked.

"Forgot to tuck in your pecker," Stone said. Ibliis looked down, and Stone turned to Buck, shouting the command to action imprinted in the dog's brain through months of training. "Green light!"

Ibliis raised the gun toward Stone, then turned the barrel to where Buck had been, but it was too late. Two strides and Buck was airborne, seeming to go for the gun at the pirate's waist, but clamping his powerful jaws on Ibliis's exposed cock instead and ripping it off along with his testicles. Ibliis roared in pain, then fell over backward, whimpering and holding his hand over the stump that had been his most prized possession, the source of so much demonic pleasure now a pitiful, flaccid piece of bloody meat in the sand.

Charlie Christmas raised the 30.30 and, for a moment, relished the notion of leaving Ibliis to die in slow agony. A single gunshot rang out behind them, striking Ibliis in the face and killing him instantly. *"Allahu Akbar,"* Amiir shouted, and dropped the pirate's smoking pistol in the sand.

CHAPTER 11

The irreversibility of it all sank into Charlie as they approached the Kenyan border. He had paid a high price, they had all paid a high price, for an illusion of a new life in America. Awil, Ebla, and Samina paid with their lives. Stone and Ademar forfeited pieces of themselves in the journey that they would always feel but never recover, like an amputee with a phantom pain in a missing limb. Guilt crept up Charlie's spine, a palpable feeling of shame and disloyalty, that settled and stayed. And with it came the scolding words of his other, Sayiid Awale.

"For what, Charlie Christmas?" the voice whispered in his ear. "Your wife dead, your niece dead, your son now a killer before his ninth birthday. What can be worth that?"

Charlie had no answer. He wanted to cry, but no tears came. Perhaps he had lost that too somewhere on the Somali savanna, buried under the tragedy of the past month. Charlie's shoulders slumped and his knees buckled from the weight of the emotional gravity.

The four of them crested a plateau on just the other side of a border crossing at dusk and dismounted in the gloaming. Four generations separated Ademar from the voyage her great-great-grandfather made from Syria with a shipload of camels, but the blood of a refugee ran in her veins. She would always be the *other* in America, in many ways a nation of *others*, and perhaps that's what imbued it with the audacity to reach beyond its grasp for purple mountain majesties above the fruited plain. Perhaps that's what draws all refugees to the idea of America, and bequeaths her with the steel forged from their resolve. The blood of a refugee also ran in Stone, the Jewish warrior, the renegade son of a rabbi whose great-grandfather emigrated from Greece for the promise of a new life in America free from the shtetl of Thessaloniki and its suffocating mythos. Charlie dropped to his knees on the plateau overlooking Kenya, and prayed. Amiir, Ademar, and Stone joined him—Muslim and Jew side by side emerging from the desert as the living embodiment of the Passover legend. Buck rested his heavy head on Amiir's shoulder as the sun pulled the last shafts of light back into itself and left them in darkness.

The Kenyan border guards went through their passports and possessions the next morning, hardly raising an eyebrow at the military-issue weaponry tucked into Stone's and Ademar's gear. The American commander in Mogadishu had alerted the US ambassador in Nairobi, and she in turn had cleared it with the Kenyan authorities so everyone throughout the refugee pipeline would be prepared for them.

"Good to go, Captain," said the border guard, waving the ragtag crew through the checkpoint and into Kenya. "Godspeed."

Charlie was the last to pass through and stopped for a moment straddling the border, half of him in Somalia and the other half in a foreign land. Charlie knew that it would always be that way, and attempted to conjure up the good memories of life in his country to carry with him like a scrapbook. But all he felt was the deep regret of that last morning at home in bed with Ebla, and her sweet, generous offer of a final intimate moment before he started his new job as a translator for the Americans. The brief interlude between wife and husband had played back in his mind over and over since she died—Ebla, languid and inviting, offering herself to him; and her words when he demurred. "Okay, Mister American Translator," she scolded in mock disappointment. "You may regret it."

Indeed, Charlie thought to himself, and crossed the burning bridge into his new life.

Stepping across the border felt like walking out of an airport terminal after midnight in Bombay, Cairo, Khartoum, New York, or some other foreign capital, with a few honest people among the hundreds of chiselers who make a living duping the uninitiated. Many a Somali refugee had traded precious shillings for a bundle of Khat, a phony identification card, or an overpriced ride to the United Nations High Commissioner for Refugees' headquarters seventy-five miles west in the town of Dadaab, where they would be processed and oriented into the ramshackle cities of despair that would be their homes for years. Stone, Ademar, and Charlie did not emanate the kind of vibe that draw con men to potential marks, but they did have the camels and sold them in no time for a few extra shillings in Charlie's pocket. Riding the UN-sponsored bus to Dadaab, Charlie began to feel his friends slipping away into their world while he and his son were being sucked into a state of suspended animation. Charlie knew he would have to maintain a façade of confidence and strength for Amiir, but he felt neither confident nor strong as they stepped off the bus into a line of displaced humans stretching as far as he could see.

"It'll get better, Charlie," Ademar said. "For what it's worth, your asylum application was marked as a priority by our commander, and the ambassador will push it as hard as she can."

"It won't be an easy time, my friend," added Stone, handing Amiir a pack of Juicy Fruit chewing gum he had been saving for just this kind of moment. "But I promise, no crocodiles or pirates."

"Captain Pro," Amiir said. "Know what I'm gonna do?"

"What, kid?" Stone asked.

"Football," replied Amiir, tapping the place in his backpack where the ball pooched out the side and smiling with a hint of the resilient boyhood innocence that may have survived.

Ademar and Stone stayed with them the entire day, provided a little American military bluster with the UN bureaucrats, helped decipher the paperwork, and ensured that anyone with any authority understood that Charlie Christmas had friends in high places. But there's no short-timers in Hagadera refugee camp, despite how much grease your friends may have in Washington. At least Charlie and Amiir were assigned their own tent, a loaf-shaped, fifteen-foot structure with UNHCR printed in blue block letters on the side so nobody would confuse the branding of their humanitarian response. Their tent was lost in a sea of tents amid several hundred thousand souls all waiting for a ticket to somewhere else.

Charlie, Amiir, Ademar, and Stone were a family, just as surely as any that had braved the journey to Kenya and survived. They all knew goodbye would be the hardest part.

"What will you do, Ranger?" asked Charlie, forestalling the beginning of the next chapter in his new life as a refugee.

"My tour's up in a few weeks," she replied. "Back to West Texas for some home leave, time with family. Get my head right."

"Cap?" Charlie asked Stone.

"I'm twenty years in," he replied. "I'm thinking this might be my last rodeo."

"Rodeo?" Amiir questioned. "Can I have your horse?"

"You got it, kid, if I had one," Stone said. "It's an expression. Means getting out of the military."

"Well, we're not going anywhere for a while," Charlie said.

"When you two get to America," said Ademar, crouching

down and folding Amiir in her arms, "come stay with me and my family in Dell City. We've got plenty of horses and rodeos."

"And a real football field with real goal posts?" Amiir asked.

"You bet," she replied. "And a scoreboard."

Amiir had one final question before they parted, but was afraid to ask because he was afraid to hear the answer. Stone was ready for it, and spoke before the words came out of Amiir's mouth.

"Buck's yours, kid," said Stone, handing the dog's leash to him. "You need a mean son of a gun to watch your backs once Zarkan and I are gone."

"Thank you, Cap," Charlie said. "Thank you, Ranger . . . for everything."

"*As-Salaam-Alaikum*," Ademar said.

"*Wa-Alaikum-Salaam*," Charlie replied.

Charlie held Amiir's hand as they watched the two Americans walk past what must have been a quarter mile of tents. Tears ran down Amiir's face, forming tiny channels on his dusty cheeks that Buck wiped away with a few slobbery swipes of his tongue. Pure canine compassion, and a fondness for the taste of salt. Ademar sensed Ebla reaching out to her from the other side and remembered how she felt that night when Samina nuzzled into her breast. At that moment, she was not a West Point graduate or a lieutenant or a sniper with almost a dozen kills. She was a mother losing a child. She and Stone stopped just before rounding the last tent and turned for what might very well be the last time they saw Amiir and Charlie. They resembled two confused shipwrecked sailors clinging to the broken remains of a ship, swept away on a storm-tossed sea. Then they were gone.

Charlie half expected it, in some ways felt he deserved retribution for their plight, and his nemesis, Sayiid Awale, did not disappoint.

"I told you so," he whispered in Charlie's ear. "This is where your punishment starts."

CHAPTER 12

Natalie Maria Bell grew up on a farm in Dawsonville, Georgia, almost sixty miles north of Atlanta, the eldest of five children born to a part-time Lutheran pastor whose wife died giving birth to their last child. Natalie, or Nat as her siblings called her, took naturally at twelve to managing an unruly brood of siblings while her father tended to the pumpkins and sheep. Natalie's mother, a former schoolteacher, imbued in her towheaded oldest daughter the curiosity of a scientist, the spirit of a saint, and the heart of a lion. Natalie was equal doses practical and frivolous, perfectly suited as the matriarch to her two brothers and two sisters. Her mother taught her everything about sheep and wool, which stood Natalie in good stead with her father, both as a helper with the animals and a seamstress for her siblings. She was an end-to-end mistress of wool—shearing, cleaning, scouring, sorting, carding, spinning, weaving, and finishing. Natalie asked her high school chemistry teacher why wool was such good insulation against the cold, and why it held colors so well. The teacher explained wool is composed of cells that form a honeycomb-like structure called a medulla, with tiny air pockets providing thermal insulation and hydrophilic qualities that enable the easy absorption of dyes. Her sisters cherished the fashionable sweaters and leggings, and her brothers strutted through school in sweaters emblazoned with the logo of their favorite football team, the Atlanta Falcons. Georgia is a football state, and the blood of the gridiron ran deep in both of Natalie's brothers, which required their oldest sister to spend hours as quarterback, coach, and trainer. It was football that initially bonded her with Amiir.

Natalie was surprised when a football dropped from the sky square on the table outside the UNHCR office, spilling her coffee and launching her papers in every direction. But not as surprised as Amiir when the attractive twenty-year-old lady with blonde curly hair swept into a bun picked up the football and told him to run a fifteen-yard post, then threw a tight spiral at the apex of his cut.

"Score!" Natalie shouted. "High five!"

"Where'd you learn that?" said Amiir, running back to Natalie and slapping hands.

"Never seen a girl throw a football?" she asked, dropping her hand for the second half of the congratulatory gesture. "Down low!"

"Only one" said Amiir, slapping her hand again and smiling a real smile for the first time in months. As different as Natalie was from Ademar in both appearance and demeanor, she reminded Amiir of the lieutenant from Texas, and how much he missed her. Amiir was in the middle of that bridge in a boy's life between youth and manhood, and, although he would never admit it openly, there were times when all he wanted was to be engulfed in the warmth of a mother's embrace. Natalie, having essentially raised two boys, sensed it instantly, but knew better than to risk a critical faux pas with any public display of affection. *That will come in time*, Natalie thought to herself.

"I'm Natalie Bell; call me Nat," she said. "What's your name?"

"Sayiid, call me Amiir," he replied. "Sayiid Awale from Mogadishu. I'm here with my father."

Natalie studied international development and peace building at St. Cloud State in central Minnesota and landed a job with UNHCR after graduation, which is why she found herself tending to Somali refugees thousands of miles from the rural heartlands of America. And she loved it. The minor inconveniences—cold showers, dirty fingernails, endless meals of rice and lentils—weren't too far from life on the farm in Georgia, and they didn't bother her one bit. Natalie came from the maelstrom and felt as if serving in the maelstrom was her life's calling. She also relished the intangibles in the margins of life as an international aid worker—passionate late-night discussions with her colleagues over a few beers or a joint, trips with them to exotic capitals every few months for mental health leave, and the first real chance to explore openly her sexuality away from her father's purview. Not that Natalie was a prude back home in Dawsonville or at St. Cloud State, but there was something about the intensity of overseas aid work that encouraged casual intimacy. She met her future husband, Sloan Allen from Minnesota, in Hagadera, and laid with him well before she loved him.

Natalie worked hard not to play favorites with the kids in the Hagadera camp. But Amiir's story, which leached out of him in tiny droplets over several months, endeared him to her in a way that she could not have anticipated. Amiir had been determined not to let any other women into his inner sanctum, that place in his heart reserved exclusively for his mother and Ademar. But he discovered that there was room in his heart for another, and before long Natalie had inched her way in. Charlie Christmas, who spent so much time chasing his tail in the asylum bureaucracy, scraping for money with odd jobs in the UNHCR office or supplementing his meager income during dice games with the other men, liked Natalie and was grateful for the attention she lavished on his son. By the end of their first year in the camp, due primarily to

Natalie, Amiir spoke perfect American-accented English, had read ten books—including J. D. Salinger's *Catcher in the Rye* and Stephen Crane's *Red Badge of Courage*—knew his multiplication tables, and could placekick a football thirty yards.

"Know what today is, Nat?" Charlie asked.

"No, Charlie. What?" she replied.

"Today is our anniversary here," he said. "One year in hell."

"I know it sucks," she said. "But you're dealing. Amiir's okay. And I have a little bit of good news. Nothing dramatic."

"Hit me," he said.

"All your paperwork's done, no dings in the background investigation, and it's been shipped to Washington for the suits to bless. Don't start packing for a trip, Charlie, but you're on the people mover now."

That was good news for Charlie, the first real sign of movement since they arrived in the camp. And yet, he couldn't help but temper his expectations with the doubts sown by his *other*, who visited him so regularly during those long nights that he seriously thought he might be slipping into insanity. At times like this, when a ray of hope cast a thin sliver of light into his darkness, Sayiid Awale crept in to snuff it out. "She's full of shit," his alter ego whispered. "She's lying. You're never leaving; neither is your boy."

Charlie and Amiir had settled into a routine that resembled a life by the end of their second year at the refugee camp—weekdays filled with work, school, meals, and evenings watching videos on the Web with laptops the Gates Foundation provided to UNHCR. Sundays, however, were reserved for prayer and, in Amiir's case, football—starting with a game in the afternoon and NFL highlights in the evening with Natalie. Amiir's knock on her door at noon on Sundays marked the beginning of a day that resembled life back home in some ways, and she was concerned on this early November day when he showed up an hour late with a bandage on his left hand.

"What's up?" she asked.

"Nothing much," replied Amiir, at nearly eleven years old starting to exhibit what Natalie recognized as the early signs of pubescent sullenness.

"Your hand?" she said, taking it into hers for a closer look.

"Oh, that," he said, trying to pull it back from Natalie, who held it firm with the concern of a mother.

"Yes, this," she said.

"It's nothing," he said.

"Amiir!" Natalie said with enough tension in her voice to let him know she was not taking no for an answer this time.

"Okay, okay," he said. "There's an older kid, Hamza—fifteen, I guess—who I've been hanging out with. He's really close with the Imam, and he got pissed at me for talking during prayer this morning—said I had to be punished. Told me to put my hand on the door frame with the door open. I thought he was kidding. But no joke. He slammed the door on it."

"Where was the Imam?" Natalie asked.

"There. Didn't do anything. Kinda smiled like I deserved it."

"That's not all right, Amiir," she said, dropping it for a later discussion with Charlie Christmas.

Under the tutelage of Osama bin Laden, the Saudi extremist who had made a name for himself during the guerrilla war in Afghanistan against the Soviet Union, Al-Qa'ida, the Base, had buried deep roots in the Middle East and North Africa. His tentacles had not yet stretched into Europe and the United States, but bin Laden's violent Salafi brand of Islam found fertile ground in East Africa, particularly amid the simmering cauldron of chaos in Somalia. The Islamic Courts Union, opposed to the Transitional Government in Somalia and espousing the strictest application of Qur'anic law, had begun to take hold in the grassroots under the leadership of the charismatic Imam Sharif Sheikh Ahmed. And it would only be a matter of time before the union morphed into Al-Shabaab, a violent offshoot of Al-Qa'ida specializing in kidnapping, abusing, and brainwashing Somali youth. The marginalized masses of refugees in Kenya, particularly young men with nothing better to do than stew in resentment at the injustices that had landed them in a life of shit and misery at camps like Hagadera, were dry tinder for the spark of violent radicalization. And the Imam at Hagadera had identified young Amiir as a first-round pick in the radicalization draft. The CIA and its counterparts throughout the world had shared intelligence with UNHCR and other refugee agencies to be on the lookout for any hint of Al-Qa'ida in the camps. And Natalie, standing on the sideline of the usual Sunday football game, made a mental note to inform her superiors at Hagadera about the incident with the Imam.

Amiir had built quite a following for the SFL, the Somali Football League, and had no trouble fielding enough players for two full squads, composed of boys and girls, on Sunday afternoons. In the nearby town of Dadaab, Natalie identified a source for wool that she wove into headbands for all the players, emblazoned with SFL and its trademark crescent-shaped lightning bolt. She had become something of a corrupting presence to the nefarious schemes of the Imam, and he confiscated the headbands any time one of the players wore it to the mosque tent.

Naturally, Amiir's team was the Cowboys, named for the Dallas team in Ademar's home state of Texas, and they lined up today against the Pirates, an unfortunately ironic name given the contempt with which most Somalis held actual pirates. Natalie, the Cowboys' coach, tossed Amiir the football for the kickoff.

"That's the guy," Amiir said to her.

"The one that mashed your hand?" she asked.

"Yep," he replied. "Payback time."

"Amiir, wait." But he had already trotted onto the field.

The older kid from the mosque tent, who was playing for the first time and clearly uninitiated in the dangers of tackle football, lined up as the designated return man. Amiir usually booted the ball and hung back as a safety while his teammates made the tackle. This time, he lingered for a moment after a solid thirty-yard kickoff, just long enough for the opposing team to discount him, then drifted down the opposite sideline unopposed. The mosque kid fielded the ball, reaching full speed within a few steps, and seemed to find daylight until Amiir delivered a classic blind-side hit, knocking him ass over teakettle and causing a fumble. Amiir smiled as he trotted to the sideline, where Natalie huddled with the defense.

"Blew him up," Amiir chuckled, high-fiving teammates and avoiding the glare of disapproval from Natalie.

"Keep it clean, guys," said Natalie, glaring at Amiir, but feeling a touch of pride at how he handled the bully.

The Cowboys, with Amiir dominating at quarterback and linebacker—just like Ademar's boyfriend, Deuce, and her brother, T2—won as usual. Both teams congratulated each other, except for the mosque kid, who threw his headband to the ground and sulked away. The weekly football games were a welcome break for many camp denizens, and they gathered in a festive atmosphere afterward for something resembling a picnic. Amiir enjoyed the post-game celebration almost as much as the game for the opportunity to talk football with Natalie, who, along with Charlie, sat on a blanket in the shade.

"Cowboys tied with the Eagles," Amiir said. "Aikman's killing it. Bets on Super Bowl repeat?"

"Don't count your chickens before they hatch," Natalie said.

"What you talking 'bout, Coach?" Amiir replied. "Chickens? What chickens?"

"Smith messed up his neck, Haley's hurt, and Michael Irving was suspended," she said. "Watch out for my Falcons."

"You kidding?" Amiir laughed. "Lost eight straight. Hebert stinks at QB, and June Jones is about to be fired."

"Changing the subject, Amiir," said Natalie, suddenly serious. "Your dad know about the incident at prayers . . . with your hand?"

"No," Charlie answered as Amiir hid his bruised hand under the edge of the blanket and scowled at Natalie. "But I've heard a few things about that Imam. We've all heard a few things. Keeping an eye on it."

"No problem," Amiir said. "See how I took care of that guy on the field? Just like Captain Stone taught me."

"It's bigger than that," said Natalie, careful not to presume a parenting role she didn't have, and handed the conversation off to Charlie with a sideways glance.

"It's hard to explain, Amiir," Charlie said. "You know danger, after all we've been through—crocodiles, pirates. There's danger with that Imam. Keep it to yourself, son. Remember your mom. Hopefully we'll be in America soon."

"And?" Amiir questioned.

"And what?" Charlie asked.

"Going to a Cowboys game with Ademar and Stone!"

"*Inshallah*," said Charlie.

CHAPTER 13

December 25, 1996

Dear Ranger,

Today is my forty-fifth birthday, the second at Hagadera. Happy birthday to the Muslim boy born on Christmas day! Charlie Christmas; makes me laugh every time. When it doesn't make me cry. Does finding Charlie Christmas mean losing Sayiid Awale? It's like my old self is my new self's enemy. I try to hold on to what's important from before, but time passes and so do the connections to the old Somalia—as dead as my poor wife Ebla. So much of what's happened the past two years has been hard to shake, particularly the way Ebla looked when I found her—so peaceful I thought she was asleep. I dream all the time that she was just sleeping, playing possum you call it in the States, and she wakes up. Islam says our spirits will be rejoined in the afterlife, but that seems like a fairy tale, and I doubt whether Malak al-Maut, our angel of death, would let me into paradise after all I've done.

Speaking of Islam, there's a lot of pissed-off Muslims in Hagadera, upset at their situation and at the US, and powerless to change anything. It's like we're non-citizens here—no voting, no working, no justice. And the only hope is that some other country will allow us in, but not as us, as a bleached-out version of us. It's not so bad for me, but for kids like Amiir it's dangerous—as we say, "life on the fingertips," meaning life as it happens every day. I'm worried about him. As an American military officer, I know you're on to Al-Qa'ida and bin Laden. He's like a rock star here, especially to the young men, who spend a lot of time following him on those computers Mr. Gates donated. And there's an Imam here who preaches openly about support for bin Laden and a war against the "infidels." That would be you, Ranger, even though you're a Muslim, and your entire country; Europe too. He invited Amiir to join a youth prayer group, but he doesn't go because it's at the same time as his weekly football game. Whatever works, for now, but it won't work forever. Life is cheap here, and there's been a few people opposed to the Imam who have disappeared or turned up dead. I don't put up with any of that Imam's crap, and I could be the next one on his list. And then, I'm afraid, Amiir would be lost. We can't let that happen, Ranger.

So, seems like it's either out of here in a wooden box or on an airplane to America with Amiir.

There's an American woman here, Natalie Bell, who's about your age and reminds me of you, and not only because she plays football. Natalie works for the UN. She's good people, a friend and very close to Amiir. She's tracking our asylum application and trying to push it, but nothing's happening. She was telling me that refugees who somehow get across the border are allowed to stay while their cases are considered. I've been trying to figure out how that could happen, but it's a long shot without any real money for bribes and travel. I've got to figure something out for me and Amiir, before it's too late.

Don't mean to burden you with all this, Ranger,
but I don't really have anyone else, except for Stone, and
I don't know how to reach him. Please fill Cap'n Pro in
on all of this if you talk to him.

As-Salaam-Alaikum,
Your friend Charlie Christmas

CHAPTER 14

Irish blood ran in Jack Laws' veins, and he didn't know what it meant to back down from a fight. It saved dozens of men on his boat off the coast of New Guinea during World War II when he shot down a Japanese Zero on a kamikaze mission, a singular act of bravery that cost him a thumb. And it would have cost his life on the business end of a switchblade if Ali Zarkan, who survived months of jungle warfare in the Western Pacific and helped Jack build a farming empire on the high desert of West Texas, had not happened to be in a Juarez cantina to fight off three drunk *rhinestone vaqueros* determined to gut Jack for the kind of minor insult that so often escalates after a few too many shots of Mezcal.

Texas was built by men like Jack Laws—men with a fire in their bellies that either landed them under unmarked gravestones in the middle of nowhere or elevated them to the highest reaches of their chosen endeavors. Jack belonged to the latter, due in large part to having enough smarts to follow the advice of his wife. Marcelina Laws was an agronomist with Archer Daniels Midland who possessed an innate sense for negotiating corporate politics during a time when most women were reduced to fetching coffee, typing memos, or enduring pinched fannies. Marcie, who was raised in West

Texas, convinced Jack to stake his claim outside godforsaken Dell City on top of the Bone Springs–Victorio Peak Aquifer, a decision that reaped them hundreds of millions of dollars years later when they sold the water rights to El Paso after an epic legal battle that ended with a landmark ruling by the Texas Supreme Court. Jack and Marcie had two kids, Ray and Eulalia, Eula for short, who was a thorn in his side her entire life, and the apple of his eye. Eula inherited Marcie's brains and Jack's vinegar, a potentially lethal mix that often as not landed her in trouble, serious trouble. She survived a brutal rape in an alley behind the Kentucky Club in Juarez at the hands of three men, all of whom Jack and Ali killed during a daring nighttime raid deep in Mexico, and went on to found the Karma Cowgirls, a wildly popular band out of Austin that soared to the top of the music charts with their unique fusion of country and rock.

But the song that brought Eula immortal fame, and a Grammy nomination, was "The Ballad of Charlie Christmas."

Charlie's story first tickled Eula's inner muse around the fire on the farm in Dell City with all the Laws and the Zarkans gathered for a barbecue to welcome Ademar back from Somalia. Pretty much every successful country song includes a broken heart, a dog, Mom, a pickup truck, and a good fight. The story of Charlie Christmas had all of it, except the truck, and a few extras, like crocodiles, pirates, and camels. Eula wrote the story down in her music journal at first light the next morning, then rolled on top of Captain Stone for a morning ride. Stone had decided to cash in his military chips after two decades of service, and took Ademar up on an offer to visit Dell City to explore whether desert life suited him. Hooking up with Eula was the last thing on Stone's mind. But he hadn't been with a woman for months, and Eula had a way about her that made even the most righteous men, much less one fresh from the front lines of war, putty in her hands.

"That's one helluva story," Eula said the previous night around the fire, placing a hand on Stone's arm and leaving it there long enough to erase any doubts about her intentions. "I could conjure a song out of that."

"Ademar left some of it out, but I'd be happy to fill in your gaps," said Stone, smiling at the unintended double entendre.

"I'd be appreciative, Captain Stone," she said with her best imitation of a coquette. "How about we mosey over to my place after the party?"

"I'd like that," Stone said.

Eula was a voracious lover, and Stone a grateful beneficiary. It was enough to hold them together for a few months while Stone figured out the rest of his life, but not enough to span their considerable differences over the long run. He accepted instantly Jack's offer of work, slipping easily into the routines of farming and life on the high desert of West Texas. Accustomed to working with and leading people from all walks of life, he quickly became a valuable part of the operation and friends with all the Zarkans and the Laws. Even Anil, Ademar's taciturn twin brother who spent hours studying the Qur'an or surfing the Web since losing his hand in a farm accident, seemed to accept Stone without reservation. But Stone was a wandering Jew with a restless heart who'd made peace with what he'd done in the Army, but not with his father or his faith. And he knew nothing would work permanently until he'd done so. Stone also had unfinished business with Charlie Christmas that ate like a parasite at both he and Ademar.

Charlie's letter from Hagadera after more than two years in limbo left them with little doubt that his situation was coming to a head. As a battle-hardened Muslim woman who spoke perfect Arabic, Ademar was a valuable asset in many of the Pentagon's most discreet and risky operations against extremists in the Middle East, South Asia, and Africa. Stone was gratefully out of that loop, but Ademar kept him apprised within the boundaries of classified protocols. Both of them knew that young Amiir could succumb to the siren call of violent radicalism that drew so many disenfranchised, alienated, powerless youth, and they were determined to prevent it.

"But how?" asked Ademar, who had called Jack, Marcie, Ali, and Stone together to read them Charlie's letter and to seek their help in finding a solution.

"What about the State Department?" Marcie asked.

"Zip," Stone answered. "Frozen as tight as an Eskimo's backside."

"We owe him," Ademar said. "Risked his life to save us. Wouldn't be here today without him. Unfortunately, Charlie couldn't save his wife. Ebla gave up just before Charlie came in guns blazing with Buck. She gave up; just closed her eyes and went to heaven. Strange."

"His kid saw it all," Stone said. "Not even ten years old. Watched his mother die, then shot that pirate dead, straight through his ugly face. Finished the job Ademar started a few months earlier."

"Any options other than the bureaucrats?" Jack asked.

"We have our share of migrants come across the border illegally," said Marcie, who'd been discussing it with Ademar and studied alternatives to legal immigration. "If Charlie and his boy make it into America, they can stay. Then we pull some of those strings in Austin and Washington for a green card. After that they're golden."

"Whoa, Nellie," Jack said, peeling off his Marfa low crown, pushing his hair back, exhaling, and staring at the ground.

"Jack Laws?" Marcie said in a tone that her husband had heard so many times when he was on the cusp of inevitability with a decision she had already made for them.

"Guess that's decided," Jack said. "We extract them from that refugee camp and bring them back. We'd need somebody on the inside—somebody to work the angles back here too in case something goes wrong. And some muscle."

"There's this American woman, Natalie Bell, who works for the UN. Good people," Ademar said. "She's willing to help, but we'd have to bring her out with us. Probably lose her job. Worse, end up in a Kenyan prison. Don't need to tell you what that would be like for a pretty blonde American girl."

"I'm in," Stone said.

"Same," said Ademar.

"Thought I was done with this kind of shit at my age; guess not," Jack said. "One last rodeo for me and your granddad, Ademar. Ali and I make a pretty good team. He hasn't used that trench knife since we took down Eula's rapists in Mexico."

"Don't worry, *patron*," Ali said. "I keep it sharp."

"Too bad Deuce and T2 can't help," said Jack, fit as a fiddle at almost eighty. "But they're active duty; would land them in a world of hurt. Crockett and Tam will stay back to look after the farm, the kids."

"I'll work Austin and DC," said Marcie, who had forged some powerful political alliances during their legal battles over water rights in West Texas. "Wish Ann Richards was still governor. Suppose I'll have to deal with W. Too bad John Tower is not in the Senate anymore. But Kay Bailey's there, and we go way back. Plus, she's tight with the military. We'll need that."

"We'll also need a plane that can fly from West Texas to Kenya, some kind of jet, and an airstrip to accommodate," Jack said.

"I got that," Marcie said. "We'll pay Bobby McKnight a visit up the road near Fort Davis. They've got a paved strip at the Jeff Ranch that could work."

CHAPTER 15

M ilitary muscle memory took over for Stone. He designed a table-top exercise for them to rehearse the entire operation and to anticipate wild cards that might come up. Stone cleared the immense oak poker table in Jack's study, employing twelve-gauge shotgun shells to represent people and constructing an airplane and a replica of the refugee camp out of Lego pieces from several generations of kids and grand-kids. Quaint, in a morbid way.

Overwhelming force is the guiding principle of American combat, but Stone and Ademar went old school with 30.30s and commando knives. Jack opted for the close-in punch of the .45-70 long gun he used for hunting grizzly bear in Mon-tana, and Ali stuck with the *knuckle duster*, the trench knife with the brass knuckle handle that tore the life out of so many Japanese soldiers in the jungles of the Western Pacific during World War II. Men who kill rationally are men of habit, and it was no coincidence that Jack and Ali had used those exact weapons to take out Eula's rapists during a midnight raid in Mexico more than a decade ago. Jack double-tapped two of them from a distance while Ali silently passed the blade across the throat of the third. A shootout at a Kenyan refugee camp by a bunch of renegade Texas cowboys had a certain visceral appeal to all of them, but they knew it would trigger an international incident and jeopardize the goal of their mission.

"Dad," Ademar said. "You're not Wyatt Earp, and this is not the OK Corral."

"I've been told I favor Doc Holliday," Stone joked. "Or in my case, Doc Hanukkah."

"Okay, gentlemen, cut the shit," Marcie said. "Ademar is right. Y'all need to be in and out fast; no drama. Grab Charlie and his boy, scoot to the airport, and wing it home."

"You take care of the paperwork, Marcie?" Jack asked.

"Not yet, but I'm meeting Kay Bailey in Austin tomorrow. I think she'll come through, but she's gonna want something in return—politics."

"You'll figure it out, Marcie," said Jack, flashing those sparkling green Irish eyes that won her heart so many years ago. "You always do."

"We'll see, Jack Laws," she replied, tugging gently on his long earlobe in the way she did when expressing her affection for the Irish rascal in him.

"Stone and I set it up with Natalie and Charlie," Ademar said. "They're both good to go."

"And the boy?" Ali asked.

"In the dark," Stone answered. "Safer that way. He's just a kid. Might slip."

"Run us through it one more time, Prometheus," said Marcie, who had a huge soft spot in her heart for the same kind of rascal in Stone that she found so endearing in Jack, and took undue pleasure in using his full first name.

"Yes, ma'am, Mrs. Laws," Stone said.

The plan was painstakingly orchestrated, but simple. Marcie had called in a favor with Bobby McKnight, whose family owned the Jeff Ranch in Fort Davis, related to the huge financial windfall they received as a result of her work behind the scenes on the water-rights case. McKnight agreed to lend them his Cessna Citation and a pilot, providing they take full responsibility for replacing or repairing it should anything untoward happen. They'd fly out Wednesday night, which, with a refueling stop in Khartoum, would put them on a small airstrip near Hagadera just as the sun was setting on the Muslim Sabbath. A group of Namibian mercenaries, friends of Stone from the Liberian civil war, were happy to help their old drinking buddy by securing the airstrip and providing transport to the camp in exchange for two cases of Lone Star and a case of Macallan Rare Cask single malt scotch. With most of the camp shut down for worship at various makeshift mosques sprinkled throughout the sprawling tent city, Natalie would start a small fire on the opposite end of the camp from the barbed-wire fence where they would enter, which would create confusion and distract attention away from them. Natalie and Charlie would meet Ademar, Stone, Jack, and Ali at the fence, and they would fetch Amiir from the service presided over by the militant Imam. The group would quietly make their way out of the camp and back to the airplane—mission complete in thirty minutes.

"*Enshallah*," Ali said.

"*Enshallah*," Ademar replied.

"What she said," Stone remarked.

"Good luck with Senator Hutchison tomorrow, Marcie," Jack said. "Our last piece on the chessboard."

Marcie was a West Texas ranch gal through and through, spending much of her time the last few decades in faded jeans and dusty cowboy boots. But she flew in some rarified air sometimes and understood the importance of the right costume. She would be all business for the lunch with Senator Kay Bailey Hutchison at the grill in Austin's iconic Driskill Hotel, where cattle barons, wildcatters, lawmen, and politicians had parleyed for more than a hundred years. Marcie liked what she saw in the mirror at her suite in the Driskill.

She wore a dark blue fitted double-breasted wool blazer from Tom Ford over a simple black cashmere turtle-neck sweater from Ralph Lauren and black crepe astor pants from Veronica Beard, with a pair of dark blue Salvatore Ferragamo low-heel pumps. Her only jewelry was a single strand of white South Sea pearls with a pair of matching earrings set in gold, all of which Jack had given her for their fiftieth anniversary. Kay Bailey Hutchison wore nearly the exact same outfit, although her blazer was a beige one from Georgio Armani and her cream-colored shoes with nearly three-inch heels came from Fendi. The two broke into the easy, self-effacing laughter of confident old friends when they met in the hotel grill.

"Courtesy of Stanly Marcus," said Marcie, referring to their mutual friend and founder of Neiman Marcus in Dallas.

"Cream always rises to the top," the senator replied. "Drink?"

"It's early, Kay Bailey, but must be five o'clock some-where," said Marcie, turning to the waitress. "Stoli martini, neat, please. How about you?"

"Same," Hutchison said. "I'll be a little naughty with you, Marcie. Us old gals have earned it. And a dozen Oysters Driskill, please."

"Naughty indeed, senator," Marcie said.

The conversation darted in an out of substance—political dealings in Washington, the oil business, family, and Hutchison's potential run for governor—for the better part of two hours, both of them dancing around the primary reason for the meeting.

"Let's get down to it, Kay Bailey," Marcie said over coffee. "Fish or cut bait."

"Sure," the senator said, reaching into her purse for some papers. "I appreciate the thorough briefing you gave my chief of staff, and I'm happy to help someone who's been such an asset to us. And saving Ademar; that's big."

"Knew I could count on you, Kay Bailey," Marcie said.

"Same," Hutchison said, handing Marcie the paperwork she had processed for Charlie's and Amiir's visas. "And I can count on you."

"Naturally," Marcie replied, handing her an envelope with a generous check for Hutchison's political war chest, which the senator did not need to open to know that it would suffice.

"It's always a pleasure, Marcie," she said. "Please keep me posted on how it all goes. Hope I don't read about it in the newspaper."

"From your mouth to God's ear," Marcie said.

They were predators and meat-eaters, all of them—Ademar and Stone by training; Jack and Ali by nature. And like predators, they tensed for the inevitable as they gathered outside the barbed-wire fence on the perimeter of Hagadera just after dark. Ademar and Stone wore camo and black skullcaps with 30.30s slung over their shoulders and commando knives on their hips. Jack had his .45-70 at the ready, and Ali's knuckle duster was strapped to his ankle. They both wore *the uniform*—jeans, cowboy boots, and the sweat-stained Marfa low-crowns he and Jack put on every day of their lives. The adrenaline of battle is one hundred proof, and the sweet, bitter taste for it endures. Some associate it with service, others with something more primitive and savage in their souls. The end result is usually the same.

Stone smelled it a thousand times, crouched in the dark, soldiers on the muscle for what was to come, like thoroughbreds in the starting gate milliseconds before the bell.

"Stop," Stone whispered just before Ali cut the barbed wire. "I know what you're feeling. It's in me too. But one gunshot and we're in it, probably done. If it comes to that, so be it. Couldn't ask for a better crew. We all know why we're here; not to fight. I don't know about you, but I don't need any more blood on my hands.

"Cut it, Ali," said Stone, motioning to the barbed-wire fence.

Ademar made sure Charlie and Natalie had a transmitter, and she signaled them to start the fire as they crept through the hole Ali cut in the barbed wire. The strategy worked like a charm. Kenyan soldiers and camp security streamed toward the blaze through the lanes between endless rows of combustible tents while Charlie and Natalie wiggled through them in the other direction like salmon fighting upstream. They reached the rescue party within a few minutes, and, although it had been more than two years, there was no hugging or any conversation between Charlie, Ademar, and Stone. That would come later, although Ademar smiled after Charlie whispered one word—"Ranger." Natalie had felt danger before, but she was a peacemaker, not a soldier, and had never tasted blood. The Georgia farm girl wasn't sure what she was feeling, not dissimilar from the anticipation before all the first-times in her life, and she liked it, particularly the notion of slipping one by the condescending, inefficient UN bureaucracy that warehoused these hundreds of thousands of refugees. Charlie smiled a little inside when he saw the 30.30s slung over Ademar's and Stone's shoulders. They reminded him of happier times hunting pigs with them from a Blackhawk, and desperate moments during the Battle of Mogadishu when he shot that Somali boy under the streetlamp with Stone's 30.30. He half expected his dark partner to emerge, to offer some cynical, soul-rattling words to shake his confidence, but the *other* remained silent. Despite their differences, Charlie Christmas and Sayiid Awale seemed to agree on the primacy of this mission, and on the bleak downside of failure.

"Here," said Charlie, pulling back the flap on the mosque tent where Amiir and a few dozen others gathered to worship with the militant Imam. Stone and Ademar stepped through first, Amiir smiling immediately from the front row at the sight of his beloved friends. Jack and Ali were next, two out-of-place old cowboys the likes of which nobody in that room had seen outside of an American Western.

"What's the meaning of this," the Imam shouted.

"This," growled Jack, shouldering the .45.70 and leveling it at the Imam. "The boy, Amiir, he's coming with us. Not a damn thing you can do about it."

"Come to me, Amiir," said Charlie, holding out his hand for the boy.

Amiir stood up and walked by the Imam to make his way toward Charlie, but the Imam grabbed him by the shoulder and pulled him close. Jack cocked his rifle as Stone and Ademar began to raise theirs.

"What do you cowboys think you're doing?" said the Imam, speaking as much to the marauders as to his congregation. "This is not bloody Texas. This is a religious service. Amiir belongs here with the observant.

"You and your country put us here. You and your country keep us here in this . . . this prison. You have made an enemy out of Islam. Allah, blessed be his name, has warned us of the Crusade against us, the Crusade that left all of us in these unholy cages to rot. Rise up! Rise up and fight them! Do not be afraid to die a martyr's death!"

The entire congregation stood as if on cue and turned menacingly toward Jack and the others. "Steady," Stone said to the others. "Wait for me; hold your fire."

Ali was a man of few words, but he knew that words from him at that moment were all that stood between them and a bloodbath. *"As-Salaam-Alaikum,"* he said.

"Wa-Alaikum-Salaam," the Imam replied.

"Not about us and you," Ali said. "It's about the boy, about one of you getting out of here to a place of freedom. Imam wants a war between us and you. He won't be doing the fighting and dying. You will. His words are not the will of the Prophet. We will leave here with the boy. I hope you will all leave here one day too, and find a safe place for your family. But if you follow him, the only place you'll end up is a grave."

The Imam sensed the congregation siding with Ali and drew Amiir even closer, removing a sharp four-inch needle that secured his Taqiyah and pushing it into Amiir's jugular sharply enough to elicit a whimper from the boy. Ali knew it was the moment of truth, turning away from the Imam to face Ademar and Charlie. *"Allahu Akbar,"* he whispered to them, and in one seamless motion yanked the knife from his ankle holster and wheeled around to throw it at the Imam.

"Shit," said Stone, curling his finger around the trigger and bracing for the gunplay that would inevitably follow.

Ali was fast, particularly at his age, but Ademar was faster, grabbing his arm at the wrist a split second before he released the knife.

"Wait," she said to Ali and, holding up her other hand, addressed the Imam. "Nobody has to die. Not you, not Amiir, none of us. Nobody."

Sometimes the knife that isn't thrown or the gun that isn't shot can change the course of history. Ademar's quick thinking and quicker hands bought her a moment to defuse the tension, to walk away without bloodshed and with Amiir.

"But you will die," she said to the Imam, "if you don't release Amiir. He is not yours."

"You are wrong, woman," the Imam said. "The Prophet Muhammad said, 'Each of you is responsible for his flock. The ruler is a shepherd and is responsible for his flock.' This is my flock; the boy is in it."

"Muhammad also said, 'A man is the shepherd of his family and is responsible for his flock,'" Ademar replied. "His father wants him to go."

"Do you not fear Allah?" the Imam questioned. "The Qur'an says, 'Whosoever obeys God and his messenger, fears

God, and keeps his duty are the successful ones.' God speaks through me. And he wants the boy to stay."

"The Prophet Muhammad said, 'Fear God and treat your children fairly,'" Ademar replied.

An old man in the front row shouted, "Let him go," and murmurs of assent rippled through the congregation. The Imam knew he was caught on the horns of a dilemma—accede to their demands and lose face or kill Amiir and trigger a firefight in which many would die, starting with him.

"Let the boy decide then," said the Imam, lowering the needle from his throat. "Just know, Amiir, that Allah wants you to stay. It is a sin to disobey."

Amiir brushed the Imam aside and walked back to Charlie. "My God doesn't kill children," he said.

"That was close," Stone said. "Nice work, Ademar. Let's get the fuck out of here."

"Not without Buck," Amiir said, "and the football you gave me."

"Really?" Jack said. "We've got plenty of dogs and footballs back home."

"Really," Ademar replied.

"Don't worry," Natalie said. "Amiir and I taught Buck a trick; watch."

They all stepped out of the tent, relieved to see that it was quiet with most of the people at the fire. "Go ahead, Amiir," Natalie said, and the boy gave two short, high-pitched whistles followed by one long one, like Awil had taught him. Within a few seconds, Buck, football in his mouth and tail wagging, loped down the pathway between the tents to them, dropped the ball, and jumped up to greet Amiir. "Good boy," he said. Dogs never forget smells; they simply catalogue them away for future reference. Buck's ears, the whole one and the one with the tip lopped off in the storm, perked up when he caught the scent of his two old friends, Ademar and Stone.

"I'll be damned," Stone said as Buck jumped up to greet him and Ademar. "Let's git while the gitting's good. Plenty of time for ear scratching on the plane."

The seven of them, and Buck, made their way through the camp and back to the airplane without a hitch. Unbeknownst to any of the others, Stone had kept one bottle of the Macallan single malt to celebrate a successful rescue or to drink themselves numb if they had failed. He placed five glasses on the table in the middle of the Gulfstream once they were safely in the air, each one with a single ice cube, and a few drops in Buck's bowl over a dog biscuit.

"A toast," Stone said. "To us. Just my kind of mission. Successful without firing a single shot."

"All that biblical talk back there reminded me that this is the Sabbath. Not supposed to do much, certainly not raid a refugee camp. But there is a loophole in the Torah called *Pikuach nefesh*. Means Jews have a duty to save a life even if they break another rule to do it."

"Here's to both our faiths," said Stone, raising his glass and downing the shot of Macallan in one swig.

"I don't have the words to thank all of you," Charlie said. "For giving us a life."

"Nonsense," Jack said. "You saved Ademar's life. You deserve better than that back there. My wife got visas for you, and the two of you are welcome on the farm as long as you want. You too, Natalie."

"Is there a real football field in Dell City?" asked Amiir, rolling the ball back and forth to Buck.

"You bet," Jack answered.

It didn't take long for them to polish off the bottle of scotch, and all of them except for Charlie fell into a deep sleep over the Atlantic. He reflected on what was behind him—the war in his homeland, the boy under the streetlamp he had killed, the tragic trek into Kenya, the death of Ebla and Awil, the rescue from Hagadera—and the unknown path in front of them. Memories of Alaska and Utah were all Charlie really knew of America. Fond memories, he thought, touching the tiny replica of a willow ptarmigan on his necklace and smiling at the thought of Hanna and Pia. But this wasn't a summer trip; it was forever. A profound sense of loneliness settled on him as the plane rocketed through the inky darkness at almost six hundred miles an hour and forty thousand feet. Charlie was in limbo—a stateless, penniless widower with a young son and no roadmap for the future. But his dark shadow, Sayiid Awale, was never far away, and this night was no different.

"Don't be too proud of yourself," Charlie's other hissed in his ear. "The Americans won't be waiting with open arms for a Black African with no money and no job, much less his son. You've traded freedom in Somalia for slavery in America. Sound familiar?"

CHAPTER 16

The only airplanes young Amiir knew were the instruments of war that disgorged foreign troops at the Mogadishu airport or snatched lives out of thin air from a distance with missiles and guns that fired chunks of steel the size of branding irons. To him, being inside the Cessna Citation was as if he had landed on another planet—a planet of whispers with heated leather seats, plush carpet, a movie screen, a soda fountain with all the Coke or root beer he could drink, and a refrigerator stocked with smoked fish, cold cuts, and tapioca. Amiir had never eaten tapioca, couldn't even pronounce it, but the creamy, sweet texture of the tiny cassava pearls tasted like heaven. From that point forward, forever, he associated them with his freedom, and with the United States. He spent hours slurping up bowls of tapioca and staring out the window at the world so far below him, so benign and pleasant after the savagery and chaos of what he left behind in East Africa. It was as if his entire existence had slowed down so that he could somehow catch up with himself, at least for a few hours wrapped in a cocoon of luxury. Amiir saw and reacted to the world as a man, a man who had killed, seen death, and plumbed the depths of evil. But he was still a boy, and so many times on the plane he reached out excitedly to the empty seat next to him where Ebla should be to point out a cloud, a mountain, or some other feature far below. Instead of Ebla there was Buck, Charlie, Ademar, or Stone. And if he couldn't have Ebla, they were enough.

Ademar scratched Buck under his chin, gently nudged the dog out of the seat next to Amiir, and sat down beside him as the Cessna flew over the skyscrapers of El Paso on the approach to the remote airstrip at the Jeff Ranch.

"Texas," said Ademar, pointing out the Rio Grande River that ran through the heart of El Paso and Juarez. "Mexico. A lot of our nation, and almost half of Texas, are Hispanic. They all came here like you, refugees, immigrants. Remember the story about my ancestors—came to Texas from Syria with those camels? America is a nation of us. You and your father are welcome here. Don't let anyone tell you otherwise."

Amiir listened intently as he stared out the window at the sun setting on the high desert, the final particles of light scattering across mesas and arroyos in shafts of vivid orange, yellow, violet, and blue as it surrendered to the horizon. There was so much he felt, so much he wanted to say, but Amiir was too young to have found the relationship between complex emotion and words, and could not articulate what was in his heart.

A simple "Thank you, Ademar" was all he could manage.

The pilot made the final approach to the Jeff Ranch in darkness, with the illuminated runway stretching into the high desert like quicksilver. The matriarchs, Marcelina Laws and Sana Zarkan, stood shoulder to shoulder by the last step of the jet ladder as the triumphant rescue party emerged from the Cessna. All twelve members of the two clans stood just behind them, holding their hats down in a stiff wind. They looked every inch like the returning warriors—Jack, Ali, Ademar, and Stone, unchanged, unwashed, and toting their weapons—and the two women embraced each of them with the relief of a mother whose child has survived the crucible.

"You're a sight for sore eyes, Jack Laws," Marcie said. "Aren't you and Ali rather long in the tooth for these escapades?"

"Maybe," Jack replied.

"Definitely," said Ali, one arm around Sana to support his arthritic left knee.

"Mom, Marcie, this is Charlie Christmas and his son, Amiir, " Ademar said. "And this is Natalie Bell."

Marcie and Sana had raised their share of boys, and they recognized when one needed a mother's hug. Marci bent over a little so her eyes were at the same level as Amiir's, shook his hand, and wrapped him in her arms.

"So pleased to meet you, Amiir," she said. "We've heard so much about you and your father."

"*As-Salaam-Alaikum*," said Sana, hugging the boy as if he were her own and placing on his head a straw cowboy hat just like the one Ademar always wore. "Welcome to Texas."

"Sayiid . . . sorry, Charlie Christmas," Charlie said, stumbling awkwardly over his identity and shaking hands with the two women. "Thank you."

"No, Mr. Christmas," Sana said. "We're the ones who should be grateful—saving my great-granddaughter's life from that pirate."

"You're welcome to stay with us as long as you want," said Marcie, handing him a cowboy hat. "And you'll need this if you're looking for work here on the farm."

Charlie and Amiir would have those hats the rest of their lives.

"This is Natalie Bell," said Amiir, reaching back to pull Natalie next to him. "My friend."

"Couldn't have done this without her," Stone said.

"We're grateful, Natalie," Marcie said. "That offer extends to you as well.

"Let's head back to Dell City. We've got some celebrating to plan."

Amiir awoke at dawn the next morning, fed Buck, grabbed his football, and headed downstairs, where Ademar; her brother T2; and her fiancé, Deuce, were drinking coffee at the big table in the Laws' kitchen. Amiir had one thing in mind, and one thing only. He dreamed about it the night before, and so many other nights the past two years as he lay awake in Hagadera imagining a day when that dream might come true.

"About those goal posts, Ademar," said Amiir, tossing the football from one hand to the other. "Remember?"

"Oh yeah," she replied with a smile. "I figured that one would come early. Eat some of these cheese grits and *huevos* before we go."

"*Huevos?*" Amiir asked.

"Eggs," said Ademar, ladling a gooey blob of steaming cheese grits and scrambled eggs on a brown clay plate for Amiir. "Spanish."

Dell city is a small town of about five hundred people that doesn't take up much more than four square blocks, and a big chunk is composed of a school that serves all twelve grades, the Two T's Grocery, Rosita's Café, Perry Hardware, and Donnie Ziler's Cut and Curl Beauty Shop. Ademar, Amiir, Stone, T2, and Deuce drove to the school from the family compound outside of town in less than ten minutes, pulling around back to the football field where Coach Billy Tarnowski, Coach T, fiddled with a broken sprinkler. Amiir loved *The Wizard of Oz*, and seeing a real football field for the first time reminded him how Dorothy felt when the yellow brick road finally ended at the Emerald City. No matter where he found himself in the future, Amiir would wish he could tap his heels together three times and magically return to the Dell City football field. Dorothy's magical incantation from the movie that *there's no place like home* played over and over in his mind during those brief seconds before they climbed out of the pickup.

"Ademar, Deuce, T2," Coach T said to his former play-
ers. "And this must be Amiir, the legendary soccer-style
Somali kicker. Already have a nickname for him, the *Somali
Sidewinder.*"

"Perfect," Stone said. "Ademar and I taught him everything he knows."

"Let's see what you got, Amiir," Coach T said.

"Yes, sir!" said Amiir, sprinting with Buck to the fifteen-yard line and handing the kicking tee to Ademar. "You
mind holding?"

Amiir drilled the goal posts with four consecutive kicks,
after which Buck dutifully retrieved the ball, and he split the
uprights from the twenty and twenty-five. But he was wearing
worn-out Converse high-tops, and Coach T could tell his toes
were hurting.

"He's got game," Coach T said. "But he needs something
besides those sneakers if he intends to be a real football player.
Give me a minute."

Coach T returned from the equipment shed a few minutes later with a pair of brand-new Nike Sharks. "Try these,"
he said. Amiir slipped them on and laced them up, thinking
to himself that these shoes really would bring him back to the
Dell City football field if he tapped them together three times
like Dorothy in *The Wizard of Oz.*

"They fit perfect; thank you," Amiir said, and started
to unlace the cleats so he wouldn't scuff them. "But I can't
afford them."

"What are you talking about, son?" Coach T said. "That's
my gift to you. I hope you'll be kicking for me, like Ademar.
But even if you're not, you think about ol' Coach T every time
you drill one."

Amiir spent most of the next few days helping out around
the farm, riding horses, plinking rattlesnakes or jackrabbits with
Jack's .22 pistol, and of course, kicking field goals and learning

the fine points of football with Stone or one of the others. As delighted as he was with life on the farm, Amiir was equally disturbed by the time he spent with Ademar's twin brother, Anil. The bitter, radicalized message of hate from the Imam in Hagadera seemed as far away from him as Kenya is from Texas. But Osama bin Laden had created a global franchise in Al-Qa'ida, and its tentacles of violent extremism stretched as far as West Texas, due in part to how the Web enabled recruiting efforts. Al-Qa'ida graduated to the big leagues of terrorism in 1998 with its near-simultaneous bombings of US Embassies in Kenya and Tanzania, which killed 224 people. In many ways, their virtual campaign exceeded the deadly effectiveness of their actual efforts, and recruiters navigated the cloaked chat rooms of multiplayer video games to ferret out potential Muslim youth they could procure for their cause. Anil was a classic case—undersized, bullied, ostracized, and disabled as the result of a farm accident that took his right hand. He was the antithesis of his beloved twin sister, Ademar—heralded athlete, champion barrel racer, West Point graduate, and war hero. Although his family had deep concerns about Anil and the hours he spent alone in his darkened bedroom illuminated by the fluorescent glow of a MacBook Pro, they had no idea how deep he had been drawn into the world of violent extremism. Anil was a valuable asset in the heart of America to Al-Qa'ida, and his mastery of digital tools helped them immeasurably in producing content suitable for reaching typical young American Muslims. Amiir was young chronologically, but his journey in life had instilled a hard maturity far beyond his years. Anil recognized a good target when he saw one.

"Take a look at this," said Anil, displaying a video from the popular porn site Ass Parade. "Look at the tits on that blonde."

"What!" said Amiir, blushing at the only bosoms he had ever seen that did not belong to a family member nursing a baby, but clearly not entirely immune to the titillation.

"These American chicks are trash," Anil said. "Good for only two things—fucking and killing."

"Killing?" questioned Amiir, imagining what Natalie might look like nude, and how absurd it was to even think about murdering her.

"Look, man, America may seem like paradise to you, especially after Somalia," Anil said. "But Americans treat Muslims the same way here as they do there. They look at you and see a nigger, a nigger with a funny accent."

Amiir didn't have the words to dispute any of it, backing out of the room deeply conflicted and full of questions. But he could not erase the memory of the naked blonde women, or the notion that Ebla's death might have been avoided if the Americans had not invaded Somalia.

Several hundred thousand Somali refugees had settled throughout the United States since the war, with the majority in Minnesota, Washington State, Ohio, and Maine. More than fifty thousand of them put down roots in Minnesota, building successful careers in every sector of society. They have served in the state and federal legislature, sat on city councils, run nonprofits, headed successful businesses, and managed meatpacking plants. Natalie's fiancé, Sloan Allen, and she planned to settle in St. Cloud, where she intended to establish a nonprofit focusing on social justice and community resiliency. She had connected Charlie with several Somali leaders in Minneapolis, and, although the winters would take some getting used to, he leaned toward relocating there. Such decisions could wait, at least until Charlie, Amiir, and Stone had the full dose of Texas hospitality they deserved.

Lou Lambert and his sister, Liz, were as typical of West Texas royalty as West Texas is atypical of the other forty-nine states. The notion of royalty is the embodiment of anathema in Texas, which fought and bled for independence from three foreign sovereigns over two hundred years. But if there were such a thing as Texas royalty, Lou and Liz would be it. Their families—the Lamberts and the McKnights—had no overt political aspirations or the casual disregard for rules the rest of us have to follow, like the Kennedys of Massachusetts. They saw all people as their equals and treated everyone, from their housekeeper to their foreman, with noblesse oblige. It may have been this sense of serving others that drove their success in the hospitality industry. Fueled in part by the conquests of their forefathers in oil and ranching, Liz made her name developing elegant, funky hotels like the San Jose in Austin and the lux-bohemian trailer park El Cosmico in Marfa. And Lou, a master chef trained in the classic tradition of the Culinary Institute and under Wolfgang Puck at Postrio in San Francisco, built a Texas food empire one smoked brisket at a time. Naturally, Lou could not have been happier to oblige when Marcelina Laws asked if he might consider a full-on Texas barbacoa feast to welcome Charlie and his son to the United States.

No real Texas hoedown is complete without music, and Eula was all over it with the unique blend of East she had learned studying the sitar in India after her rape, and West that was her birthright. The other three women who helped her found the hugely successful Karma Cowgirls were not there, but Eula preferred the whole spotlight to herself anyway. The lonesome ballad of Jerry Jeff Walker's time in the UK, "London Homesick Blues," spun out of her sitar, and pretty much everyone around Lou's smoke pit that evening, particularly Charlie Christmas, could relate to Jerry Jeff's lamentations on bad luck, loneliness, poverty, and homelessness.

For convenience, cooks rarely prepare barbacoa the traditional Mexican way—brisket and beef cheek wrapped in banana leaves and wet burlap buried in a pit with charcoal and mesquite so its smoked and steamed at the same time over the ten or so hours it takes to render the crown jewel of barbecue. They use industrial smokers and ovens most of the time, but Lou wasn't cutting any corners for the new Americans. Charlie had no idea what to expect when Lou interred that morning a bundle of beef about the size and shape of a body, but he got religion with the first whiff of what rose out of the smoke that night like a gastronomic deity. They'd all been kicking around the farm most of the day, riding horses, swapping outlandish stories, or listening to Eula break their hearts with every strum of the sitar, and by dinnertime most of them were a few Lone Stars past their cruising speed. Lou didn't want any of them messing with the meat or with the razor-sharp tools he used to carve it, although he liked nothing more than baptizing new worshipers into his church of barbecue. But he invited Amiir, who was too young for alcohol, to the carving block for a short lesson in cutting and pulling a brisket.

"The deckle," said Lou, holding up what most aficionados considered the diamond cut of beef that emerges from the black crust of a smoked brisket. "This here's the rib and the fat cap. After a day underground at 230 degrees, the fat and connective tissue melt into the meat." Lou pulled off a small piece of beef, wrapped it in a warm flour tortilla topped with green chili salsa, and handed it to Amiir. "Don't get much better than this, Amiir," Lou said.

"Looks like he died and gone to heaven," said Stone, laughing at the look of pure ecstasy on Amiir's face as he ate it.

"Texas is all about dying and going to heaven," said Lou, raising his Lone Star longneck for a toast.

PART
TWO

CHAPTER 1

Stone did most of the driving as they snaked their way across the Great Plains from West Texas to Minnesota, although he'd occasionally let Amiir take the wheel on barren stretches of highways so long and so desolate that Hank Williams must have traversed them as he conjured the *midnight trains* and the *empty silence of shooting stars* that inspired his paean to melancholy, "I'm So Lonesome I Could Cry." There was plenty of room in Ademar's white Chevrolet Silverado to accommodate the four of them on the 1,400-mile journey. But Amiir, Buck by his side with the one intact ear sideways in the wind, would occasionally lay in the pickup bed, lost for hours imagining animal shapes in the towering cumulus clouds floating overhead like cotton candy.

They were all inside the truck the first time Charlie Christmas and his son witnessed a murmuration. They had just crossed through the Llano Estacado in northwest Texas, where the half-breed Comanche Chief Quanah Parker led the last pocket of free Indians until the late 1870s, and had passed through that narrow slice of western Oklahoma just north of the border. The late spring sun was melting into the high desert behind a shimmering palette of primary colors.

Jackrabbits and coyotes seemed to have forged a conditional truce to drink from puddles of cool water after a brief popup thunderstorm, and an occasional pronghorn antelope or javelina darted across the plains. In the distance, a black cloud flowed toward them, folding on itself, oscillating and billowing like a bedsheet tumbling from a clothesline in a stiff wind. The four of them were hypnotized by the shape-shifting cloud, and, as it neared, they could see clearly that it was thousands of starlings somehow bound together by a silent, ethereal rhythm. Two peregrine falcons circled menacingly overhead, diving for prey into the flock of starlings, which magically expanded, contracted, or opened to avoid the predators' talons.

"What's that?" asked Amiir.

"A flock of starlings," Ademar replied. "It's called a murmuration: a flight path only they know that helps protect them from predators like those two falcons."

"Like swarming?" Amiir asked.

"Not exactly," Ademar replied. "Sort of the opposite. They're not attacking, more like escaping."

"Defense," Stone chimed in, citing a sports metaphor he thought Amiir might more easily understand. "Not offense."

"There's a lesson there to remember," Ademar said. "Safety in numbers, particularly for migrants to a new country—like my people to Texas, Stone's to Israel, or you to Minnesota. Remember when you asked me *why Minnesota*, and I said you'll see? Well, that's why. It's safer than traveling alone."

"Until it's not," said Stone, just as one of the falcons plucked a starling from the flock, driving it to the ground and tearing away feathers, bone, and flesh. "That's the other side of the coin. Ademar's right about safety in numbers, but numbers make you easier to find. Always watch your back, particularly when someone tells you they've got it."

Charlie remained silent, even though he had seen a breed

of starlings, known as glossy starlings in East Africa because of their iridescent plumage, murmurate when he was a boy. "What are you thinking, Dad?" Amiir asked.

"Beautiful and tragic, like so much of life," Charlie replied. "They come together by the thousands in a masterpiece of nature, instinctively risk their lives knowing a few will die. It is a breathtaking act of communal loyalty. We could learn a lot from the natural world, but we don't. In the world of people, mostly, a community picks a scapegoat and pushes them to the predator in hopes he will stop at one victim. Doesn't work that way in Somalia, and, from what I can tell, not in America either. That's the lesson of the murmuration to me, Amiir. The universal lesson."

Charlie wrapped his arm around Amiir, and they all sat in silence for many miles. He hadn't meant to be such a downer on an otherwise upbeat day, and Charlie perked them all up when they passed a sign for a Waffle House, an iconic American institution he had heard several soldiers mention wistfully over a plate of powdered eggs at the mess hall in Mogadishu. "Anybody hungry?" he said.

The concept of a waffle fascinated Charlie and Amiir almost as much as an entire house constructed of the doughy breakfast confection, and the last-chance Waffle House on their trip was thirty miles west of Kansas City in Shawnee. Nothing is more American than a Waffle House, 2,100 of them spread across twenty-five states, nearly identical one-story diners with yellow roofs, black lettering, and red awnings. And you can be sure that each one will have a cook cracking eggs and flipping hotcakes in front of a sizzling griddle, two haggard but solicitous servers slinging plates to diners seated in an L-shaped array of booths, a half-dozen stainless-steel swivel stools with red padded seats, and the ubiquitous Wells WB-2E double waffle maker. To really understand what's going on in the United States, forget the politicians, the public opinion research polls, and the talking heads on Fox, MSNBC, or CNN, and simply spend an hour at a Waffle House in rural America.

"Time for a lesson in Cap'n Pro's waffleology," Stone said as a perky Black waitress in a blue shirt and dark smock placed four menus on the table.

"I'm Birdie," she said. "Where y'all from?"

"All over, ma'am," Ademar said. "Mainly Texas."

"I'm from Somalia," young Amiir chimed in.

"Switzerland?" said Birdie, thinking she might have misunderstood the boy.

"No, Somalia," he said

"Right," she said. "Missouri?"

Ademar and Stone had a sixth sense for trouble, and they sat as far away as they could from two middle-aged white men who looked as if they might have played defensive end or linebacker on a college football team one hundred pounds or so thinner and twenty years back in their rear-view mirrors. But they sat close enough for the two men to overhear the conversation.

"Somalia, Birdie," said the man at the next booth who was wearing a baseball cap adorned with a Red Man chewing tobacco logo. "That's in Africa, where all of y'all come from."

"And could go back to as far as I'm concerned," said his companion, who didn't have a baseball cap but was in the process of jamming a plug of Red Man into his left cheek. "More illegals coming in for our jobs."

"I'll order for us," said Stone, ignoring their comments. "The works for everybody—eggs over easy, crispy bacon, waffles and cheesy hashbrowns on the side. And a chocolate milkshake for my young friend."

"A chocolate milkshake for the little chocolate boy," the man in the baseball cap said, emphasis on *boy*.

"You got it," Birdie said, leaning close to them and whispering so only they could hear. "Ignore those ol' boys. They got something up their asses they can't push out."

The rest of breakfast went without incident, and Amiir finished off the scraps from each of their plates as if it was his last meal, except for a slice of bacon he took out to Buck, napping in the back of the truck. Charlie went to the men's room as Stone and Ademar tended to the bill. The man with the cap tripped him on his way back, and Charlie stumbled into a waitress carrying three bowls of steaming grits, which splattered all over the two strangers.

"God damn, Birdie!" the one in the baseball cap yelled.

"So sorry," she said, trying to wipe the grits off but only spreading the grease on their white T-shirts.

The man with the cheek full of Red Man grabbed her hand and started to force it into his jeans and down his crotch. "How about a hand job, Birdie, as long as that hand of yours is all lubed up." Ademar took three steps from the cash register to their table, grabbed his hand in the thumb lock she learned at West Point, and twisted it until he squealed. "Uncle!" he screamed.

"Damn, you got some spunk," he said, shaking his hand. "Where you from, little lady? You got some color to you."

"Texas, asshole," Ademar said. "Unless you want some more, we'll be on our way."

"Nice work, Ranger," Charlie said to her as they walked to the truck.

The two men followed them out to the parking lot, itching for a fight, but Stone stepped in front of them before they reached the truck.

"Wait a second, fellas," he said. "I got a joke for you."

"What the fuck you talking about?" said the one with a tobacco plug the size of a chestnut in his cheek.

"Two Africans, a Muslim, and a Jew walk into a Waffle House," Stone said.

"Jewboy," Red Man said. "I knew you a Jew."

"Pay attention," said Stone, slapping him on the cheek hard enough that a few drops of brown spit dribbled down his chin. "Two Africans, a Muslim, and a Jew walk into a Waffle House. What did they forget?"

"Fuck you," he said, reaching into his pocket and flicking his wrist to open a Hawkbill knife with a razor-sharp crescent-shaped four-inch blade. "This here's what I gut deer with, but today I might just gut me a Jewboy, a dune coon, and a couple of African niggers."

Amiir noticed that 666, the sign of the Antichrist, was tattooed down the middle finger of his right hand, and it took him back to Kenya, to the dead pirate with the same ink under his eye, and to his mother's death.

"You didn't answer the riddle," said Stone, ignoring the threat. "They forgot the dog."

"The dog?" he said.

"Yeah, the dog," Stone said, and shouted, "Buck, green light!"

Like an apparition, Buck rose from the back of the truck. Before the two men could lift their eyes, 110 pounds of snarling, snapping combat-trained canine was on them, clamping down hard on the wrist of the man with the knife and shaking it until they all heard the sharp snap of a broken bone.

Buck released the man's wrist, raised his leg to piss on the other one, and jumped nonchalantly back into the truck like a dog that's returning home from a brisk walk in the park.

"You can't forget the dog," Stone said to the two men. "Never forget the dog."

Stone, Ademar, Charlie, and Amiir drove off before the law arrived, and left the two men in the parking lot, steaming with anger, impotence, and revenge. "You ain't seen the last of us," the one with the cap yelled through a cloud of dust. "Not by a long shot."

Which turned out to be true, appropriately enough, in the Badlands of South Dakota.

CHAPTER 2

Ademar's great-grandmother, Sana Zarkan, had given Amiir a laptop and a smart phone as a going away gift, like Marcie Laws had done so many years ago with Anil, and as an easy way for him to stay in touch. Technology tends to take a person down the path of least resistance toward their basest instincts, as it had sucked Anil into a portal leading to the world of violent radicalism. Amiir felt burned by the introduction Anil had given him to radicalism and its kindred spirit, pornography, and jihad or naked blondes on the Web were the last thing on his mind as they took a left on Interstate 90 at Sioux Falls, South Dakota. Charlie had spent a few days hiking the slot canyons of the Badlands on his way to Alaska more than thirty years ago, and he wanted to share that with his son since it was not far off their path to Minnesota. Ademar and Stone had never been there either, and they were game for a side trip into the legendary territory of the Sioux Indians, who named the parched, rugged territory *mako sica*, or Badlands. Amiir surfed the Web for hours researching the region during the long drive from Kansas to the Black Hills in South Dakota, and he made them stop at the Adams Museum in Deadwood to see grainy black-and-white daguerreotypes of Wild Bill Hickok and Calamity Jane, who reminded him of Ademar. But nothing could have prepared them for the paleontological grandeur of the one-hundred-mile Wall that stretches from the town of Scenic on the western edge of the national park to the town of Kadoka on the eastern boundary. Or for the brothers who had tracked them like rabid bloodhounds from the Waffle House in Shawnee.

The Turner brothers had first names, but they went by Burl and Goose for most of their lives, Burl with the Red Man cap and Goose with the broken wrist. They seemed like caricatures of ignorant country rednecks to Ademar, a true daughter of rural America who knew that growing up in small-town America had nothing to do with intelligence, grace, sophistication, or fate. Burl and Goose were far from stupid, but they had been radicalized and altered by abusive parents, perceived injustices, substance abuse, and poverty, just like thousands of other violent extremists in places like Somalia, Syria, Belgium, or Charleston. The ideologies run the gamut, from Islam to white supremacy, but in the final analysis, those who fall prey to it are victims of a few powerful megalomaniacs running global criminal enterprises. It's the same bullshit promise of epiphany and eternal glory preached by the Yemeni-American Imam Anwar al-Awlaki on bootleg videos distributed in the chatrooms of video games or hung on virtual chalkboards in the Dark Web by white supremacists like Richard Spencer. After their humiliation at the Waffle House, Burl and Goose launched their own personal jihad.

It wasn't rocket science to track down their prey. Ademar had paid for breakfast with a credit card, and the brothers managed to steal the receipt from the restaurant in all the mayhem after the dustup in the parking lot. Less than an hour on social media yielded them a photograph of Ademar's truck that revealed her license plate, and a few snippets of conversation they overheard in the restaurant about where they might be headed led the brothers a few days later to Ademar's truck in a parking lot at Badlands National Park, where the four of them had gone for a hike in a slot canyon. Goose dispensed with the Hawkbill blade in favor of the Aero Precision AR-15 assault rifle with the legal extended ammunition clip that he purchased for $575 at a gun show in Nebraska, where the dealer required no more than a valid driver's license. Burl had a concealed carry permit, despite a criminal record, and slid his Beretta 9 mm semiautomatic pistol into the Western-style holster embossed with a Confederate flag.

"Lock and load, brother," Goose said to his younger sibling as they started down the trail into the slot canyon, mimicking Tom Berenger's call to the troops in his favorite movie, the 1980s Vietnam classic, Platoon.

"Teach those assholes a thing or two," Burl replied, running a hand through his greasy hair and sliding the Red Man cap over it.

The sky was overcast as Ademar, Stone, Charlie, and Amiir started down the trail into the slot canyon, confident they'd be out before the thunderstorm forecast for later in the day. The parking lot was empty, except for a broken-down pickup truck and a few Indians drinking coffee in the bed. "We better lock the car," said Amiir, who's only experience with Indians came from old westerns in which a brave cowboy rescued a woman and her children from a howling, blood-thirsty pack of savage warriors.

"Of course we'll lock the car," Stone said, "but not from them. Some of the bravest, most loyal men I ever served with were Indians. They stick to their tribe, whether it's a group of Indians or their platoon. Remember what your dad said about those starlings. The Indians are close to nature. They understand something most of us don't. You can do a lot worse than having one of them on your side in a jam."

Slot canyons can be a deathtrap, with steep walls that obscure any sudden changes in weather and narrow passages that transform dusty trails into raging rivers within minutes during fast-moving storms. The Park Service forbade dogs from the fragile canyon ecosystems, and Buck was none too happy at being left behind in the bed of the truck with no more than a rawhide chew bone and a musty old serape to keep him company. But he was nothing if not obedient, and he stayed put with his chin resting disconsolately on the bone in his best effort at laying a canine guilt trip on his companions. Buck's mix of breeds render an intensely empathetic, protective dog, and his training had honed those characteristics to a sharp edge. Danger has many smells, and a dog like Buck never forgets. Buck lifted his head when Goose and Burl walked by the truck, and he peeked over the side, careful not to alert the two brothers. The dog whined and fidgeted a bit once they were out of earshot but, like a good boy, remained in the truck for the time being. He was confident enough in that psychic connection dogs have with their masters that he'd know if there was trouble.

A few raindrops drifted into the bottom of the slot canyon on the return trip from the hike, but Ademar and the crew had no choice at that point but to keep moving and hope for the best. "Keep an eye out for a little stream of water on the trail," Stone said. "Means trouble; means water is building at the other end of the canyon. Could mean we need to start climbing."

They couldn't have known that was the least of their troubles, until they came around a narrow bend thirty minutes later and ran straight into Goose and Burl, who had been lying in ambush drinking airline bottles of Wild Turkey.

"Well, well, well," said Goose, "looky what we have here."

"Genius, bro," Burl answered. "A little dark meat for lunch."

Despite their battle-hardened sixth sense for danger, Ademar and Stone had been caught off-guard, and they didn't have too many options at that point, short of divine intervention. Charlie pushed Amiir behind him with one hand and tapped his empty pants pocket where the knife he left in the glove compartment of the truck should have been.

"So much to do," Goose said. "So little time."

"Not so tough now, little missy," said Burl, putting his face so close to Ademar's that she could smell the sweet stench of chewing tobacco. "Might have to get my dick wet with this one."

A few benign drops of rain had turned into a cloudburst, and the canyon was nearly dark except for a periodic flash of lightning that illuminated the brother's faces and reminded Amiir of the fake vampires and werewolves that jumped out of the shadows at the House of Horrors exhibit in Mogadishu. But the darkness and the storm had taken the edge off the brother's tactical advantage, much more than they realized after four miniature bottles each of one-hundred-proof whiskey. Ademar and Stone felt the increased water flow at their feet and knew that within minutes a churning river of mud and boulders could come crashing around the corner.

"Remember Awil," said Stone, hoping his companions would make the connection between the river in Somalia and the one that was closing in on them at the bottom of the canyon. Ademar thought she heard what sounded like rushing water, but she and the other three knew they needed to buy some time. Charlie understood and moved closer to Amiir so he could grab him once the torrent burst through the narrow passage.

"Lady or the tiger?" Stone said.

"Another riddle, Jewboy?" Goose said.

"An old parable about a man who has a choice," he replied. "He had to choose which door to open. Behind one was a beautiful lady; behind the other a deadly tiger. Salvation or death; your choice."

"Mighty bold talk for a dead man walking," Goose said.

"The water's coming up," said Burl, who could barely keep his head up dogpaddling at their local swimming hole, much less the torrent churning through the slot canyon behind them.

"Lady or the tiger, asshole," said Stone, who seemed to know something the rest of his crew did not.

"Forget that shit," said Goose, shouldering the AR-15 and pointing it at Stone's face. "How about lady or a bullet in the head?"

Stone laughed and looked at the ground, then up to the rim of the canyon at least fifteen feet overhead. "Guess it'll be the tiger, then," he said. "Green light!"

On command without a thought for his own safety, Buck launched himself from the rim like a feral missile square at Goose, just as a wall of water burst around the corner. "Climb!" shouted Ademar, pushing Charlie and Amiir to one side of the canyon as Buck went to work on the two brothers. Then something happened that may well have been divine intervention—three ropes dropped magically from the canyon edge. Charlie, with Amiir clinging to his back, Stone, and Ademar saved any questions for later and started climbing. The bottom of the canyon was too dark to see what was happening, until a flash of electric blue from a single bolt of lightning cracked overhead and illuminated the struggle below them.

"Nooooo!" shouted Amiir, turning around to see the two brothers helplessly washed down the canyon as Buck barked, ripped at their faces, and pushed them underwater with his paws. Buck took one mournful look back, locking eyes for a brief, final moment with Amiir, then he was gone.

The climb was difficult, but not as difficult as it would have been without the ropes, and all four made it to the top. None of them had any idea what awaited as they crested the edge, but the last thing they expected to see were the four Lakota Sioux tribesmen from the nearby Pine Ridge Reservation steadying the ropes around a rock. Another moment of biblical proportion for Stone, standing on the edge of a South Dakota canyon with Ademar, Charlie, Amiir, and four mysterious Indians in a driving rainstorm amid bolts of ground lightning and cannons of thunder.

"Close call," said the apparent leader of the group. "Those other two are finished, and the hound too, I'm afraid. I know a military dog when I see one. Figured something was wrong, and we followed him. You owe the dog your lives."

"More times than you can imagine," Ademar said.

"Thank you," said Amiir, turning toward the leader, then to Stone. "You were right."

CHAPTER 3

Almost thirty thousand Native Americans live on Pine Ridge, the largest reservation in the United States, roughly the size of Rhode Island and Delaware combined. Home to the Lakota Sioux, Pine Ridge, as much or more than any other chapter in American history, epitomizes injustice toward Native Americans dating back to the 1800s, when they were deemed wards of the nation and forced to live on reservations like refugees in their own country. They are some of the poorest, sickest, and least educated people in the nation, and women are two and a half times more likely to be raped than women in any other American minority community. Reservations are like petri dishes for violent extremism, and two of the most deadly, radicalizing incidents involving Native Americans took place almost one hundred years apart on Pine Ridge at Wounded Knee Creek. A failed attempt to disarm a Lakota Sioux encampment there in 1890 led to the US Seventh Cavalry opening fire with four Hotchkiss revolving cannons and killing nearly three hundred men, women, and children. Several dozen troopers were killed or wounded, most by friendly fire from their own cannons, which shoot 37 mm rounds sixty-eight times per minute. And in the early

1970s, Wounded Knee was a flashpoint for deadly violence between the American Indian Movement, a grassroots organization founded to defend Native American rights, and law enforcement officials. Even though Wounded Knee has been designated a National Historic Landmark, it is shamefully barely a footnote in the education of most Americans.

White Eagle, Wambleeska in the Lakota native tongue, was an elder of the tribe and led the rescue that snatched Charlie, Amiir, Ademar, and Stone from the jaws of death in the flooded slot canyon. He invited them to spend a few days on the reservation to regroup and to recover from the incident, a welcome respite, particularly for Amiir after the loss of Buck. While some of the marginally prosperous Lakota live in relatively modern prefabricated houses on subdivisions like Thunder Valley, most reside in old mobile homes or ramshackle houses that barely insulate them from South Dakota's harsh weather. This was a special time of year for the Lakota, and hundreds of them, including White Eagle and his wife, Shappa, or Red Thunder, camped for a few weeks near Wounded Knee Creek for their summer Sun Dance.

"We call it the *Wiwanki Wachipi*," White Eagle told them as they ate breakfast a few mornings later on a bluff overlooking preparations for the sacred ritual. "It cleanses us, renews us, reconnects us with nature and ourselves.

"Life has been unjust to us, as it could have been for you a few days ago. The Sun Dance restores balances," he said, extending both arms like the scales that symbolize justice. "As refugees and minorities, I'm sure you know injustice."

"I'd never been called a nigger until I came to the United States," Charlie said. "And they tried to kill us because of it."

"We are the original niggers," said White Eagle's wife, Red Thunder.

"Speaking of justice," Ademar said, "shouldn't we tell the police about the slot canyon incident?"

"No," White Eagle said. "We'll end up in jail, or worse. There's no justice for Indians or Blacks."

Charlie's inner demon, Sayiid Awale, ridiculed him for hours the past few nights in dreams or hallucinations that induced sweats, sleepwalking, and agonized wails that awakened his companions and White Eagle. The messages from his nemesis were variations on familiar themes, but they struck deep into a wounded heart that had lost so much to gain so little. He felt ripped apart inside, violence and death at every turn the past few years, and a son from whom the world took what he loved most—his mother, his dog, his country, his youth, his innocence. Charlie felt possessed, desperate to exorcise the demon within.

"I hear you at night, Charlie Christmas," White Eagle said. "Sounds like torture. Your path back to yourself will be long, hard. The Sun Dance heals. That is why you are here."

The ceremony was to begin at dawn the following morning, preceded several hours before dawn by *Inipi*, a rite of purification in a sweat lodge constructed of willow saplings covered with hides to block out the light. The Lakota consider the sweat lodge a metaphoric womb of the universe from which participants emerge with fresh souls after several hours meditating, chanting, and sweating in temperatures well over one hundred degrees from heated stones placed in the middle of the structure.

White Eagle took one drag from a ceremonial pipe as he emerged from the sweat lodge and passed it to his guests, each one taking a small puff before passing it on to the other and back to White Eagle, who placed it on a small mound of earth meant to represent a crescent moon. Amiir had never smoked before and felt a little wobbly until Red Thunder steadied him with a gentle hand on his shoulder. A cloud of steam escaped the sweat lodge when White Eagle threw back the flap and ushered them inside, and they sat on sage in the withering heat. Stone flinched the first of four times the door was thrown open, and Amiir, who was having a hard time with the heat, began to stand so he could leave.

"Sit and I will tell you about the white buffalo calf woman," Red Thunder said. "We open it four times for her. We come out after the fourth, leaving behind all that is dark and impure in us.

"Hundreds of years ago a chief sent two scouts to hunt for food during a famine. A beautiful young woman draped in white buckskin emerged from a cloud, reducing one of them to a pile of bones for impertinence but sparing the other because she sensed his heart was pure. The woman explained that she had supernatural powers, and imparted the seven sacred ceremonies to protect mother earth and gave him a sacred ceremonial pipe."

All four fell into what they could only describe afterward as a dreamlike state, weightless and content when the door was thrown open the fourth time so they could emerge into the light from the vivid yellow orb of the rising sun.

"It's only the start, Charlie Christmas," White Eagle said. "Now you're ready for the Sun Dance." He was a Somali, not an Indian, and the notion seemed frivolous to Charlie. But there was something in White Eagle, a deep spiritual connection different from the close friendships he had with Ademar and Stone, that drove him to the Sun Dance. Perhaps the medicine man knew how to exorcise demons. White Eagle extended a hand to Charlie. "Come," he said, and Charlie took it.

The outside circle of the campsite surrounded the inner circle of the Sun Dance lodge, with an opening facing east, which enabled prayers to flow unimpeded toward "all the created world," White Eagle explained. It was not lost on Charlie or Ademar that Muslims pray facing east in the direction of Mecca. Charlie had some idea of what's involved in a Sun Dance but wasn't sure he would participate, until that moment and the realization that there were divine bonds between him and the American Indians that stretched back to the beginning.

White Eagle led Charlie to the tent where the other Sun Dancers prepared for a painful trial of flesh and spirit that required humility, perseverance, and faith. Charlie stood naked in front of the chief, his coal-black skin in sharp contrast to the light brown of the other dancers, and donned an ankle-length, skirt-like fabric attached at his waist by a sash. White Eagle handed him a whistle with an eagle's plume attached that was carved from the longest bone in the mythical raptor's wing, which the dancers would blow continuously in concert with drumming and chanting from outside the circle that helped carry their prayers into the *universe of all medicine.*

Amiir gasped when his father emerged from the tent with the other Sun Dancers, all of them barefoot, shirtless, and wearing a simple wreath of sage on their heads in a symbolic gesture of naked humility. The Sioux women around the dance circle wore modest handmade cotton dresses as they drummed and chanted the dancers into the sacred inner circle. A fifteen-foot cottonwood tree that had been cut for the dance stood in the middle of the circle with rawhide strips almost as long as the central pole, and a Bison skull on top as if presiding over the ceremony. Each dancer had a mentor to lead them through the journey, and White Eagle would serve as Charlie's guide. *So far so good*, Charlie thought to himself, until White Eagle opened his hand to reveal two sharpened pegs of bone.

"There is no healing without pain, Charlie Christmas," said White Eagle as he applied a numbing salve a few inches below the collarbones on either side of Charlie's chest. Stone, Ademar, and Amiir flinched when White Eagle sliced deeply into Charlie's chest, piercing the bloody gashes with the sharpened bone, then attaching them on either end with the rawhide strips hanging from the cottonwood tree. "Now dance, my Black brother," White Eagle said, "until your flesh gives way, and you are released."

Charlie had no time to process the pain from the piercing before the other dancers leaned their full weight back against the rawhide strips, stretching the skin several inches away from their chests, and blew their whistles in rhythm with the drumming. A primeval instinct stretching from South Dakota up to Alaska and across the Bering Straits down into Africa—a spiritual, genetic pathway—gripped Charlie as he leaned back against the rawhide strip and began to sway with the other Sun Dancers. Charlie felt excruciating pain for the first few hours, nearly passing out twice, and all he could think about was a cool drink of water and the tines tearing from his chest inch by agonizing inch. The physical pain faded as the sun crested high noon and the temperature neared one hundred degrees. But a sharper, more subtle misery throbbed like fever through Charlie's psychic wounds, oozing the pus of a deeply infected soul. The ancient beat of primitive rawhide drums—*thump, thump, thump*—passed through Charlie in waves, and he focused on breathing through the torment by exhaling into the eagle-bone whistle around his neck—*wheet, wheet, wheet.*

Charlie felt as if he might be dying, as if his spirit might be leaving his body. But it was not his spirit, rather the tatters of other spirits he carried in his heavy heart—Ebla, Awil, Samina, his father, and all those travelers in him who had died or been left behind on his trail of tears. They all stood around Charlie, simultaneously propping him up and pushing him back against the rawhide anchors. The skin closest to the pegs puckered and tore like cracks in a sheet of ice. *Thump, thump, thump. Wheet, wheet, wheet.* There was still one more spirit that had not been released from the darkest recess of Charlie's dharma, his haunting mirror image, Sayiid Awale. Charlie imagined that releasing Sayiid Awale was like exorcising a demon, euthanizing a hellhound. Charlie Christmas looked at Sayiid Awale from the end of a long tunnel with no reference to time, distance, or dimension, only the drumming and whistling tethering him to the earth. *Thump, thump. Wheet, wheet.* "You are free, you bastard," Sayiid Awale cackled. "But not your son; he will be mine. You will see." Charlie's flesh popped as the pegs tore free from his skin, and he fell unconscious to the ground.

Charlie dreamed that a moist cloth was moving across his feverish forehead, and awoke to a cool muzzle and a gentle lick from Buck, battered but unbroken, looking as if he'd returned from the dead.

Amiir smiled as he cradled his father's head. "Buck's alive."

CHAPTER 4

As they hit the outskirts of Minneapolis on Interstate 35, Charlie tapped the eagle-bone whistle that now hung on his necklace along with the other totems of his life—the Somali flag, an Islamic crescent, the gold letter *S*, a 7.62 mm shell casing, and the wood carving of a snow-white willow ptarmigan. What he knew didn't hang on him like a yoke anymore was his *other*, Sayiid Awale, which Sigmund Freud would have referred to as Charlie's id, in constant conflict with his superego over attempts by his ego to mediate between them. Instinct versus culture with reality officiating in the match for his soul. Some shrinks might have labelled it emerging schizophrenia—the tics, the nightmares, the voices. Viewing Charlie's condition through the prism of the ancients, White Eagle never named it because he knew that giving something a name meant that it lived as a being distinct yet dependent on the host, like a parasite. But he knew it was there and knew how to heal it. He was a medicine man.

"You are whole now, my Black brother," White Eagle told Charlie before he and the others left Pine Ridge. "A new person who we call Black Eagle—the bird that keeps balance in the universe between the sun and the moon."

Natalie was obviously pregnant with her first child when she met them at the East Village Grill in the Cedar Riverside neighborhood of Minneapolis, otherwise known as Little Mogadishu. Almost ten thousand Somalis live within the four square blocks that compose Little Mogadishu, four thousand of them in Riverside Towers, directly across from the Riverside Mall and catty-corner to Hubert Humphrey Stadium, home of the Minnesota Vikings. Amiir could not have been happier when Natalie told them she had arranged an apartment facing the football stadium in one of the six buildings that make up Riverside Towers, built during the early 1970s in the German Brutalist style with exposed structural elements, appropriate for a community that wears so much of its heart on its sleeve. Charlie could imagine he was back in Somalia when he looked down South Fourth Street, full of Somalis in typical Somali clothes speaking his language. But that bubble, like so many glimmers of hope in his life, nearly burst when he saw a tag on the wall across the street spray painted by the Somali Hard Boys, a local gang of small-time thieves and drug dealers. *A pirate by any other name*, Charlie thought to himself.

"Don't fret," said Abdi Salah, a rising political star in the civic government who Natalie had brought along as part of the welcoming committee, when he noticed Charlie looking at the gang graffiti. "We keep an eye on them."

Charlie shifted nervously in the booth of the restaurant and looked at his son, then back to Abdi.

"How old is he?" Abdi asked.

"Eleven," Charlie replied.

"The Hard Boys like to get them when they're young," Abdi said. "But not that young."

"Eleven in years," Charlie said. "But not so innocent after the last two. He was old enough to remember Mogadishu. The war. The day his school closed. The exodus. His mother's death. The refugee camp. I mean, he killed a man at nine. Just a boy; then he wasn't. I don't know how he's stayed so good."

"I can imagine," Abdi said. "Ten of my family fled Somalia; seven of us made it. Dangerous, but in some ways simpler. You could see the bad guys coming. Over here, forget it. Minneapolis police, not exactly sympathetic to people of color. Plus, all that shit on the Internet. The Internet of ideas. Hah! What a bunch of camel shit. More like the Internet of jackals. Trust your instincts. Hold him close, with an open hand. Hold the line, brother."

"Keep him busy with school, sports, anything that keeps him off the street," said Mohamed Farah, head of a local NGO that worked with Somali youth and the government to bolster community resiliency against extremism. "And send him to us if he has any free time. Arts, sports, learning; we have something for everybody. And we know who the bad apples are."

"Idle hands are the work of the devil," said Stone, who perked up as the waitress, Amina, a young Somali woman, asked for their order.

"What'll it be, gents?" said Amina, whose willowy Nilotic beauty and pearl-white teeth took his breath away.

"Uh," Stone stammered.

Awkward silence.

Ademar laughed, elbowed him in the ribs. "Cap!"

"Cap?" asked Amina, whose name means *honest* in Somali.

"We served together in the Army; Somalia," Ademar said. "He was my captain, but he's out now. Thinking about settling here. I'm still in, just taking some leave to drive our friends up from Texas. What about you?"

"My name is Amina, obviously," she said, pointing to her nametag, laughing. Not forced; true laughter. "Amina Hussein. Refugee, like everyone around here. Twenty-eight. Usual story—Mogadishu, Kenya, blah, blah, blah. Sorry, don't mean to be cynical. Everyone misses the past they thought they had. But I like it in America. I have a good job. Almost finished with my master's in computer science at the U of M, full scholarship. Go Gophers! What about you, Captain?"

Stone recovered. "Prometheus Stone, at your service."

Amina laughed—head-back laugh, hands-on-her-hips, elbows-at-ninety-degrees laugh, sassy laugh. "What should I call you?"

"Been so long since anyone called me anything but Captain, Cap, or Stone."

"You're a funny guy," she interrupted. "I'll call you Cap. At least that's what I'll call you if I see you again. You can call me Sam, if you see me again."

"Suits me fine, Sam," he said.

Awkward silence. Stone stared at Sam; everyone stared at Stone.

"Well, Cap?" Amina said.

"Well what?" he said.

"Okay, I'm the waitress, you're the guest, and I'm taking your order," she said. "Capeesh?"

They all needed a good laugh, and they all did at the expense of Stone, who was actually blushing.

"Jesus, Stone!" Ademar said. "Love at first sight, or what?"

They all laughed again, the kind of laughter that is the cousin of crying—that comes from somewhere deep and has been waiting to come out for a long time and wants to stay out, that can't be pulled back in. Hilarious crying laughter. Shaking laughter that infected the entire restaurant.

When the laughter finally stopped, a man in his thirties at the next booth leaned over and extended his hand. "She's my little sister. I'm Samikab. Just bring them the breakfast special, the Somali one."

Stone didn't realize it. Men like him, accustomed to keeping score in all things about their life, rarely do. But Ademar did. Women always know when destiny ripples through the universe, particularly in affairs of the heart.

"Wish I was sticking around to watch this one," Ademar said.

"Huh," said Stone, not sure what he was feeling.

"I'll be back for the wedding," Ademar said.

After they'd had their fill of mascharo yariis, laben, and sabaayad muqmad iyo ukun—mini rice and coconut cakes, yoghurt with sumac, pomegranate and basil, and flatbread wrapped around eggs and preserved beef—Samikab noticed the dusty old football in Amiir's lap. Samikab grew up in nearby St. Paul and played tight end for the Arlington High Phoenixes, although he preferred basketball. A former schoolmate was the equipment manager for the Vikings, and during the offseason they played pickup games in cavernous Humphrey Stadium just outside the boundaries of Little Mogadishu.

"That Somali food is heavy," Samikab said to Stone. "You and the boy want to run some of it off? My buddy works at Humphrey. We can go over there and toss the ball around."

"Really?" said Amiir, remembering the field in Dell City and the notion that clicking the heels of his Nike Sharks together three times would take him there like Dorothy in *The Wizard of Oz*.

"Sure, why not?" Samikab asked.

"I'm in," said Ademar, also a little excited to kick a few through the goalposts on a real NFL field.

"Be over in a bit," said Stone. "Gotta take care of the waitress."

"I'll bet you will," Ademar replied.

"I'll stay with him," Charlie said. "You know, chaperone, matchmaker, troublemaker."

The next few days were as happy as any of them could remember when they reflected back over the past few years. Their routine consisted of meals at the East Village Grill, Stone flirting with Amina, goofing at the Humphrey, and helping Charlie move into his new place and adjust to his new circumstances. Days can seem like years to a refugee, and roots grow fast. But Ademar's and Stone's departure at the end of the week reminded them that there was a new life to construct, new schools to attend, new jobs to find. And all of it would be without Ademar. They stood around her truck Sunday morning, Buck on his back legs in the bed with both front paws on the top of the tailgate one last time.

"What's next for you, Ranger?" Charlie asked Ademar.

"A little time in Dell City, catch up with Deuce," she said. "Then ship out somewhere. Middle East, Europe, who knows?"

"I'll miss you, Ranger," Charlie said.

"Me too," said Amiir, hugging Ademar as hard as he could while Buck wagged his tail and pawed at her arm resting on the side of the truck.

"Me too, LT," Stone said, which did not come as a complete surprise to any of them.

"If Charlie and Amiir will put me up at their place. Whaddya say, Kid?"

"Yes!" Amiir blurted out.

"You don't have to ask," Charlie said. "Stay as long as you want."

"I'm thinking about studying to be a rabbi," Stone said.

"I can see it now," Ademar said. "The rabbi of Little Mogadishu, married to Sam, and several little chocolate Stones running pass patterns at the Humphrey. Perfect."

"One step at a time," said Stone. "But that don't sound half bad to me."

"Okay, time to saddle up," said Ademar, opening the driver's door as everyone moved away from the truck and she climbed in, starting the engine and shifting it into gear. Ademar stopped for a moment and rolled down the window, motioning to Charlie. "Almost forgot this," she said, handing Charlie a check for $25,000.

"What's this," said Charlie. "Charity?"

"Not hardly, my friend," she answered. "You earned it. The Dell City crew wanted you to have it. I'd be a bag of bones back in Somalia if not for you, twice."

"And I you," Charlie said.

"This is not the end, Charlie," she said. "You and I; it's written."

"*Enshallah*, Ranger."

"*Enshallah*, Black Eagle."

CHAPTER 5

Charlie, Stone, and Amiir had it pretty good in Minneapolis. The money from Ademar's family gave Charlie a little breathing room to help Amiir adjust to a more normal life in America, with normal day-to-day routines like school, sports, and just being a twelve-year-old kid who doesn't have to worry about air strikes, alligators, or pirates. Some of the best Jewish mothers are Jewish fathers, and Stone held his own in that regard, cooking, cleaning, coaching, educating, and nagging. Stone was an Army combat officer for twenty years, and what he maintained was a cross between a proper American household and a military base—efficient, wholesome, clean, and nutritious but a little short on affection and motherly nurturing. Buck was as good as it gets with war zones and bad guys, and a cold nose with a few sloppy licks could go a long way with Amiir, but their dog was a little rough around the edges when it came to domestic life. Amiir didn't shed tears, not an uncommon symptom of post-traumatic stress in children who experience the type of horrors to which he was exposed. But that doesn't mean they don't need the kind of warmth, comfort, and nonjudgmental empathy that only a mother can provide. That perhaps was one reason the universe had brought Amina into their lives, but far from the only one.

"Can you get that, Amiir?" Stone asked when someone knocked on the door. "Keep the chain on until you see who it is."

"Aye aye, Cap," Amiir said, opening the door six inches, then undoing the chain and pulling it all the way open when he saw who it was. "It's Sam."

"I come bearing gifts," she said, laying out an assortment of Somali dishes from the East Village Grill. "I got dinner tonight, Cap. Take off that apron, as fetching as you look, and let me show you what a Somali woman can do."

"Did you bring the Xalwo?" asked Amiir, referring to the glutinous cardamom-flavored Somali confection that was his favorite.

"Didn't have time to make it, work, school, and all," she said. "But I picked some up at Riverside Mall."

"Glad you didn't hide the Xalwo on me," said Stone, winking at Charlie and using a humorous Somali expression for someone who elopes.

"Very impressive, Cap," Amina said. "Impressively forward."

"Doing my best, Sam," said Stone, untying the apron and tossing it at her.

They were such an unlikely pair on the surface, Stone and Samina—Jew and Muslim, white and Black, Somali and American—and impossible back in Somalia. But, as Stone so often told Amiir, anything is possible in America. After their first encounter at the East Village Grill, and the obvious chemistry between them, Ademar had asked her to keep an eye on the three of them. Amina had spent most of her life in the United States, no stranger to romance at twenty-eight, but she was still a Somali and a Muslim with all the cultural baggage that comes along with it. She liked that Stone, with regular mentoring from Charlie, was taking his time, and she was reassured by the bird's-eye view of his domestic side. Within the context of Islam and a highly traditional society, Somali women play a powerful role in their communities.

They are full partners in nearly every marital decision, which Charlie explained to Stone when advising him to let Amina drive the pace of their relationship. "You're not charging a bunker, Cap," Charlie said.

The first time they kissed was magic. The top note of her body infused Stone, settled deep in him—mesmerizing, titillating, unforgettable. During the middle of a brutally cold Minneapolis winter, six months since they first met, Stone walked Amina to her car after an evening at the apartment. Amina dropped the car keys, and they bumped heads stooping at the same time to pick them up. They came up slowly, and their faces were inches apart, their eyes locked all the way up. Amina leaned into Stone, turning her head slightly, coquettishly, holding his cheek in the palm of her hand and brushing her lips lightly, provocatively against his. The slight kiss, the cloaked sensuality that traveled with it, caught him by surprise. Then she ran her tongue slowly, tenderly along Stone's lower lip and pulled him closer.

"I'd never hide the Xalwo on you, Cap," said Amina, smiling, tugging his ear affectionately, stepping back, the steam of their breath spiraling into the night sky as she climbed into the car, leaving Stone in stunned silence and taking his heart with her.

Money was not an immediate issue for Stone, but deciding how he planned to spend the rest of his life was. Tending to the house, keeping an eye on Amiir, and courting Amina were not the answer, as pleasant as they were compared to life with a bunch of grunts in overseas war zones. Stone had spoken with his father, a third-generation rabbi, about it several times since leaving the Army, and he had urged him to consider what he referred to as "the family business." Stone had doubts, did not feel called to the rabbinate like the other men in his family. A life without the hot rush of adrenaline that came with combat might not be enough to satisfy his inner warrior, and Stone was nothing if not a warrior.

"Son, our history is full of warrior-priests: Moses, Judah Maccabee," his father said over the telephone from Arizona. "Life is combat for Jews, but it's not always fists or weapons. It's the cleverer one that wins the war without pulling the trigger."

"I hear you, Dad," Stone said. "I've about decided you're right."

"Mazel tov!" his father said.

"Don't be mazeling your tov so soon, Dad," Stone said. "I've found the woman I want to marry."

"Double mazel tov!" his father said. "All good news today."

"She's not an American," Stone said.

"No problem," his father replied.

"Or a Jew," Stone said.

"She can convert," his father said.

"Unlikely," Stone continued. "Or white."

"What else?"

"Amina, that's her name. She's a Somali migrant, a Black woman, and a Muslim."

"Wow, the trifecta," his father said.

Silence as his father covered the phone, but not enough to muffle the conversation with Stone's mother.

"Dad?"

"It doesn't matter; none of it matters," his father said. "If you love her, we love her. The rest will work itself out."

It was not as easy for Charlie Christmas, with no family business and no father to consult. But a growing circle of friends had his back, foremost among them Natalie Bell, who had an idea for Charlie and a friend to help make it happen. Minnesota fit the resettlement profile for groups like the International Rescue Committee and Catholic Relief—low unemployment in a large, seemingly progressive state—and nearly one hundred thousand Somalis put down roots in the northern plains. The young Somalis, those with skills suited to the modern job market, gravitated toward the Twin Cities, but those with an agricultural background migrated to cities like St. Cloud or nearby Willmar and found work on farms or in meat-processing plants. That's why Natalie arranged for Charlie to meet Marley Wittenberg, an executive with a large turkey-processing plant in Willmar. Marley trusted Natalie, understood the nuances of managing Somalis after five years at the plant, and offered Charlie a line job during breakfast at Frieda's Café in Willmar. The money was decent, $14.75 an hour to start with regular increases and full benefits, but he'd have to commute two hours back to Minneapolis on the weekends.

"It will do for now," Charlie told Stone. "As long as you and Sam keep a close eye on Amiir back here."

"No worries, Charlie," Stone said. "Between Sam and I, we've got it covered."

"Settled, Cap?" Charlie asked.

"Settled," Stone replied.

They could not have known then how their world would change when the sleeping dragon awoke.

CHAPTER 6

A succession of American and world leaders knew the dragon was in the cave, watched it cautiously and tried to wall it in with years of costly overseas aid programs intended to build strong, resilient democracies where women are empowered, children are educated, and rule of law prevails. But dragons are mythical and won't be bought off by some Western model of a civil society that seemed more like a business development project than a sincere humanitarian mission. Throw in a heavy dose of official corruption that siphoned aid off to strongmen like Hafez Assad of Syria, Sani Abacha of Nigeria, and Saddam Hussein of Iraq, all of whom Washington held its nose and danced with, and the dragon not only awakens but rises up, soars out of its cave, and leaves behind a trail of scorched, smoking, red-hot earth. Ashes are like fertilizer for new growth, and what grew out of this dragon's infernal breath was the fire of radicalism and its evil twin, violent extremism. The dragon spawned Osama bin Laden, the Saudi necromancer who brought down the Twin Towers; Anwar al-Awlaki, the Yemeni-American Imam who reached into the heart of Western Civilization through the Web to radicalize a generation of young Muslims; and Abu Bakr al-Baghdadi, who presided over the ghoulish ISIS

Caliphate in parts of Syria and Iraq that inspired violence as far away as St. Cloud, Minnesota. Add to that list the American white supremacists and veiled bigots brought to power by a society as profoundly radicalized by perceptions of injustice as any disillusioned Somali kid in Minneapolis. September 11, 2001, was not the beginning, but it gave birth to an era of violence and instability around the world and in the heart of America that seems biblical in its breathtaking ferocity and size. Several years after 9/11, Charlie Christmas, Ademar Zarkan, and Prometheus Stone were about to feel the heat of the dragon's breath.

Ademar had lost count of how many people she had killed—dozens in the battlefields of the Middle East and Africa as an Army sniper, and at least three more since being detailed to the CIA as an undercover assassin in black operations. Given her job, Ademar feared that she might one day find her brother, Anil, in the crosshairs of her scope, particularly after the discovery that he was involved in the unsuccessful kidnapping of her fiancé, Deuce Laws, in Afghanistan. That episode might have ended with a gruesome video of a masked ISIS executioner hacking off Deuce's head were it not for his daring escape and the sharpshooting of Ademar and her older brother T2, all three of whom were stationed together at Forward Operating Base Fenty in eastern Afghanistan. She would never forget the image of Deuce, the gunslinging West Texas quarterback, tossing a grenade forty yards into a jeep full of ISIS militiamen and his last desperate sprint from the rocks a few hundred yards outside the base with two more of them hot on his tail. Ademar and Deuce would not have married, would not have created the purest expression of their family's partnership, their son Tamerlane Laws, if she had not taken both of them down with a shot that rivaled *The Shot* from the wave-tossed ship off the Somali coast. Deuce told them afterward that Anil, who had fallen for the online ISIS siren song and disappeared into South

Asia, was set to film the video of his execution until he realized who it was and secretly abetted his escape.

Her undersized, introverted, bullied twin brother, Anil, whose hand was torn off in a farm accident, blamed the entire world for his troubles, except for Ademar, T2, and Deuce, who did everything they could to protect him growing up in West Texas. But it was not enough, not even close, and the runt of Dell City found the stature he craved as the digital wizard behind the ISIS propaganda machine. And he had Amiir in the crosshairs of his weapon, the network of chat rooms and multiplayer games at his fingertips on the World Wide Web.

Anil had stayed in virtual touch with Amiir, and his pet project was the recruitment and radicalization of the Somali immigrant. He was in no hurry, and the foreplay of the recruitment process aroused Anil in a way that no woman or man could. What began as the brief encounter with online pornography when Amiir first arrived in Dell City from the Kenyan refugee camp had flowered over the years into a rich relationship between them in late-night chats, videos shared through bulletin boards on 4chan and multiplayer video games like Spyro the Dragon. But Amiir, battle-hardened at sixteen, was not your usual suspect, and the love of his father, Stone, and Amina kept him away from the edge of the abyss. Anil was nothing more than a diversion for Amiir, and in some ways he felt that ignoring him completely would be tantamount to disrespecting Ademar. Although he had been exposed to many of the influences that drive violent radicalism—injustice, violence, and poverty—Amiir's prowess as a star kicker at South High School elevated his self-esteem, provided entrée to almost every clique on campus, and caught the eye of several college football coaches. Anil was frustrated by his inability to find the one chink in Amiir's armor, until he connected him with Violet Cremona, the purple-haired vixen of South Fourth Street.

Violet Cremona was not her real name, her Italian accent was fake, and her hair wasn't naturally purple, of course. Nobody actually has purple hair. Yasmine Ait was her real name, Morocco her native country, and her hair was naturally jet black, as anyone could clearly see in the ample, unshaven nest under her arms. Violet's cover was that she studied at the Minneapolis School of Art and Design and, after graduation, hoped to work on architectural restoration in her hometown of Venice. All bullshit—cleverly crafted bullshit, but bullshit nonetheless. Underneath her bohemian funkiness, at the root of her dyed hair, behind the phony Italian accent, she was a succubus—the chimera of the Kabbalah spawned in the underworld to seduce men, consume them, extract their essence, and ultimately, kill them. Violet Cremona was no legend. She was a skilled ISIS recruiter trained by Anil and smuggled into Minneapolis like a Trojan horse to infiltrate the Somali community. She may have been Anil's most prized creation, carved in all ways to mesmerize young, impressionable Somalis. The Italian accent, which seemed so welcoming to Somalis given their nation's history with Italy, was the kind of attention to detail that made Anil such a diabolically effective asset to the global terrorist enterprise. Violet had been working a dozen or so young Somalis, whom she acquired in the teen hangouts of Minneapolis, and funneled them for further radicalization to the Egyptian Imam at the Dar al-Farooq Mosque and Islamic Center in the Minneapolis suburb of Bloomington. Several of her recruits had disappeared from their families, traveling illicitly through Turkey to fight in Syria on behalf of the ISIS Caliphate—good, pure souls lost forever amid the kidnappings, rapes, beheadings, and terror done in the name of a deity who clearly condemns such crimes as blasphemy.

Saturday afternoon, and Amiir, along with a few friends, was hanging out at the Electric Fetus, since 1969 an iconic Minneapolis music store and counterculture hub on the corner of

South Fourth and East Franklin. The Fetus was the only place in town that stocked bootleg copies of music from concerts in Africa by Keinan Abdi Warsame, the charismatic Somali-Canadian rapper and poet known as K'naan, whose international hit Wavin' Flag would be selected by Coca Cola as its promotional anthem in the 2010 FIFA World Cup. Violet and Anil found the coincidental symbolism between the name, Electric Fetus, and their activity, conceiving little extremists, intensely amusing.

Amiir was thumbing through some vinyl, K'naan pumping through the earphones connected to his smart phone, when Violet made a nonchalant pass. She counted on her funk—a mix of patchouli, sour apple lipstick, and grunge—catching his attention.

"Oops, sorry," she said, brushing his shoulder with hers as she feigned interest in a stack of recordings next to him.

"No problem," grumbled Amiir, whose demeanor transformed immediately when he laid eyes on the purple nymph in the black leather biker jacket with a scent that traveled like a lightning bolt from his nose to his crotch.

"Is that K'naan?" she asked.

"What?" Amiir asked.

"K'naan," said Violet, pointing to her ear, then to his phone.

"Yeah, you know him?"

"Dude, are you kidding? He's the shit."

"Word," said Amiir, trying to remain as chill as he imagined K'naan might be in this situation.

"Can I listen?" asked Violet.

"Um, sure," Amiir said, and in an instant Violet had removed a bud from his left ear and placed it in her right ear so that they were standing shoulder to shoulder, hip to hip, knee to knee.

"Righteous; so cool," she said after a few minutes, leaning into Amiir, wrapping one arm around his hip and swaying to the music. "I could dance to him all night."

Target acquired. Amiir was a goner, like any sixteen-year-old who thinks with the wrong head most of the time.

"Listen to this," said Violet, fiddling inside Amiir's jeans pocket to extract his smart phone, acting as if she didn't notice his obvious and instantaneous tumescence, and cueing "Purple Rain" by Prince, a legend in his hometown of Minneapolis. "Know him?"

"Seriously?" asked Amiir. "Didn't just get off the boat."

She punched him playfully in the arm. "Dude, JK."

It went like that for almost an hour, the two of them swapping tunes from their playlists, goofing on each other, and swaying to the music, and Amiir hoping it would never end.

"What's your name, by the way?" she asked. "I'm Violet. You might have guessed by the hair. Violet Cremona."

"Sayiid Awale. But they call me Amiir, prince," he said, extending a hand to shake as awkwardly as any teenage boy in the history of the universe.

"Pleased to meet you, Mr. Awale," said Violet, lowering her voice to a serious baritone, bowing slightly, laughing, and shaking his hand.

Amiir held her hand for what seemed like a proper amount of time, but Violet did not loosen her grip when he did. "Do you feel it?" she asked.

"Feel what?" Amiir replied.

"It's like electricity," said Violet, pulling him closer to her until they were just inches apart, blushing, then abruptly dropping his hand and pulling away. "Sorry, Amiir. I'm not usually this forward. It's just that . . ."

"What?"

"I don't know," Violet said. "Weird. I just felt something between us."

"Same," he said.

"Speaking of princes, you won't believe this, but I have some intel that Prince is playing a set or two at First Avenue tonight," she said. "I know we just met and all, but, well, you wanna go?"

It was Amiir's turn to land a playful, very, very light punch on her arm. "I'm down."

The night was one that Amiir could not have conjured in his wildest dreams, a night of firsts for the Somali teenager, and most of it did actually seem like a dream after he smoked his first joint on the way to the club. Prince did show up at First Avenue, the iconic music venue in the heart of downtown Minneapolis, and played "Purple Rain" and almost every other hit as the two of them moved together like they'd known each other forever, not for the six hours since Violet sidled up next to him at the Fetus. Amiir didn't quite know what to do when the music stopped and the lights came up, but Violet, after more of these encounters than she could remember, knew exactly where it was going.

"That was amazing; you're amazing," she said encircling his neck with her arms and kissing him. "Go to my place? Just a few blocks away."

"Sure, of course," said Amiir, trying not to sound as if this was his first rodeo.

"Good," said Violet, grabbing his hand and leading him the entire way to her apartment, resting her head on his shoulder at red lights, and squeezing his hand as if the two of them were in the midst of a private conspiracy.

"Sorry it's so messy," she said when they walked up the two flights of stairs to a simple studio with a kitchen, a lounge chair, a bed in the middle of one small room, and a poster of Bob Marley illuminated by a fluorescent black light. "Water?"

"Please," said Amiir, unsure whether he should take the only chair in the room.

High on weed, everything seemed surreal to Amiir, slower, distorted. He heard the mechanical whirring of an ice machine pushing cubes out of the slot on the refrigerator door and the clinking as they struck the bottom of the glass, then the splashing of water over them. Violet had taken her biker coat off in the kitchen and lit some sandalwood incense, and Amiir was not sure if the scent that trailed her into the room was woman or smoke.

"Sit," she commanded, motioning to the one chair and handing him the glass of water.

"Thanks," said Amiir, obediently sitting because he didn't know what else to do, grateful to douse the fire in his scratchy throat with some cool water.

"Can I kiss you?" Violet asked.

"Please."

A first real kiss for Amiir, so different from the tentative bashful pecks he'd given to a few teenage girls at the doors of their apartments after high school dances. Her lips tasted like apples and her tongue felt slippery, juicy like tapioca in his imagination.

Violet pulled back after a few minutes. "Give me a second." She turned off the lights as she headed for the bathroom, the only illumination the electric fluorescence on the Bob Marley poster—orange, yellow, and green with his name on the top, him in the middle, and *One Love* emblazoned on the bottom. Amiir heard the bathroom door open, but he could not see Violet. She was just a shadow on the wall crossing the room, passing like a ghost over Bob Marley until she stood directly in front of him, wearing only a smile. Her breasts brushed his face as she placed buds in their ears and cued up the iconic Rastafarian anthem "One Love." With the skill of an experienced courtesan, no fumbling with shoelaces, belts, or jeans, Violet had Amiir completely naked on the chair in no time, his manhood the only thing standing between them. She stepped back so Amiir could see her full body, breasts like perfect ripe pomegranates with one erect nipple pierced by a tiny gold spike, and a trail of hair that began light as lint at her bellybutton and ended in a dense black triangle between her legs.

"Twist it," said Violet, bringing one of Amiir's hands to the spike in her nipple while she straddled him, mouthing Marley's words—*one love*—as he slipped into the warm moistness of her womanhood. "Twist it harder," she hissed like a rattlesnake, forked tongue flitting out, flitting in to capture the hidden essence of fear or danger before a strike, before a deadly injection of venom into its prey. "Harder!" Feeling like a scolded child, Amiir, at least ten years her junior, obeyed and twisted the spike so hard a droplet of blood oozed from her nipple. "Like that, boy, just like that," Violet moaned, arching her spine, throwing her purple hair back, thrusting her hips in violent spasms of ecstasy and delicious pain like a madwoman, an animal, a witch, a succubus.

"Remember," she whispered in his ear as they climaxed together, "remember."

Amiir stumbled home well after midnight, his father, Stone, and Amina sound asleep but Buck on him immediately, exploring the strange, foreign smell all over his best friend.

As soon as he left the apartment, Violet sent Anil a two-word note on Skype, an encrypted messaging service used by those who want to evade surveillance by intelligence agencies.

"He's ours."

CHAPTER 7

Lilith Poe's father was a Minneapolis beat cop who shot first and asked questions later—a brutal man, a racist, with hands like truncheons, a bulbous, grotesque nose spread across his face like dimpled Silly Putty, and a spider web of broken capillaries on either side from too many vodkas and too much ranch dressing on his deep-fried cheese curds. He once caught Lilith and a high school boyfriend making out on the living room couch after a date and slapped him so hard that blood ran from the seventeen-year-old's ears. Lilith's mother learned the hard way not to question her husband, and barely stirred from her crochet when he reeled and stumbled upstairs to "tuck in" Lilith, cowering under the bedcovers when she heard the heavy thump of his boots ascending the wooden stairs. She knew what was coming, once or twice a week, and lay quiet as a mouse under the sheets she tucked tightly around her body in a child's futile attempt to protect herself from the demons of night terror. Her father slowly opened the bedroom door and a triangle of light crept across the floor, over the stuffed animals, and stopped. "There's my little lady," he whispered. She smelled vodka on his breath as he leaned over her and cigarette smoke on his fingers when he pulled back the sheets to fondle her with one hand and pleasure himself with the other. Lilith never told anyone about the abuse, rationalizing that it was her duty. She hated him with every fiber in her body, and loved him in the same way a condemned man yearns for his executioner. She followed in her father's footsteps, in all ways, joining the Minneapolis police force after graduating from St. Cloud State. But she was forced to resign following two suspensions for excessive use of force against detained black men, venting her conflicted feelings for her father and repulsion for people of color. Lilith had not been procured into radicalism by some Svengali of the Internet or by some older seducer, but the illness grew organically in her like a runaway virus and infected everything she touched.

The Latin root of radicalism is *radix*, literally translated as *root*, and a perfect, elegant articulation for how hatred and violence is transported through the vascular system of a person in the same way the xylem and phloem of a tree conducts nutrients from the ground and air to its trunk, branches, twigs, and leaves. Extremism is not a psychological diagnosis. It's a sickness, a tangible, physical malady with primary, secondary, and tertiary symptoms. There is no vaccine to prevent it. And like a diseased tree, extremism can't be cured by snipping off a few leaves. Those who specialize in behavior-change programs for outbreaks of violent radicalism jibber and jabber about foreign aid programs that mitigate it in ISIS hotbeds like Belgium's Molenbeek quarter, Bosnia-Herzegovina's Salafi-dominated gated communities, and Pakistan's remote frontier provinces. They seek to replicate the broken American system of democracy in them and award multimillion-dollar contracts to private companies or nonprofits like Common Ground, Creative Associates International, M & C Saatchi, and Palladium to build programs that nurture governance, rule of law, female empowerment, and education to create strong, resilient communities. While they interpret mountains of ambiguous data supporting their theories of change for programs that counter violent extremism, radicalism continues to metastasize throughout the world. And in their hubris, they fail to see that the emperor in the hall of Western power has no clothes, that the pot is surely calling the kettle black, and that the most well-armed, best organized, most dangerous and radicalized groups reside in the homeland. Under the guise of restoring America's greatness, their leaders are voted into office and spread hate to their followers in coded language and dog whistles. They develop policies that promote racism, fan the flames of anti-Semitism, stoke the fires of nationalism, and deny basic constitutional rights to minorities, migrants, and the bottom 1 percent. Their followers seethe with righteous indignation in almost every American community, pretending to exercise their constitutional rights by spreading vile messages on the Web, placing polished opinion pieces in the media, defacing houses of worship, and stockpiling military-grade weapons. Groups like the National Socialist Movement, the successor to the Nazi party; QAnon; The Base; C-Cubed; and Alt-Right Minnesota are dug-in and pissed off in even the most progressive states. And they are funded in part by illicit activities led by people like Lilith Poe.

Lilith, who moved to St. Cloud and joined the police force, formed a group of like-minded citizens calling itself C-Cubed, or Concerned Community Citizens, which met regularly at Culvers Restaurant off Interstate 10. She married George Barker, a reticent, bespectacled pharmacist, and they had a son, George Jr., whom she nicknamed Georgi because it sounded to her like someone who might have been an adjutant to Hitler. She cuckolded her husband regularly with liaisons at Americas Best Value Inn across the highway from Culvers and forced him to help her cultivate a profitable trade in Oxycodone. Her acolytes pedaled the deadly opiate to young, affluent junkies hanging out at counterculture hubs like the

Electric Fetus in Minneapolis, and she in turn financed the activities of C-Cubed from the illicit proceeds. The irony tickled her every time she walked into the basement of a fancy neighborhood to find a teenager in a puddle of vomit slumped over dead from an overdose purchased with an allowance that was more than she made in a week as a cop. The cultural elite would pay the price for snubbing her from their sororities, lake parties, and country clubs. Lilith Poe would make them pay. Her other target was the growing Somali-Muslim community, hundreds of whom worked in meat-processing plants around rural Minnesota. And C-Cubed helped Lilith weaponize her seething anger. The agenda for their upcoming meeting included the development of a drone fleet to help them monitor the Somalis, hoping one day to retrofit the pilotless aircraft with weapons.

"Calling this meeting to order," said Lilith, banging her nightstick on the plastic table in the corner of the diner around which the leadership of C-Cubed had gathered. "I'd like to call on our treasurer for a report on finances. James?"

"Not much update since last month, Lilith," said James Palmer, a retired teacher known for disrupting City Council meetings with diatribes on drunken driving or conspiracy theories about the local Somali population. "Were down to $6,300 since we spent $940 on that drone, the DJI Mavic Pro."

"Shit," Lilith hissed. "We'll need more than that for the concert and march against Unite Cloud. Bunch of nigger lovers and Jews. Take care of it, George. You know what I mean?"

"Yes," said her husband, fidgeting uncomfortably in his chair and making a note in the minutes she forced him to take at every meeting.

"Thanks, hon," said Lilith, with a conspiratorial wink at her partners in crime. "Speaking of Unite Cloud, what are we gonna do about that bitch Natalie Bell; thinks she's Martin Luther King or some such."

"I expect she'll be keeping a lower profile since we threw a brick through her front window the other night," said another member. "Otherwise, well, she has those three kids."

"Cool," Lilith said. "Anything to share before we adjourn?"

"I've got something," said Olaf Schneider, the great-grandson of immigrants, forced by circumstance to work slaughtering turkeys side by side with dozens of Somali immigrants at the turkey-processing plant when the government cut corn subsidies and repossessed the family farm.

"I'm tired, goddamned tired of those Somalis. Work next to those stinking niggers all night—they don't wear deodorant, you know—and watch them drive off in new trucks after the shift. I can barely put gas in my fifteen-year-old Ford. I served two tours in Iraq, took a bullet in the shoulder for our country so those Somalis can take our jobs and soak up welfare.

"Shit, when I was young, we learned that racism was the supreme evil, and for a long time I more or less believed in it. As I got older, I kept noticing more and more of the lies being pushed by those New York Jews in the media and academia about race. Obvious lies. Why don't other people notice these things? I also noticed how anybody who disagreed was labelled a horrible person only worthy of contempt and violence. I also got reading human biodiversity blogs, especially Steve Sailer. He's right! Race is real and races are different. Why work so tirelessly to bring in low IQ immigrants when we know the effect they will have on the country, in every way? Why is there such nonstop hatred for straight white men in mainstream culture?

"Whose country is this, who decides? If the alt-right is anything, it's acknowledging how important race, identity, and immigration are to our country and telling white people they can, and should, act in their interests again. Otherwise, tribal people like the Somalis will take everything from us, and our country will devolve into third world status."

"Wow!" said Lilith. "Well said, O."

As the crowd began to filter out, Lilith held up her hand. "Let's all come out Friday night for the football game; cheer on the Eagles and my boy, Georgi."

Karma is an unforgiving mistress. She empowered Jonas Salk to discover a vaccine for polio and brought Barack Obama to power, but she also enabled Robert Oppenheimer's development of the atom bomb and seemed to look on with callous disregard as the modern plague, AIDS, ascended from hell. She manipulates the universe in ways that place stars on cataclysmic collision courses for unfathomable reasons that become fathomable only in the rear-view mirror of history. And in 2015, she brought a Somali refugee who could kick a football like a dream to the St. Cloud Apollo Eagles. It was an unfortunate development for Georgi Poe.

Stone and Amina found Amiir inaccessible, reticent, and belligerent after his encounter with the purple-haired vixen. Amiir spent more time than seemed healthy at the Dar al-Farooq Mosque in Bloomington, and a new circle of friends he met there were surprising in their strict adherence to Islam. He continued to do well in school and was a star kicker on the South High School football team. But he sat like a zombie in front of his laptop well past midnight on most nights, and immediately shut down the screens whenever Amina or Stone entered his bedroom. Amina, who had a good job as a software developer at a promising Minneapolis startup, found some troubling crumbs when she examined Amiir's browsing history. She dismissed the visits to porn sites as typical for a teenage boy, but the repeated hits on a link to videos from Anwar al-Awlaki, the radical Yemeni-American cleric, and encrypted downloads were more than troubling. Stone's rabbinical responsibilities at the Shir Tikvah synagogue and his growing stature as a community advocate left him little time for Amiir, and what free time he had was spent nurturing his recent marriage to

Amina. Stone, Amina, and Charlie Christmas, who made it in from St. Cloud on weekends when he didn't pick up overtime shifts at the turkey-processing plant, decided that removing Amiir from the temptations of Minneapolis would be best for him given the circumstances. Amiir's creeping radicalization did not diminish his love for the three of them, and shame ate at his heart after every encounter with Violet Cremona, every viewing of an ISIS beheading, every memory of his dear, dead mother, Ebla. Amiir didn't fight too hard against moving to St. Cloud, hoping, like a serial pedophile or habitual wife abuser, that a few minutes in the confessional booth would bestow absolution. But none of them, least of all Amiir, had any idea how deep into him the claws of the dragon had dug.

The Eagles' football coach, Matt Korn, knew from the first practice that there would be trouble between Georgi and Amiir, both of them kickers. Georgi was a decent high school talent, and started the previous year, but Amiir had a leg like a cannon that fired pigskin bullets through the uprights from distances worthy of a standout Division 1 college player.

The politics of high school football, particularly in an incestuously small town like St. Cloud, can be a perilous high-wire walk for coaches. Presiding every Friday night in the fall over a three-ring circus, they must be equal part diplomat, dictator, and therapist, and their decisions determine whether they will wake up Saturday morning with a fresh tuna fish casserole or a paper bag of dog shit on their front doorstep. Korn, thirty-four, a former assistant at Texas powerhouse Odessa Permian who doubled as a math teacher at St. Cloud Apollo, had built his program the past three years around nine "cornerstones"—Attitude, Team, Hope, Faith, Responsibility, Dedication, Discipline, Excellence, and Work. His formula seemed to work, producing three straight winning seasons and a trip to the Minnesota state semifinals the previous year. His players reflected the diversity of the St. Cloud community, mostly white but with many Hispanics and Somalis.

Nothing prepared him for the cyclone of controversy that blew on to the field with Amiir the first day of summer practice, which fell during Ramadan, the month of dawn-to-dusk fasting for Muslims. School administrators bent over backward to accommodate their students, providing a private space for observant Muslims to pray and permitting female athletes to wear the hijab head covering during competitions. The students seemed tolerant, and the previous year they had elected a Somali girl as their homecoming queen. But managing Amiir, the first truly devout Muslim to play for him, stressed the system to its breaking point. It all started in summer practice, when Amiir refused to drink or eat during grueling two-a-day practices and passed out the second morning. Like a skilled diplomat shuttling between the capitals of warring nations, Korn convinced the local Imam to grant Amiir a Ramadan waiver to eat and drink during the day. But there was only so much Korn could do to manage Amiir—a man among boys, a battle-hardened refugee, a killer who had tasted the sex of an older woman, and a true believer in the hollow rhetoric of violent radicalism. He wasn't about to let a pudgy, obnoxious racist like Georgi disrespect him. He made that more than clear in the locker room on the fifth day of summer practice when Georgi made a crack about deodorant, and Amiir held his head in the toilet so long the other players thought he might drown. Amiir's obvious superiority as a kicker didn't make things any easier for Coach Korn, who chose discretion over valor in starting Georgi the first game.

As usual, the stands were packed for the home opener against their cross-town rival, the St. Cloud Tech Tigers, and Lilith Poe sat in her usual seat directly behind the bench so she could hector Georgi if necessary. It was a close game that the Eagles would have been leading had Georgi not missed two extra points. Lilith stormed into the locker room at halftime, still in her police uniform, and interrupted Coach Korn's pep talk.

"What the fuck, Georgi!" Lilith shouted, grabbing her boy's shoulder pads and jacking him up against the lockers. "Folding like a camp chair under the pressure, a pussy just like your father. Get your head right or else!"

"Mrs. Poe, please," said Coach Korn, who she shoved out of the way as she stalked out of the room, leaving her son in tears.

As karma would have it, the game came down to a final field goal—fourth down, Eagles on their opponents' thirty-yard line, and down two points. Georgi didn't have a prayer of making the kick, and Coach Korn knew it as he motioned to Amiir. "Your chance, son," he said.

"No problem, Coach," Amiir replied. "I got this."

All six hundred fans were on their feet chanting "Somali Sidewinder" as Amiir strapped on his helmet, trotted to the field, and shouldered his way into the huddle. "Laces forward, bro," Amiir said to his holder. "The Mogadishu madman is in the house!" Amiir surveyed the players lined up for the final play of the game under a dense cloud of steam, sweat pouring from their twenty-two bodies and dripping off their facemasks. "Check 51," Amiir shouted to the left when the opposing weak-side linebacker, number fifty-one, shifted to the line, creating an imbalance in which the Tigers had more rushers than the Eagles had blockers. "Blitz!" Amiir was pumped, totally focused as he envisioned the ball splitting the uprights and his teammates carrying him off the field on their shoulders.

The eerie silence of history in slow motion was interrupted by an unfamiliar voice in Amiir's head—the long-dormant tormentor of his father. The *other*. Sayiid Awale, true to his word, had come to claim Charlie's son. "Just like your father," the voice whispered. "Playing their game on their terms. Show them you're not their nigger; miss it for Violet."

But Amiir, who had stood up to a murderous pirate, shook it off. He imagined the steely resolve of Stone in his mind's eye, and the football sailed dead center through the goalposts as time expired. Just like Amiir had fantasized the first time he drilled one on the field in Dell City with Ademar, the crowd erupted, and his teammates piled on him in an exuberant explosion of congratulations and joy. All but two people on the Eagles' side of the field shared in the celebration. Georgi felt his mother's eyes drilling like lasers into the back of his helmet, and he imagined the red-hot anger coursing through her veins. He turned around, and when their eyes met, Lilith shot him the middle finger, mouthed the word "pussy," and marched out of the stands with her husband meekly toting their seat cushions several steps behind.

Bleary eyed from a few too many Pete's Wicked Ales, Coach Korn found a burning brown paper bag on the steps when he opened the door to retrieve the *St. Cloud Times*, and he didn't realize it was full of dog shit until he stamped it out with his slippers.

CHAPTER 8

Stone didn't carry himself like a rabbi—far from it—more like the former athlete and warrior of his past, still tightly muscled, coiled even in repose, as if he might strike at any moment. That's why his lopsided smile and wry humor when he unpacked it disarmed people and made them feel as if they had narrowly avoided something unpleasant. Burl and Goose Turner trifled with Stone and learned the hard way at the Kansas Waffle House and at the bottom of the slot canyon in the South Dakota Badlands just how unpleasant Stone could be. FBI Special Agent Peterson Jeremiah had poked around in Stone's background before their meeting in his office at Shir Tikvah synagogue, and knew he was not your run-of-the-mill liberal Minneapolis rabbi. But Jeremiah, the son of Haitian immigrants, who, like his biblical namesake and like Stone, detested false prophets and condemned idolatry, was still taken aback when he walked into the rabbi's office to find him in faded Levi's 501s and a black T-shirt with his bare feet propped on the desk.

"Rabbi Stone?" asked Jeremiah as he tapped the open door and flashed his badge. "Peterson Jeremiah, FBI special agent."

"Jeremiah," Stone quipped. "The ancient prophet in the flesh."

"Save it, Rabbi," Jeremiah laughed. "I've heard it all before."

"What can I do for you?" Stone said.

"Is this a good time?" said Jeremiah, dropping his eyes to the football emblazoned with a red C from Stone's days at Cornell prowling Schoellkopf field and lighting up ball carriers from sideline to sideline. "Cornell, huh?"

"Yeah, long ago and far away," Stone replied. "Please, sit down; just call me Stone."

"You know this boy?" said Jeremiah, holding up his smart phone to show a photograph of Amiir and a group of Somali boys about his age walking out of the Bloomington Mosque.

"Amiir," said Stone, who knew from experience when the field of battle was shifting in unpredictable ways. "Known him for years. His father is one of my best friends. Brought them out of Somalia during the war, helped settle them here."

"Amiir?" asked Jeremiah, scrolling to another photograph of him outside the Electric Fetus with the purple-haired hippie chick Amina found on his laptop.

"Same," Stone said. "He in some kind of trouble?"

"To say the least," Jeremiah said. "We need your help."

"Anything," Stone said. "He's like my own son."

"We have a CI," Jeremiah said.

"CI?"

"Sorry, confidential informant."

"Right," Stone said. "Go on."

"Somali acquaintance of Amiir's, goes by the nickname Cali. I know you've done some work in the Somali community with young men at risk for the dark side—you know, radicalization, ISIS."

"That's right," Stone said. "Where does Amiir come into all this? I mean, he's been up in St. Cloud for eighteen months."

"Not exactly," Jeremiah countered. "Both of these pictures were taken in the last six weeks."

"What the fuck?" Stone said. "Who's that woman with the purple hair?"

"Calls herself Violet Cremona," he replied. "Her real name is Yasmine Ait, a Moroccan, ISIS honey pot, a real black widow, and she's got Amiir in her web. Speaking of the Web, we also have strong evidence of her connections to Anil Zarkan—Internet chat rooms and the like."

"Anil Zarkan, as in the Zarkans from West Texas?" Stone asked. "As in the brother of Army Lieutenant Ademar Zarkan?"

"Yes."

"Shit, Ademar is another good friend, fought together in Somalia. She helped me extract Amiir's family," Stone said. "How's Anil mixed up in all of this?"

"He's the Josef Goebbels of ISIS," said Jeremiah, confident that Hitler's chief propagandist needed no introduction for Stone. "Master of online recruiting. He's got Amiir in his sights, has for years."

"And?" Stone said.

"This young man, Cali, we put a wire on him. Seems Amiir and eight others are planning a trip to Syria to help ISIS build the Caliphate."

"Fuck me!" said Stone, slamming his hand on the desk, hard.

"Exactly."

"And how do I come into all of this?" said Stone.

"You're going to save his life."

Stone and Amina left their one-year-old son, Noah Warsame Stone, with some of her relatives at Riverside Towers and drove to St. Cloud the next day to meet with Charlie Christmas. They timed their visit so they could talk to him during a lunch break at the turkey-processing plant, not at the apartment with Amiir there, and nobody was more surprised than Charlie when his two friends showed up.

"Climb in, Charlie," Stone said after a few hugs and pleasantries with Stone and Amina. "Taking your sorry ass to lunch, after you wash off the fruits of your labor."

"Any good Thai here?" Amina asked. "Some place we can talk?"

"Sawatdee Thai on St. Germain, downtown, not too far from the river," Charlie said. "What's up?"

"We'll tell you when we get there," Stone said. "Kosher?"

"When did you start keeping kosher, Cap?" Charlie asked.

"He doesn't," answered Amina, poking Stone in the ribs. "Just another one of his non sequitur-ish jokes."

Charlie was at peace. He had settled into something of a routine in St. Cloud, not exactly exciting but normal, which is all he wanted after the chaos and heartbreak of the last decade—his dark alter ego banished long ago, friends with whom he visited whenever he wished, and solitude when he wanted to disappear. He worried about Amiir, but no more than most parents, and he knew Stone and Amina were doing at least as good a job as he could with parenting the teenager. The tension between the concealed but growing white supremacist element in St. Cloud worried him, yet he managed to ignore the racist comments and steer clear of any confrontations. But the sands of fate had begun to shift in the silent, imperceptible way that sand moves, particle by particle until a few grains form into a hill and then into swirling, blowing, nearly unscalable dunes that suck at your feet with every step. Charlie knew, from the first words out of Stone's mouth, that a reckoning was coming.

"I'm not gonna BS around, Charlie," said Stone, fiddling with his food in the tedious, almost comical attempt to eat rice with chopsticks. "Amiir's in trouble, deep trouble."

"He's still that good kid we know," Amina added. "But he's lost his way."

"If you mean partying, grass, alcohol, sex, isn't that the American way these days?" said Charlie, hopeful but knowing full well how far that was from the truth by the way both Stone and Amina dropped their eyes to avoid his stare. "What?"

"I'm sure you've been following all the terrorist recruitment out of Minneapolis," Stone said. "ISIS, Al-Shabaab, Somalis going to Syria?"

"Yeah," Charlie said. "What's that got to do with my boy?"

"FBI paid me a visit, agent named Peterson Jeremiah, Black guy, Haitian, solid," Stone said. "They turned one of Amiir's friends, calls himself Cali, put a wire on him."

"Damn!" Charlie said. "I knew that crowd at the Bloomington Mosque was up to no good. But he hasn't been around them for almost two years."

"Illusion," Amina said. "He's been going there on the sly every few weeks. There's also some hippie chick, the FBI says she's an ISIS recruiter, who's, well . . . let's just say Amiir has found it hard to resist that version of Eve and her poison apples."

"Ademar's twin brother, Anil, he's involved too," Stone said. "Big time ISIS guy now. Handler for that woman in Minneapolis, Violet Cremona. Runs a network of them. Works through the Web. Been chasing Amiir ever since they met in West Texas.

"Violet Cremona," Charlie said. "What kind of name is that?"

"A fake one," Amina said. "Her real name is Yasmine Ait, Moroccan. Skilled predator, procured several Somalis to her cause."

"Shit, what am I supposed to do?" Charlie asked. "Ground him?"

"Way past that, brother," Stone said. "Amiir could be going to prison, or worse, escaping to Syria. I'm going undercover for the feds. Hopefully we can save him before it's too late."

Amina had adjusted the defaults on Amiir's smart phone so they could track his movement, and Stone had begun to tail him on secret visits to Minneapolis, each one involving a rendezvous at the Electric Fetus with Violet Cremona, and a tryst at her apartment. He even managed to conceal a camera in her flat, but the sex had become so sordid, so unlike the boy Stone knew, that he never shared the footage with anyone except for Jeremiah, and then only in hopes it might be used as evidence of Amiir's temporary insanity at a future trial. Stone concealed his commando knife in an ankle holster during the covert surveillance of Amiir, and a small derringer on a slide around his wrist, and many a night he felt like going postal on Violet or one of the other adults that had taken his boy. He thought of them as vampires, the armies of the night. They preyed on the weak, the dispossessed, the radicalized. They sank fangs into the young recruits' necks and sucked their blood, leaving only a brittle, desiccated shell, like the exoskeleton of a locust stuck to a tree. Stone was determined, even if it cost him his life, everything, to save Amiir. This was one Somali that the United States would not abandon.

CHAPTER 9

October 4, 2015

Ranger,

As-Salaam-Alaikum.

No idea where you are, but wherever this letter finds you, I hope you're well. I called that office at Ft. Bliss where you're stationed, but they wouldn't give me an address, said you were TDY and they'd forward it. Not sure what TDY means, forgot all those Army codes, but I'm sure they're taking advantage of what you do best. Bad news for the other side.

I'm still working at that turkey slaughterhouse in St. Cloud, good money but up to my knees in bird guts all day long. I used to enjoy American Thanksgiving, but I'll never look the same way at a drumstick. Think I'll just go with the cranberry sauce and dressing, and that pecan pie at the end. I see Captain Pro all the time, the rabbi of Little Mogadishu, and he's making a name for himself in Minneapolis, kicking ass and taking names as always.

I'm sorry to say everything is not going so well with Amiir. He's doing okay on the surface—good grades and a full scholarship to kick for St. Cloud State. But the boy we knew for so many years seems to have gone somewhere else. Like those sea turtles we used to watch on the beach in Mogadishu, he's crept slowly down the beach into the ocean and disappeared underwater. He's fallen into a bad crowd, that same crowd you're chasing around the world, and I don't know what to do. Amina went through his computer and found all kinds of ISIS stuff, even some coded messages from your brother, Anil. He sneaks off to Minneapolis almost every weekend, and we're sure he's spending time with that radical Imam at the mosque in Bloomington. There also seems to be some older woman—calls herself Violet Cremona, looks like one of those purple-haired hippies you see hanging out over on Fourth Street in Minneapolis—but I know an Arab when I see one. Nothing wrong with Arabs, some of the best people I know, but that Arab is trouble in a shoebox, as we say in Somalia. Amina found a photo she sent to Amiir, and she's not wearing any clothes! What would his mother have said?

Stone consults with that nonprofit in Minneapolis, Ka Joog, that works with young people to keep them away from the radicals, and they told him they're worried about Amiir and ten other boys he's hanging out with at the mosque. As we both know, since they take money from Washington, the feds must be tracking him, and they've talked to Stone about it. A bunch of young men AND WOMEN in Minneapolis have slipped off to Syria to join ISIS, that gang of criminals pretending in the name of Allah to recreate the old Caliphate. What a bunch of camel shit! They're no better than that mafia in the US, or the cartels in Mexico. I've been through a lot, we've been through a lot, and I've never been afraid. But I am now. It's like that time we crossed the river in Somalia when that damn crocodile leaped out of the water and bit Awil in half. I can feel those ISIS reptiles circling Amiir. He has no idea, blinded by the open legs of that purple-haired woman. I'm afraid that you'll look through the scope of your rifle and my sweet boy will be in the crosshairs. You or some other sharpshooter.

Something else. You know all that stuff the resettlement people told us about Minnesota being such a progressive state? More camel shit. Sure, there are kind, open-minded people here like our friend Natalie, but there's also a bunch of white radicals who've crawled out of their caves since that "Tea Party" political gang started raising so much hell. I thought this country was way past that when they elected a Black brother as president. No way! Somebody threw a brick through Natalie's window, must have scared her kids like hell, and I'm sure it's that group that calls themselves C-Cubed, Concerned Community Citizens. Bunch of them work at the turkey plant, and they give me a lot of shit.

Enshallah it all blows over, but I'm not hopeful.

Your friend,
Charlie Christmas

November 19, 2015

Charlie,

Wa-Alaikum-Salaam.

I feel you about those turkey parts, but with Thanksgiving just around the corner, I wouldn't mind sitting down to a big old gobbler with all the fixins. Snowball's chance in hell of that happening where I am. Can't say much about what I'm doing, but sounds like you have a pretty good idea.

It's ugly out here, my friend, and dangerous. What you said about the crocodiles is right on target. At least in Somalia we knew who the bad guys were. They're everywhere. Not surprised they're popping up in Minneapolis. I don't fault Amiir; what boy his age could resist a woman like that Violet Cremona? My twin brother, Anil, went down that same path, and it kills me that he's the predator in the background with Amiir. I worry every day that he'll show up in my gunsight one day. What would I do? You know I'd come there if I could, and I'll take some leave when I'm back, whenever that is. You, Stone, Sam, and I can try to intervene with him before it's too late. Do you think it's too late? Don't answer; it would break my heart. I still see him on Jack's plane out of Kenya, slurping tapioca with old Buck's head in his lap. Sweet boy, caught in the undertow. I wonder if he was looking out the window that night, or at the reflection of a stranger.

Those white supremacists, ugh! Not so much of it in Texas, but some, and they're a nasty crowd. Watch your ass with them, Charlie Christmas. God forbid if one of them ever gets to the White House. I've seen some stuff about them in the intel, how embedded they are in places like police departments, and seems to me that we should be putting more energy into rolling them up. I just found out that many police departments started as "slave patrols." I mean, there's plenty of good cops, many of them my friends, but I'm not surprised there's racists in there too. They're everywhere, and you're right, our political system has drawn them out of the sewage drain.

So happy for Sam and Stone; those two were destined to be together. Remember how love-struck the good rabbi was when they first met at the East Village Grill? Hah! Never seen Stone at such a loss for words. I'm also a little jealous. Haven't seen Deuce for more than a few days at a time since we were married two years ago. We're thinking about calling it a day in the full-time Army. Might be boring, but boring is just what I need.

I miss you, Charlie, and hope to see you soon. Keep the faith. There is no God but God.

Ranger

CHAPTER 10

On a late summer afternoon in 2017, Amiir and a few friends from his inner circle at the Dar al-Farooq Mosque in Bloomington gathered around a picnic table at Lakefront Park in St. Cloud. They were seething over the bombing of the mosque a few weeks earlier by three men from the White Rabbit Three Percent Illinois Patriot Freedom Fighters Militia, which derives its name from what they claim were the 3 percent of American colonists who armed themselves against occupying British troops. The ringleader, Michael Hari—a former sheriff's deputy and an acquaintance of Lilith Poe—and his two associates said they wanted to "scare" Muslims out of the country with the bombing, which caused considerable damage but no injuries, because "they push their beliefs on everyone else." The pace and severity of racist and anti-Semitic acts in Minnesota had quickened since the election of President Barack Obama in 2008, including Ku Klux Klan graffiti painted in elevators at St. Cloud State, the firebombing of the Adas Israel Synagogue in Duluth, and the defacement of mosques with pig's blood, considered unclean to both Muslims and Jews. One of their friends, Dahir Adan, a twenty-two-year-old security guard who had recently flunked out of St. Cloud State, was incensed by a comment on the mosque bombing from President Trump's deputy national security advisor, Sebastian Gorka, who insinuated that it was a fake hate crime "propagated by the left." Adan was a few years older than Amiir, but they were friends and teammates at Apollo High School and at St. Cloud State. Adan had been on the glide path to violent radicalism for months—prone to outbursts of anger, disassociating himself from his family, losing weight, and spending hours in Internet chat rooms with the likes of Violet Cremona and Anil Zarkan. They had expertly enabled the radicalization of Adan, and the disease had reached its terminal stage.

Adan was a ticking time bomb, an ISIS foot soldier waiting for an opportunity to attack. And he'd decided September 17 would be his day to enter the halls of martyrdom, to strike a blow against the Western Crusaders, to follow in the hallowed footsteps of all the holy warriors before him, and to take his place in heaven with the seventy-two virgins that the Prophet Muhammad promised for *shahids*, those who die defending their rights or property. Adan called his boss at the security company to inform him that he would not come into work, tucked two kitchen knives into the pants' pockets of his dark blue uniform, and headed to the sprawling Crossroads Mall a few miles from downtown St. Cloud. His last words of conversation, uttered to a clerk at a convenience store where he stopped on the way to the mall, were "You won't be seeing me again."

Adan was a nervous assassin. He tapped his pockets dozens of times, like a madman scratching a phantom rash until it bled, reassuring himself over and over that the nine-inch serrated knives had not somehow fallen out. It's impossible to unravel the last thoughts of one who thinks of himself as an Islamic holy warrior. Those who carry out attacks and survive have described a feeling akin to an out-of-body experience in which they see each moment, each gunshot, each slash, each explosion as if they are watching themselves in slow motion, stalking from victim to victim, waiting to die, to ascend. Robots of mayhem, angels of death, servants of God, shahids. Although Adan had planned to launch the first attack inside the mall, he nonchalantly slashed a man standing outside the GNC store on his way inside. Adan seemed confused, charging in one direction and then another amid a few shoppers and elderly mall walkers wearing track suits and jogging shoes, asking people if they were Muslim and muttering *Allahu Akbar* to himself. Ultimate Electronics was his first stop, and a young male clerk was the second of ten victims, all of whom survived the attack with the comically puny domestic kitchen knife.

Slash. The clerk falls to the ground with an obvious head wound, scrambles around racks of computer games. Adan pursues amid the clutter of fallen electronics, stab, stab, slash. The victim cowers, covers his head, scoots away on all fours like an animal on fire. Adan rushes out, past H&M, reassures himself, *Allahu Akbar, Allahu Akbar.* He charges into Northwood Candy Emporium, pulls out the other knife—slash, stab, slash stab—slips on the faux linoleum tile floor slick with blood. He strides down the mall, leaving red footprints in front of Macy's. Thinks, *Macy's, yes, Macy's, where my mother couldn't afford to shop, the belly of the Western beast, the embodiment of the oppressor, the Crusaders, the heretics.* Adan is methodical— slash, slash, slash. Children scream. Someone chases Adan. Shots echo off the hard tile floor, off the ceiling. Adan's chest burns. He falls down, stands up, turns away, backpedals at a full sprint toward the gunfire, arms pumping. Two more shots. Adan feels something explode in his chest. He falls. Dying. He struggles to breathe. *Allahu Akbar.* Breath. *La Ilaha ilAllah.* Black. Nothing. Dead.

Lilith Poe was just starting a meeting of C-Cubed at Culvers when static from the transmitter on her belt crackled—*10-64 at Macy's Crossroads Mall. Possible 10-67. Crime in progress, report of death*. "Sorry, folks, meeting adjourned. Live one at the mall," said Lilith, rushing out of the restaurant and calling dispatch with her mobile as she turned on the siren in her cruiser and sped the two miles to Crossroads Mall. She felt important, indispensable, and everyone better get out of her way, or else.

"What the fuck's going on?" she barked at the dispatcher.

"Terrorist attack," the dispatcher replied. "Somali went postal with a knife. Multiple victims. Sounds like an off-duty officer took him down."

"Jesus F Christ," she hissed. "En route; I'm close."

Lilith was among the first officers on the scene, parking near the Macy's entrance, inching into the store gun barrel first like a lioness stalking through the tall grass. Adan lay on his stomach in a puddle of blood next to the men's discount suit rack, knife still in his hand and Jason Falconer, an off-duty cop and firearms instructor, standing over him. Ambulances and police cars, sirens blaring, converged on the mall, and paramedics with gurneys rushed around, searching for victims.

"Good job, Jason. One less *NWG*," said Lilith, using the racist acronym for *nigger with a gun*.

"Jesus, Lilith," Falconer said. "Cut the racist shit. He's Somali, American."

"Whatever. Same thing," she said. "When did you become such a pussy?"

Lilith, without putting on latex gloves to preserve the crime scene, pulled the victim's wallet from his pocket to check the driver's license. "Dahir Adan, University Place Apartments, 7C. Anybody asks, I'm going over there to check it out."

"Call it in," Falconer said. "Wait for backup."

"Relax," said Lilith, holstering her pistol and running to her car. "I've got this."

This was the opportunity she'd been waiting for her entire life, one on one with the Black enemy, a family of terrorists—Somalis, no less—and no witnesses. *No fucking way*

I'm calling it in, she thought to herself. Lilith silenced her siren as she pulled into the parking lot at the apartments, popping the trunk of her cruiser to don full battle gear—body armor, Premier Crown riot helmet with face shield, and two extra clips of hollow point ammunition for her Glock 9 mm pistol. *Locked and loaded*, she muttered to herself, feeling like the bad-ass cop she'd always wanted to be. *I'm going in.* She prowled around the garden apartments until she found a sign pointing to the C wing and the hallway leading to apartments one through seven. But there was a problem—the numbers on the apartment doors were missing, except for the one in the middle of the hallway with number four. Lilith, who had never been that good with math or reasoning, was flummoxed as a single bead of sweat ran down her back and into her butt crack. She paced up and down the darkened hallway several times, counting the doors with each pass in a vain attempt to determine which apartment was number seven. She figured out that it had to be on one end or the other; the question was which end. *When all else fails*, she whispered to herself, walking slowly past each door as she recited her favorite nursery rhyme. *Eeny meeny miny mo, catch a nigger by his toe. My mother told me to pick the very best one, and that is you.* Lilith stopped in front of the door to which she was sure fate had led her and, without knocking or shouting a warning, lowered her shoulder and attempted to smash it open. But the door didn't give way, and she fell backward with her feet in the air like an upended doodlebug. *Shit, shit, shit*, she mumbled, her shoulder barking with pain, then stood up and tried again. This time the door flew open, and Lilith charged into the room. The first thing she saw was a large dog, one ear, which appeared to have been torn in half, standing straight up, the other one flat against his head. It was an old dog, crippled by arthritis, hips buckling sideways, barely able to stand. "Police!" shouted Lilith, one eye on the dog as it snarled and dragged himself toward her, threatening and pitiful at the same time. Lilith shook her head, sneered, and fired two rounds into the dog's chest, killing it instantly. *Later, Fido*, she chuckled to herself.

Amiir and Charlie rushed into the living room of their apartment from their bedrooms in the back. Buck, their faithful guardian—Buck, their best friend—dead on the floor with two gaping holes in his chest and blood sprayed all over the wall behind him. "Buck, no!" wailed Amiir, rushing to the dog's side and cradling his big head, eyes closed forever.

"Hands on your heads!" shrieked Lilith, pointing the gun at Amiir, at Charlie, then back at Amiir. "On your stomachs, now!"

"Dad!" Amiir yelled. "Do something!"

"Do what the cop says!" Charlie replied. "Stay calm. Just do what she says."

"Damn straight do what the cop says!" Lilith yelled. "Or you terrorists are following your retard mutt straight to hell!"

Lilith handcuffed them both, twisting her face in disgust and wiping her hands on the leg of her pants as if she'd come into contact with some hidden germ, some hidden Black germ.

"You failed," said Lilith, dropping one knee hard on Charlie's throat and holding it there to cut off oxygen. "Dahir Adan is dead, killed in a terrorist attack at the mall. Son and brother to you two. Don't try to hide it. You're both under arrest."

"I can't breathe," Charlie wheezed, barely able to get the words out.

"Too fucking bad," Lilith said. "You're next, kid! Unless you spill all the beans about the plot."

"He can't breathe!" Amiir yelled. "My father can't breathe!"

". . . Can't … breathe . . . can't . . . ," Charlie repeated, starting to lose consciousness.

A neighbor rushed down the hallway, into the room, and Lilith wheeled toward him with her finger on the trigger. "What about Dahir Adan?" asked the neighbor, who had heard the name from his apartment. "That's my son. We live at the other end of the hall."

"Oh," said Lilith, lifting her knee from Charlie's throat and seeming to deflate like a punctured beach ball.

His father's dark alter ego, now his dark alter ego, haunted Amiir's dreams every night thereafter—stoking his anger, daring him to take vengeance. Amiir sent a two-word message the next week to Violet Cremona and to Anil: "I'm ready." Two weeks later Anil met him at Istanbul Airport, and within five days he crossed the border into ISIS-controlled Syria, a fully radicalized foot soldier of the Caliphate. Ademar, deployed in southern Turkey at Incirlik Air Base as part of a covert operation to hunt down and kill high-level ISIS commanders across the border in Syria, received a Skype call a few days later from Charlie and Stone.

"Charlie Christmas and Prometheus Stone, as I live and breathe," she said. "To what do I owe the pleasure?"

"No pleasure, Ranger," Charlie said.

"What?" said Ademar, instantly operational.

"It's Amiir," Stone said. "The FBI told us he's headed your way."

"Damn," that's about the worst news I've heard in months. "And there ain't anything but bad news around here. It happened so quick. Just got your letter a few months ago, Charlie."

"It gets worse," Stone said. "They think he's with your brother somewhere around Raqqa."

"That's a major TO for me," said Ademar, using the military acronym for Theater of Operations. "All kinds of bad guys there."

"You've got your orders, Ademar," Stone said. "Capture or kill. Emphasis on capture if you come across Amiir."

"*Enshallah*," Charlie said.

"*Enshallah*," Ademar replied.

"One other thing," Charlie said. "Buck's dead."

CHAPTER 11

Internal Affairs at the St. Cloud Police Department determined that the killing of Dahir Adan was a clean shoot, and the community hailed Falconer as a hero who saved untold lives with his decisiveness, bravery, and marksmanship. It was a different story with Lilith Poe. The St. Cloud Area Somali Salvation Organization and the Somali Student Association at the university filed a formal complaint for excessive use of force, and the Association for Prevention of Cruelty to Animals vilified her for killing Buck. A picture is worth a thousand words, never more so than the photograph a bystander took with her iPhone at the apartments—Lilith in full body armor, 9 mm in one hand, knee digging into Charlie's throat, and Amiir shattered, cradling Buck's head in one hand and pleading with the other for her to stop strangling his father. The ASPCA developed an entire social media campaign around the picture, with millions of shares and retweets echoing through the Web, generally denouncing animal cruelty and police brutality and christening Poe as the poster child for all that is wrong in America.

"You're done, Poe," the police chief told her in his office. "Violated every procedure in the book, nearly killed an innocent man in what amounts to a public lynching, double-tapped a harmless old dog, pissed off the whole city, embarrassed the department, and put every straight cop in the country at risk. You're a racist. You disgust me. Badge and gun, now."

"But," whimpered Poe, holding back tears, cheeks flushed crimson with anger and humiliation.

"No buts!" said the chief, removing his glasses, standing to his full height, and extending his hand. Lilith, an unrelenting narcissist, mistook it as a gesture of reconciliation and reached out to shake his hand. "You're a piece of work," said the chief, who pushed her hand aside. "Goddamn badge and gun, Poe. You're lucky I'm not arresting your sorry ass."

Lilith dropped the badge and gun. *A nobody*, she thought to herself, what she feared most, what she fought so hard to avoid, and what her monstrous father called her as a child when she was in tears after he had satisfied himself and wiped his hand on her hair. Nobody. A powerless, radicalized nobody. Like a feral lab animal freed to the wild, Poe stalked on pure instinct. She climbed into her car, took a breath, checked the glove compartment to make sure the Smith & Wesson snubnosed .38 was still there, and sent a text to the C-Cubed group chat. "Emergency meet. Culvers, 7 PM." Lilith knew she had to prime the pump before the meeting to ensure her compatriots were appropriately indignant. She sent another text to Olaf Schneider, the failed farmer working at the turkey-processing plant who had spoken so eloquently about his resentment for Somalis, and an easy mark for a predator like Poe. "America's Best Value Inn, room thirty-seven, 6 p.m. Important!"

There's nothing sexy or romantic about a thinning shag carpet; a leaking, rusty AC unit in the window; and the smell of disinfectant at a broken-down highway motel—seedy and taboo like a grainy black-and-white porn movie from the 1950s, titillating to some, but not even close to sexy or romantic. It didn't seem to bother Schneider when he walked into room thirty-seven, Poe buck naked on the stained sheets, beckoning him with one hand and rubbing herself with the other. "Hop on cowboy" was all she said, and Schneider obeyed. It was over in less than a minute, but Schneider, who hadn't been laid in more than a year, was spent and compliant.

"You hear?" Lilith asked.

"Miscarriage of justice," Schneider said. "Should have shot 'em both, like the dog."

"You see?"

"Got hard when I saw that photo," he grunted, smiling and clearly contemplating another ride on the bucking bronco.

"Whoa Nellie," Poe said. "It's all yours, but you have to back me at the meeting. Help stir up that crowd."

"Always, Lilith," said Schneider, with the mad, desperate look in his eyes of a male dog catching the whiff of a bitch in heat.

"No bullshit!" Lilith hissed, slapping him on the ass as she climbed on top for another lightning round.

"Yes, ma'am," he replied obediently.

Word of her termination had spread like wildfire through the small, insular St. Cloud community, with most people applauding the decision. Naturally, most people did not include the Culver's crowd. Within minutes, abetted by Schneider, Lilith had whipped them into a frenzy. She didn't exactly have a plan, Lilith wasn't big on details, and she knew that her fingerprints couldn't be on anything that happened after her pep talk. She only had to set the table and let others serve the meal. And she knew from the heated discussion, in which her son, Georgi, was among the loudest voices, that the kettle was boiling.

Marley Wittenberg was a good person, a smart soldier who had worked her way up the executive ladder in an industry dominated by men. She didn't mind working late—the price most women pay for advancement in an American company—without complaining and without demanding overtime, but she missed dinner with her two children and husband.

Shedding her corporate armor, trading the mundane stories about everyone's day, and feeling the simple gratification and outright joy of just being a mom, a wife, were the best parts of her life. Sitting at her desk in the turkey-processing plant, preparing a PowerPoint about 401ks for a meeting the next day with new Somali employees, she wondered what her family was eating, what they were discussing, and what television show they would watch after the kids had completed their homework. Marley had asked Natalie Bell, a mother and wife just like her, to drop by the office to help devise the best, most culturally appropriate way to explain the savings plan to the Somalis, with whom Natalie had years of experience through her nonprofit. Natalie was a true believer, a champion of social justice, and would never pass up an opportunity to help a disadvantaged group cut the deck in a card game that was so clearly stacked against them. Marley looked forward to an hour or so with the breezy, positive young woman, and smiled when she walked into her office. The two of them were deep into the night's work when they heard a metallic snap, followed by the sound of a gate opening.

Georgi was almost twenty years younger than Schneider, but he felt they were kindred spirits, cut from the same bigoted cloth, and he sensed that his mother had anointed the older man as a mentor. Georgi had finally found a club that would allow him to join—a club with only two members but a club nonetheless. They had connected through an encrypted message board on 4chan in the weeks since the explosive meeting at Culvers, sharing their mutual affinity for shooter-survivor games, drones, mixed-race pornography, and white supremacy. It was during one of those late-night sessions on 4chan that Schneider sucked Georgi into a plan to vindicate his mother and to spark an uprising against the Somalis.

"You ever hear of Emmett Till?" Schneider asked Georgi.

"No," Georgi said. "Who's that?"

"Sixteen-year-old nigger kid in Mississippi," Schneider replied. "Lynched for getting fresh with a white girl."

"Probably deserved it," Georgi said.

"That's the thing; he didn't," Schneider replied. "She lied to her husband and half brother about it. Pissed those ol' boys off good. Beat the shit out of him, lynched him, shot him in the head, and threw him in the Tallahatchie River."

"Made sure he was good and dead, huh?" Georgi said. "What's that got to do with us?"

"I'll explain," Schneider said. "Meet me at Frieda's in an hour."

Schneider spooled out his idea to Georgi at a picnic bench in front of Frieda's Café, an iconic greasy spoon diner in the heart of Willmar, near the big Pepsi sign that hung above the glass door.

"There's this autistic girl, don't know her name, but I've been tracking her with that drone, the DJI Mavic Pro, from C-Cubed," Schneider explained. "Kind of a retard, but kinda hot too, in a retarded way. Every day after school, she stops for a few minutes by the lake, just stands there staring at the water."

"Go on," said Georgi, growing more excited with every word.

"We snatch her by the lake, wait until night, and take her to the turkey plant where I work. I've got an electronic ID to open the back gate," he said. "Here's the good part. We stick her head in the electrified water that stuns the turkeys, rape her, and leave her chained there with a sign pinned on her shirt saying the Somalis did it to get back for what your mom did. Brilliant, huh?"

"But she'll know it's us," Georgi said.

"You think I'm stupid or something?" Schneider said. "We wear masks and gloves, talk like those Africans, say stuff she can hear about how pissed off we are at how the whites treat us. She's so stupid she probably won't remember any of it. But if she does, she'll remember the Somali shit."

"Who goes first?" Georgi asked.

"First for what?"

"The fuck."

"Well, me, of course," Schneider said.

"I wanna go first," said Georgi, whose cherry was still intact at twenty-two.

"Age has its privileges," Schneider said. "But you'll get sloppy seconds, all the sloppy seconds you want. I'll have her all lubed up for you."

"Okay, I'm in," said Georgi, already hard thinking about it.

Their plan worked like a charm, and the girl didn't catch a glimpse of them when they snuck up behind her, pulled an old burlap feed sack over her head, dragged her into the car, and drove off unnoticed. She whimpered, rocking back and forth between them as Georgi drove the pickup to an old shed near the turkey plant where Schneider stored equipment from the defunct family farm. Schneider didn't make anything of the girl's odd, jerky motions, but it disturbed Georgi deeply, undercut his confidence, and cast a shadow over the fantasies of the past few days about his first sex. They locked her in the shed and went in his house until well past dark, drinking themselves almost sideways on Budweiser and Wild Turkey.

"Party time. Hoods and gloves," said Schneider as they dragged the girl to the truck for the short drive to the turkey plant. "And don't forget to talk like a Somali."

"How do Somalis talk?" asked Georgi.

"Don't worry about it; just talk like a nigger," Schneider said. "On second thought, let me do all the talking."

Marley opened a link on her computer to the plant's security cameras as soon as she heard the strange sounds coming from the back gate, and saw two men in hoods dragging a girl—wearing only a bra and panties with a burlap sack over her head—who stumbled as she tried to keep her feet every time the bigger of the two men yanked the rope binding her arms. She had as little control over her fate as a Turkey bound for processing.

"What is it?" asked Natalie, who knew instantly from Marley's reaction that it was something serious.

"What do you make of this?" asked Marley, turning the computer screen so Natalie could see.

"Call the police," Natalie said.

"We may not have time," said Marley, phoning it in to the cops and alerting the company responsible for plant security, whose guards missed the intrusion by the two men.

Marley tracked them on the security camera, through a narrowing passage funneling the turkeys into a room where the birds are attached upside down to an overhead conveyor that drags their heads into an electrified pool of water, which stuns them into submission. They hang limp as a dish towel, nearly lifeless, necks stretched tight by gravity so the auto-mated blade cuts cleanly through their throats and the blood drains into troughs underneath. Aghast, Marley and Natalie watched the girl jerk once as they dunked her head in the stun pool and collapse absolutely limp. She was splayed out like a rag doll as one of the men began cutting off her panties and bra.

"Shit," Marley gasped. "Let's go!"

Natalie grabbed a canister of pepper spray from her purse while Marley picked up a crowbar, and the two women crept down the turkey funnel leading to the processing line. The smell of birds, of turkey excrement, of death revolted Natalie as she followed behind, and she nearly retched. Marley looked over her shoulder and reassured Natalie with a light, sisterly squeeze of her arm. She motioned them forward until they were close enough to smell the alcohol on the men and feel the adrenaline of the two beasts as they prepared to mount their victim. Marley, who batted clean-up on her high school softball team, stepped forward, and if Schneider's head had been a ball, it would have cleared the center field fence by a mile. Schneider, pants at his feet and prick pushing against his tighty whities, fell limp, as limp as one of those turkeys that had just been dragged through the electrified pool. Blood pooled in the diamond-shaped divot behind his right ear and spilled on to the cement floor. Georgi, who had started to unbuckle his belt, wheeled around just as Natalie gave him a face-full of pepper spray. He fell backward against the electrified pool of water, one hand clawing at his eyes, the other falling into the stun bath. For a moment, he looked like a tap dancer on his tiptoes speeding frantically through a soft-shoe routine as if he'd fallen behind the music. He jerked against the invisible grip of electricity and bit his bottom lip so hard that spit and blood ran down his chin in frothy, crimson rivulets. Marley's second at bat was a solid double, snapping Georgi's arm above the wrist and freeing it from the electrified bath. The two women, with five children between them, stood in silence, absolute silence, stunned by their audacity, by the stark reality that violence resided in their nature alongside all the other qualities of a woman that vested them with unending patience, unselfish love, and unquenchable empathy. Nurturers and killers. Creators and destroyers.

They had tied up the two men and wrapped a blanket around the girl, confused but safe and unsullied. It was over by the time the police arrived, led by the St. Cloud chief, who had responded even though the call was out of his jurisdiction. He could imagine what had happened, but all the details would not emerge until a thorough investigation and a trial, which resulted in a guilty verdict for both men—Schneider for kidnapping and attempted rape, Georgi as an accomplice.

"I can see you ladies are okay," said the chief, lifting Georgi's head up by his hair. "Georgi Poe. Guess the apple doesn't fall too far from the tree."

CHAPTER 12

Ademar didn't see much of her husband, Crockett Laws Jr., during her time in the Army, much less her older brother, Tamerlane Zarkan II. But every now and then fate would bring them together. There was the surprise visit Stone organized in Somalia when Deuce and T2 transported Buck, and a few brief days of leave in world capitals like Istanbul, London, or Amman. They were a potent force on the battlefield—Deuce, a trusted Ranger officer; Ademar, as deadly a sniper as any who wore a Ranger tab; and T2, a hulking, good-natured presence and a bomb disposal expert. Ademar's and T2's fluency in Arabic and Muslim faith were icing on the cake in Middle East operations. For the men and women who fought alongside the Texas trifecta, a nickname given to them by Stone, it was as if the top of the Yankees' batting order, circa 1978, had been plugged into the lineup.

Istanbul was one of their favorite meeting spots, and, within the boundaries of security in a nation crawling with violent extremists and criminals who would jump at the chance to abduct three American soldiers, they would roam the storied streets of the iconic Mediterranean city. They often started the day with breakfast at one of the cafés around the Blue Mosque—fresh-baked simit bread dipped in molasses and bitter Turkish coffee. They laughed at each other like teenagers back in Dell City when the loose grounds at the bottom of the small copper kettle stuck in their teeth. It felt almost normal during these brief interludes from lives that were defined by the dangers of soldiering in Iraq, Afghanistan, and Syria under a commander in chief at the White House who dodged the draft with a diagnosis of bone spurs from a podiatrist in Queens and who wanted to ban Muslims from entering the United States. They usually ended the day in the historic Sultanahmet District, where they could always count on a gentle, salty breeze off the nearby Sea of Marmara to keep the heat at bay during the summer. The trio feasted on fresh fish, mussels, and endless dishes of garlic-infused vegetables amid the soft lights strung around the outdoor café at Balikci Sabahattin. They would stroll back to their hotel afterward, T2 excusing himself while Ademar and Deuce retreated to their room for a night of stolen intimacy on the soft, clean cotton sheets of a quiet air-conditioned room.

"What did that fortune teller say this morning when she poked around in the bottom of your cup?" asked Deuce, referring to a gypsy woman after breakfast who offered to predict their future by interpreting the leftover grounds in their Turkish coffee.

"Don't really remember. Something about danger and an evil, shadowy figure in our future," said Ademar, wrapping the sheet around herself to resemble a ghost and playfully grabbing Deuce's neck as if she might strangle him. *"Muahahahaha!"*

"I'm serious, Ademar," Deuce said.

"Lo siento, mi amor," she replied. "I don't remember the exact words, but my takeaway was caution and patience in the face of danger—a little like 'Discretion is the better part of valor.'"

"Shit, that's what I thought," said Deuce, who had a deep interest in the mysticism of the Native American and Mexican culture with which he grew up in the desert Southwest.

"I love that you're so superstitious," Ademar said. "Reminds me of you and Anil on Halloween back home, the way you two cried that time mom dressed up as a witch and threatened to make chili out of you. So cute, tears running down your cheeks until you recognized it was *mamacita*."

"Very funny," he said. "Don't be whistling past the grave-yard, Addie. Just be careful the next few months. T2 and I are going back stateside tomorrow. Won't have us around to save your butt."

"Yes, sir! Promise. No whistling. No graveyards," Ademar barked, laughing and mussing her husband's hair.

"What?" Deuce asked when he sensed a cloud cross her face.

"Nothing," replied Ademar, recalling the last day of poor Awil, the Somali whistler, eaten alive by a crocodile on their desperate journey to Kenya.

The Turkish seer's words came back to Ademar three times over the coming weeks—climbing out of a Blackhawk helicopter at Incirlik Air Base in the southern Turkish city of Adana, creeping around the alleys of an ISIS stronghold in the Syrian town of Raqqa in blackface and full battle gear, and crouching on the roof of a bombed out building with her twin brother, Anil, in the crosshairs of her scope. He was super-vising a mass execution of civilians, Amiir by his side, while hooded ISIS henchmen fired point blank into the backs of their heads or cut their throats before tossing their bodies into the Euphrates River. Anil, ever the showman, wore a black beret and Ray Ban sunglasses as he directed Amiir on the placement of the tripod, lights, and reflector disc to capture the full drama and color of his ghoulish production. Amiir looked bewildered and lost, shuffling like a zombie around the unfolding carnage, flinching with every gunshot and closing his eyes as each body dropped lifeless into the water. Anil, by turns the petulant film director and the nurturing predator, slapped Amiir when he moved too slowly or wrapped an arm around him in a phony gesture of brotherly solidarity that made Ademar's blood boil. Their orders were to assassinate a high-level ISIS operative, but Ademar had no idea Anil might be the target. She certainly didn't expect to find Amiir mixed up in the diabolical affair, although she knew he was somewhere in Syria. Ademar could barely bring herself to alert command that she was in position for a shot, fearing that she might receive a green light to pull the trigger, and for a moment she contemplated calling off the whole mission. But after watching at least a dozen murders, with what seemed like an entire village of men, women, and children standing in line like pigs to the slaughter, she put it all in the hands of Allah, of God.

"In position," Ademar whispered into the transmitter as an image flashed in her mind of Amiir kicking the football in the stadium at Dell City High School, and of a seven-year-old Anil playing with his Lego on the floor of their house. "Target acquired."

"What are you seeing, Zarkan?" her commander asked.

"Shit-show," she responded. "Mass execution, some guy in charge filming it."

"You have a shot," he said.

Ademar hesitated, anguished over how she would tell her parents, much less Charlie Christmas. "Yes, sir."

"Green light," the commander said. "Then get your ass back on the helicopter."

Ademar chambered a 7.62 mm round with enough punch to decapitate her brother, or Amiir. She took two breaths with Anil's dopey beret in her crosshairs, held the third breath, and began to pull the trigger when suddenly, out of nowhere, a black stretch limousine drove in front of him and Amiir.

"Zarkan?" the commander asked. "Status."

"Lost the shot," she said, relieved beyond belief but feigning frustration. "Something happened. They've stopped, and the primary just climbed into a car heading away from the bridge."

"Shit!" the commander said. "Wrap it up. Bug out."

Ademar didn't mention that Amiir, a minor target at best, had remained behind, and that she could have easily taken his life. There were about three hundred yards between her location and Amiir's, and she had an idea as he started walking toward her by himself. Ademar knew it was crazy, and that she'd likely be court-martialed if it went south and her relationship with Amiir surfaced. But all she could think about was how Charlie had rescued her from the pirate and how Amiir—deep down in his confused, conflicted, radicalized heart—was a good boy who could be saved. *And besides,* she thought guiltily to herself, *you took him out of Somalia, abandoned him in Kenya, brought him to America, and left him a sitting duck in Minnesota for the likes of Violet Cremona and Anil.*

"ISIS target coming our way, alone," Ademar whispered in the transmitter. "We can grab him."

"Extraction?" the commander asked. "You fucking crazy."

"My call, Cap," Ademar hissed.

"Your call, Zarkan," he said. "God help you if this goes FUBAR."

"*Allahu Akbar,*" she whispered to herself.

Ademar watched Amiir through her scope as he walked alone toward their building—a shuffling, mumbling, bearded shell of the winsome boy she first met in Somalia and loved as if he was her own. She looked at the three other soldiers under her command, pointed two fingers at her eyes and two fingers at Amiir, then pulled a plastic zip-tie out of her pack and handed it to the soldier next to her. Her men flashed a thumbs-up as they descended the stairs and made their way to a darkened corner of the street where Amiir was headed. He stopped five feet from them and pulled a hard-pack of Marlboros from inside his coat pocket. Before the flame touched the tip of the cigarette, Ademar was on him. Chokehold around his neck, commando knife at his throat, Amiir struggled, powerful despite his diminished state, and Ademar cranked the chokehold tighter to stifle a shout for help that came out like the pitiful, high-pitched whine of a dying bird.

"Amiir, Amiir," she whispered. "It's me, Ademar. What you do in the next thirty seconds will determine whether you live or die. Choose life."

Amiir stopped, stunned into silence by a ghost. "I don't understand," he croaked.

"You don't have to," Ademar replied. "This is bullshit. This is not the answer. Whatever happened to you in Minnesota, just forget it. Think about your father, your poor mother, Stone."

"Cap?" Amiir muttered, jolted from his radicalized trance as if struck by lightning, and relaxed in Ademar's grip. "Cap?"

"He knows. Everybody knows, Amiir," she said. "You're with me now. Me, Ademar. I'm taking you home."

"But I'll go to prison," he whimpered and tensed, trying to twist out of Ademar's choke hold. "Or worse."

"Whatever happens, I'll be with you every step of the way. We'll all be with you," said Ademar, tightening the pressure on Amiir's throat until he passed out.

Amiir regained consciousness a few minutes later as the Blackhawk helicopter lifted off the ground and headed back to Turkey. His hands were zip-tied behind his back, and his head was covered by a hood. "It's going to be okay," Ademar said so that only Amiir could hear over the thwomping of the helicopter blade, and he dropped his head to her shoulder, utterly, totally defeated.

An Army medic on the helicopter injected Amiir with enough Ketamine and Diazepam to float him mindlessly through the entire trip to Incirlik, the transfer to an unmarked Air Force Cessna Citation and the flight across Europe to Poland. He awoke naked, except for a diaper duct taped around his privates, and nearly comatose, chained to a wall in the windowless room of an abandoned warehouse near Szymany

Airport. He jerked to life as soon as the water, ice cold, was thrown in his face. Amiir's eyes darted around the room, like a cornered animal, barely able to focus through the pulsating strobe lights on tripods around him. Judas Priest's heavy metal classic "Thunder Road" blasted over and over from speakers on all sides, and the buckets of ice-cold water kept coming. Amiir couldn't remember the last time he relieved himself and felt like crying at the rancid, acrid smell from the soiled diaper slipping down his waist, excrement oozing from the sides, puddling in the few inches between his feet and the brick floor. The echo of his desperate screams was the only human voice in the room, except for the grinding wail of Judas Priest's front-man Rob Halford. Amiir's shoulders ached after so many hours suspended by chains a few feet off the floor, and his right shoulder dislocated with a pop as he struggled to free himself.

He was chained for days to a wall in a CIA black site—naked, cold, and soiled—with no visitors except for one: the dark shadow of his father's past, the malicious, relentless conscience of an abandoned nation, Sayiid Awale.

"I hate to say it," the spirit taunted him. "But I told you so."

Amiir prayed to himself. *La Ilaha ilAllah.*

"Haha!" the other cackled. "Words, my son, hollow, stupid words."

"*Bismillah. Bismillah. Bismillah. A oothu billahi wa qudratihi min sharii ma ajdu wa uhaathiru. In the name of Allah. In the name of Allah. In the name of Allah. I seek refuge in Allah and in his power from the evil of what I find and of what I guard against.*"

"Your America is great again, isn't it?" whispered the dark shadow. "Damn them all to hell—your father, Ademar, Stone! Where is that purple-haired woman? Where is Anil, those seventy-two virgins?"

A hand—a soft, nutmeg-scented hand, the hand of his poor dead mother, Ebla—stroked his swollen cheek, cupped his chin, and whispered through the deafening noise, "This will pass, my son. It's not your time. Remember the Sun Dance; remember your father. Free yourself from this demon. Choose life. Live." The mocking alter ego that haunted two generations of his family receded farther into the dark between each pulse of the strobe light, like an old black-and-white photograph that fades to nothing with every decade until the image disappears. Banished by the power of love and hope. When Amiir opened his eyes, there was only silence, the room illuminated by a single dim light over his head and the gentle hand of Ademar propping up his chin for a drink of cool water.

"I'm sorry, Amiir," she said. "So sorry."

"Ademar." He could barely speak. "What . . ."

"Don't try to talk. Just listen. Forget all that ISIS crap. You must tell these people everything. They are madmen, torturers, killers. I promise you won't go to Guantanamo Bay. But I have to be straight. You broke the law and must pay the price. You will probably go to prison for a while in America. We'll make sure it's in Minnesota, close to your father, to Stone, to me, and we'll take care of you. Hold your head high, Amiir. Choose life. Live."

Amiir was a low-level ISIS recruit, not really a violent extremist at all but a reluctant handmaiden to the purveyors of hate, chaos, and terror. Racked with guilt at the faces of those who perished—the faces of innocent men, women, and children flung into the river half alive with their throats slashed during the only terrorist operation he ever actually witnessed—Amiir remained resolute in his will to survive. During weeks of interrogation, he imagined that his cooperation was like those football cleats Coach T gave him in Dell City, like those sparkly red slippers Dorothy wore in *The Wizard of Oz*. And, like the three magical clicks of Dorothy's heels, his cooperation with the interrogators would magically transport him back to America.

Ademar visited him every day; so did the CIA interrogators, and the more he told them, the more his time in
captivity improved. Amiir was freed from the chains on the
wall, although they hung as a chilling reminder of what could
happen if his captors had the slightest inkling that he was
anything but transparent. He was given clothes, a mattress,
bathroom privileges, and two decent meals a day. For his birthday, Ademar brought Amiir a bowl of tapioca. He experienced
a near-religious epiphany as the sweet, silky-smooth beads slid
down his throat. She also brought a letter from his father with
a photograph of him, Stone, Amina, and their son. On what
would be the final day of captivity, Ademar came into his cell
with a Black man in a dark suit.

"Amiir," Ademar said. "This is FBI Special Agent Peterson Jeremiah from Minneapolis."

"You're going home," Jeremiah said.

"Home?" Amiir questioned.

"In a matter of speaking," Jeremiah said. "A jail cell in
Minneapolis. You're being charged with conspiring to join
a terrorist organization, maximum sentence nine years. You
could be out in two if you cooperate with investigators."

"Two years in prison," said Amiir, shaking his head.
"Well, it couldn't be any worse than this."

"It could, Amiir," Ademar said. "But it won't."

The ensuing months were a whirlwind of judicial pro-
ceedings, interrogations, and eventually a trial in which Amiir
received a two-year sentence at the medium-security prison in
Stillwater, eighty-three miles from St. Cloud and twenty-five
miles from Minneapolis. In a cruel twist of fate, Amiir shared
a cell with Georgi Poe in a wing of the prison supervised by
none other than his mother, the disgraced, racist ex-cop Lilith.

CHAPTER 13

Despite her soiled record, fired in disgrace from two law enforcement jobs over a five-year span, or perhaps because of it, the Minnesota Department of Corrections hired Lilith to serve as a supervisor at Stillwater. She was part of a major effort by Stillwater to bring in more personnel after a guard was brutally murdered the previous year in an incident that laid bare the crisis of understaffing at Minnesota prisons. Edward Muhammad Johnson, the great-grandson of Elijah Muhammad, who founded the Nation of Islam, was a child of violence and radicalization. The offspring of two Chicago police officers, an eight-year-old Johnson witnessed his father fire six bullets into his mother, killing her instantly and ending his own life with a seventh round into the roof of his mouth. History repeated itself in 2002 when Johnson murdered his girlfriend in their Bloomington apartment, and again in 2018 when he bludgeoned Correctional Officer Joseph Gromm to death with a hammer in an unsupervised shop room. Lilith, who'd worked mostly part time as a cashier at Walmart since she was fired from the police force, noticed an advertisement for corrections officers in the St. Cloud newspaper and submitted an application on her next visit to see Georgi. Warden Denver Dick, a stern disciplinarian cut from the same cloth as Lilith's father, believed in redemption almost as much as corporal punishment and decided to give her a break. Lilith was simultaneously repulsed and drawn to someone like her father whom she could easily picture molesting a young girl. If she played her cards right, Lilith thought that morning in front of the mirror, tucking her breasts into a new push-up bra, a man twice her age who spent most of his time in a prison might find her appealing. Although it would be a supreme conflict of interest for a guard to supervise an inmate to whom she was related, Lilith knew how to work a man like Dick, and she landed him like an expert angler on a Montana trout stream.

"Mrs. Poe," the warden said as Lilith entered his office. "Please, sit."

"Thank you, sir," she replied, then noticed the picture of a woman on his desk. "You're lucky to have a wife like that."

"Was lucky," he replied. "The cancer took her eight years ago."

"So sorry," she said. "I'm sure she was lucky to have a stand-up guy like you as a husband."

"It was a rough few years," Dick said. "We endured."

"I'll bet you've gotten your share of casseroles since then?" said Lilith, casting a lure on the surface of a potential relationship, which he took hook, line, and sinker.

"I don't know about that," the warden said. "Not many women understand what a job like this does to a man. Takes a special one, and I haven't found her."

"Patience," she said. "My daddy, a cop, taught me that."

"You'll need plenty of it for this place, with the trash in here," he said. "What about you? Married?"

"Are you allowed to ask?" she replied, setting the hook and reeling Dick in slowly, deliciously, and, at the last moment, yanking the line to seat the barb so he couldn't wriggle off the hook. "Just joking. Like to joke. You'll learn that about me if we work together. I'm sure you'll discover all my little secrets.

Been married twenty-five years, at least in name. A pharmacist, boring. Really boring, if you get my drift?"

"I think so," said Dick, removing his reading glasses, twirling them by one temple, placing the tip in his mouth, and staring at Lilith for thirty awkward seconds.

"Warden Dick?" said Lilith, breaking the silence.

"Yes, sorry," he said, returning the glasses to the bridge of his nose and shuffling through her application.

"I think you'd be perfect for Stillwater," he said. "But you're record is, well, blemished. And your son is an inmate here."

"All true, warden," replied Lilith, pulling her blouse tight against her ample, mechanically augmented bosom, dropping her eyes, and feigning the closest thing to remorse she could muster. "I'm not perfect. None of us are. I paid a high price for my mistakes, but I learned. You won't be disappointed. Give me a chance, please, sir. You'll see."

"Okay, Lilith," Dick said. "If I may I call you that?"

"Of course," she said. "At least when we're alone."

"Okay, Lilith," he said. "Job's yours."

Prisons are incubators for violent radicalism, particularly one like Stillwater where inmates throughout its 105-year history either joined a gang or suffered as a bitch to fifteen hundred men serving their time with no sexual release other than their hand in the jungles of concrete, steel, and diseased madness that pass for justice in America. Three gangs dominate at Stillwater—Latin Kings, the preeminent Hispanic group in American prisons since its inception in 1954; Black Guerilla Family, established at San Quentin in 1966 and a powerful political advocate for inmates' rights; and Aryan Brotherhood, which also originated at San Quentin in the 1960s and whose members tattoo themselves with a shamrock and the number 666, symbolizing the Antichrist. There are no established Muslim gangs, but they may be the most dangerous and feared in prison systems around the world.

Natural allies for Black gangs, many of which find common ground with the narrative of oppression wrapped around radical Islam, they focus on piety, abstinence, patience, and brainwashing the dispossessed into a way of life that leads to early release for good behavior, and to terrorism.

Georgi wasn't a good fit for any of them but gravitated toward the Aryan Brotherhood, AB, given his formal baptism into white supremacy at the turkey-processing plant. He didn't really have a choice after three brutal rapes in the prison shower, the last one which left him with a shank in his shoulder and a perforated bowel from the "affections" of six Latin Kings. Georgi gladly submitted to the shamrock and 666 tattoos, the latter of which an AB lieutenant insisted on inscribing under his left eye along with a teardrop, signifying that he had committed a murder. "It's a deposit," the AB tattoo artist told him at the time. "You owe us one." By the time Georgi had served two years of a fifteen-year term, he had added twenty pounds of muscle from lifting weights with his compatriots in the prison yard and could bench-press 275 pounds. Lilith barely recognized her son the first time she saw him in solitary after a brawl with several members of the Black Guerillas.

"Pussy no more," Lilith said as she walked alone into Georgi's cell, a visit Warden Dick had approved after she crawled under his desk and pleasured him with her mouth.

"Mom?" said Georgi, who had no idea his mother landed a job at the prison.

"In the flesh," she said. "I'm the new supervisor for your wing. Life's gonna get a lot easier for you from here on in."

The façade of a hardened, ripped, tattooed AB gang member dissolved, and Georgi burst into tears. He reached out for her with both arms, reduced to the crying, whining child Lilith so loathed in his youth.

"Maybe I spoke too soon," she hissed. "Once a pussy always a pussy!"

"But," he stammered.

"But nothing," said Lilith, handing him a condom stuffed with heroin. "Stick this up your ass. The ABs will appreciate it. Tell them there's more where this came from, at $200 a pop."

"My ass?" he asked.

"Yes, your ass," she barked. "I don't suppose it's the first thing jammed up there since you've been in here. Then you're coming with me to a new cell."

Georgi obeyed his mother, as he always did, and she led him in shackles to a secluded wing of the prison reserved for low-risk inmates, where he would be sharing a cell with Amiir. "But he's a nigger," Georgi said as his mother pushed him into the cell. "No shit, and a Somali. Perfect cover," she said.

Jack and Marcie Laws were politically connected, doubly so after winning the landmark water-rights case in the Texas Supreme Court, and they called in a marker to help Amiir. Nothing illegal or improper, just a discreet word to keep an eye on Amiir from the executive director of the Texas prison system to his counterpart in Minnesota, with whom he'd hunted pheasant on a few occasions in the corn fields around Eagle Bend. Eighteen months or eighteen years, it's all hard time in prison, and the desolation of a cell with only a bed, sink, toilet, and medicine cabinet for company ate at Amiir during the long days, and longer nights. He marked off each day in the human zoo with a tiny scratch on the wall next to his bed, prayed five times a day as required by Islam, and read books from the library cart a custodian wheeled around his wing every day or so. Amiir gravitated toward the classics, *The Great Gatsby*, *The Old Man and the Sea*, and anything from Shakespeare or the Somali author Nuruddin Farah, whose masterpiece, *From a Crooked Rib*, reminded him of his mother. He drew many lessons from Macbeth about honor, treachery, and insanity and found disturbing similarities between Lady Macbeth and Violet Cremona. *For a charm of powerful trouble, like a hell broth boil and bubble. Double double toil and trouble; fire burn and cauldron bubble.* Islam was in his DNA, not the radical misinterpretations of Imams aligned with ISIS, but the teachings of true holy men like Muhammad or the poet Hasan ibn Thabit. He devoured the words of all faiths, particularly Judaism out of respect for Stone, and the Vietnamese Buddhist monk Thich Nhat Hanh, whose message of mindfulness and peace helped him immeasurably in living from moment to moment without anxiety in the hell of an American prison. After the first year, Amiir began to see light at the end of the tunnel, determined to emerge a changed man dedicated to helping others trapped in the spider's web of violent radicalism.

His first client came in chains.

Amiir had grown accustomed to the rhythms of prison life—mostly eating, reading, exercising, showering, and sleeping—and had become friendly with the guards, the conductors of a twenty-four-hour symphony with more than a thousand musicians. Amiir was the opposite of a troublemaker, and prison officials had told the gangs in no uncertain terms that he was off-limits. The long arm of the law—Jack Laws. Amiir didn't expect anything out of the ordinary on a typical morning during his fourteenth month in prison, no clue that his life was about to change forever with the click of a key and the familiar metallic, scraping sound of his cell door opening. Amiir had begun to look at life as a test, one which remains ungraded until your final breath, the one you take before moving on to the place where every choice, the good and the bad, stretches before you for judgment by the one who decides whether you go back to the beginning or remain in paradise. After everything in his twenty-five years of life— war, famine, death, betrayal, terrorism—he was about to face one of those tests, in retrospect the one that determined who he would be until the end, until he cast off the weight of life on earth and ascended to that place in front of the decider.

The embodiment of that test was a tattooed, musclebound, racist prisoner in shackles, and a feared prison guard he knew only as Poe.

Warden Dick told Lilith that Amiir was untouchable when he paired him with Georgi, and she knew better than to step over a redline that extended from the Minneapolis State House to the Capitol building on 1100 Congress Avenue in Austin.

"Your new bunkmate, Awale," said Lilith, unshackling Georgi and pushing him into the cramped cell.

"Yes, ma'am," said Amiir.

"My son, don't fuck with him," she barked, and left them alone in the cell.

They didn't speak a word for two weeks, as much as he wanted to question Georgi about his mother, whom Amiir was sure he recognized. But he wouldn't find out for months that the brutal prison guard Poe was the St. Cloud cop who nearly suffocated his father and killed Buck. Although Amiir found more than odd Lilith's weekly commerce conducted through the lower cavity of her son's body, he never asked about it or about the blood-stained toilet paper that stuck to the edge of the steel commode after Georgi had delivered the package. It went on like that for weeks, not a word between the reluctant Muslim terrorist and the broken racist serving their time together in a forty-square-foot cube. Everything changed when Stone walked into the cell with a chess set.

His father, Stone, and Amina visited regularly, and Ademar managed the best she could to make the trip every month or so. As a rabbi, Stone had special visiting privileges in prisons, and he saw Amiir every week. Stone gave Amiir a chess set on his second visit and imparted the wisdom of strategy, patience, and restraint that transfer to those who study the game of kings.

"This is the pawn," said Stone. "The soldiers, the enlisted men, who guard the front lines. Expendable, yes, but a wise general knows he's lost without them."

"What's this?" asked Amiir, holding up the tallest piece on the board, the one with a cross on top.

"The king. He moves any direction, but slow, cautious, one square at a time."

"Like Jack," Amiir said, referring to Jack Laws, who built a farming empire on the high desert of West Texas.

"And this is the queen," said Stone. "The most powerful piece in the game. Moves as far as she wants in any direction she wants. The one indispensable ally to the king."

"Like Ademar," Amiir said.

"Like Ademar," Stone replied with a chuckle. "Although not as pretty."

"Can the pawns become kings?" Amiir asked. "Like in checkers?"

"No, but a pawn can become queen if it survives and reaches all the way to the other end."

"Like you?" said Amiir.

"Maybe, and like you," Stone replied. "But we haven't made it all the way to the other end yet."

"I've played," said Georgi, startling Amiir with the first words out of his mouth.

"That right?" said Stone, who had gone out of his way to avoid any contact with someone so obviously antagonistic toward Blacks and Jews, lest it inure to the detriment of Amiir. There was no room for Nazis in Stone's world, and he lumped them together with racists, anti-Semites, misogynists, and homophobes—unforgiveable, unredeemable scum.

"Yes, sir," said Georgi, in a surprising gesture of respect. "Can I play?"

Not exactly global warming, but the ice between Amiir and Georgi began to melt that day, and a crack in the cap began to open where they found common ground in their determination to overcome the radicalism that had fractured their lives. Georgi was smarter than Lilith ever imagined, which she would have known if she paid attention to his literature teacher in eighth grade when he tried to explain the insights her son had drawn from reading *The Great Gatsby*. His teacher pointed out how Georgi had equated the many references to light in the book to the battle between good and evil, and the colors of the different lights as metaphors for the ambiguous gray areas in which Daisy and Gatsby lived. Georgi even brought in a third source, Buddhism. He explained how a bright light, like the sun, accompanies transcendence into nirvana—a topic that Amiir and Georgi discussed on many occasions in the dark nights of their captivity. "Whatever," Lilith said to the teacher, rolling her eyes and deflating Georgi like a slashed tire. She grabbed the book from her son when they returned home and threw it in the fireplace. Lilith never permitted Georgi to visit an optometrist when his vision started to blur in high school because she thought eyeglasses were a sign of weakness. She said they would somehow transform him into a *libtard nerd*, that class of people she held in such acidic contempt. As a result, Georgi suffered migraines if he read too much, and stopped any reading outside schoolwork. The prison optometrist gave Georgi a pair of reading glasses, and the world of literature unfolded before him. Georgi devoured every book he could lay his hands on, but the one that he returned to time and again was *Oedipus Rex*, the tragic tale of incest and patricide written before the birth of Christ by the Greek philosopher Sophocles. It was a subject of intense discussion between Georgi and Amiir, particularly the ending, in which his mother, Jocasta, hangs herself and Oedipus gouges out his eyes in despair for murdering his father and lying with his mother.

Georgi's other passion was dogs, although his mother never allowed him to have one, and her killing of Buck may have been the single deepest cut into his soul that she ever made. Revealing to Amiir who Lilith was, and the role she played in his life that day when she burst mistakenly into their apartment in full body armor, was the day Georgi began his redemption.

"You like dogs?" Georgi asked one night as they lay in bed.

"Love them," Amiir said.

"Ever have one?"

"Only one, Buck, the best damn dog ever walked on this earth," said Amiir, and for most of that night he told Georgi every detail of their life together—the killing of the evil pirate Ibliis, his years in the refugee camp, the incident at the Waffle House, the showdown in the slot canyon, and all the times Buck would retrieve the football during endless kicking sessions.

"I have to tell you something," Georgi said when Amiir was finished. "My mother killed your dog."

"What!" Amiir said, bolting upright in his bed.

"She was that cop," Georgi said. "I'm sorry. Maybe more than anything else, that's why I hate her."

"Thought I recognized her," Amiir said, choking back the molten lava of hate rising in him.

"She knows it was your dog," Georgi said. "That's how evil she is. She'd shoot me too if she could get away with it, except that would be the end of her heroin scam."

"Pick your friends, not your family," Amiir said. "I don't hold it against you."

"Thank you," said Georgi, burying his head in the pillow so Amiir wouldn't hear him cry. "You're the first real friend I've ever had."

Their shared affection for dogs must have been some kind of divine foreshadowing for the visit the next day from Ademar, Stone, and Charlie. There were plenty of dogs in prison, the no-nonsense German Shepherds or Dobermans trained to protect the guards, and when Charlie heard the jangling of a collar the next morning, he figured it was just one of them. But he was wrong. The cell door opened just a crack, and both prisoners looked up from their daily chess game expecting a guard with one of those one-hundred-pound prison K-9s. But when the door swung suddenly open, a bouncy, floppy-eared, one-year-old mutt bounded into the room, upending their chess board in a flurry of barks, licks, and tail wags. Amiir and Georgi couldn't have been more surprised or pleased if it had been Jesus Christ, Allah, or Buddha who bounded into the room.

"New friend," said Stone, walking into the cell with Charlie and Ademar.

"She flunked out of military training," said Ademar. "So, I grabbed her for you."

"What kind of mix?" asked Georgi.

"Chesapeake Bay Retriever and Husky," she replied. "All-weather pooch, as good in Texas as she is in Minnesota."

"What's her name?" asked Amiir.

"Ebla," Charlie replied. "She's all yours when you're out of here in a few months."

For Amiir it was something to which he could look forward. But for Georgi, the release of Amiir—his friend who brought so much into his life in such a short time, the friend who taught him that love, not hate, was the path to righteousness—that day would be the saddest in his life. *Truly*, Georgi thought to himself, *suffering is measured by what we lose.*

CHAPTER 14

Their last day together began with a game of three-dimensional chess. They had become so adept after months of days in which they played up to a dozen matches that Georgi thought it should be more challenging, secretly making two sets in the prison shop and giving them to Amiir for his birthday. It was the singular selfless act of love that had mercilessly eluded Georgi his entire life, and he felt a burden lifting with every piece he carved meticulously from balsa wood. Amiir was as touched and grateful for the gift as he was for the new dog. The two boards were made from plexiglass so players could see all the action without difficulty, and fit together seamlessly by four slim pegs in the corners. He customized each back-row figure to resemble a character in one of the books they read or a mutual acquaintance—for example, Daisy Buchanan and Ademar as queens, the tower at Stillwater as a castle, Charlie Christmas as a knight, and Stone as a bishop. He carved three kings in the likeness of Allah, Buddha, and Amiir, black and fierce with one hand coiled into a fist and the other with two fingers extended in the universal sign of peace. Their last morning together, which coincided with Amiir's birthday, he awoke to find Georgi, arms folded and a broad, friendly smile on his face. The new chess set, his gift for Amiir, sat in the middle of the footlocker they used as a table.

"What's that?" Amiir asked.

"Happy birthday, brother," Georgi responded.

"Dude!" exclaimed Amiir, extending a hand for a fist bump. Then, overcome with emotion, he reached around Georgi and gave him a hug, the first hug for the son of a monster in a life bereft of affection.

"When I get out of this shithole in a few years, you better know we'll be doing hard time together in front of this chess set," Georgi said.

"Count on it," Amiir said. "Let's play one."

In the middle of their second game, the cell door creaked open for a visit from Stone, Charlie Christmas, and Ebla the dog, no coincidence that it came on Amiir's birthday. Charlie produced a chocolate cupcake with one of those gag candles that can't be blown out, and they guffawed at Amiir's efforts to extinguish it. Stone gave Amiir a bowl of his beloved tapioca, the first time Georgi had ever tasted it, which disappeared in less than three minutes amid a chorus of slurps and sighs.

"Ademar may be a little late; missed her flight. Next birthday on horseback at Rancho Seco," Charlie said, referring to a good friend's property at the base of the Guadalupe Mountains near Dell City.

Amiir looked at Georgi, eyes like mirrors into his tortured soul, knowing exactly what his cellmate was thinking.

"Your day will come," Amiir said, followed immediately by the blaring horn of the prison security system.

"Inmates clear the yard!" Warden Dick yelled over the loudspeaker. "Lockdown!"

The Aryan Brotherhood leadership had been planning a prison takeover for months, bribing Lilith for keys, establishing truces with the Latin Kings and Black Guerrilla Family, stockpiling primitive weapons, hoarding food, and hiding enough first aid gear to equip a small Marine squad forward deployed in Afghanistan. They were in it for the long haul, done with the humiliation of prison and all that came with it. If it took weeks to air their grievances, so be it. They chose only lifers, prisoners sentenced to life in prison as violent repeat offenders, because they had nothing to lose from kidnapping or killing a few guards. The face of the revolt was MacDougal Bohannon, who went by Mac, a former middleweight boxer who'd spent most of his sixty-three years behind bars for a string of crimes that included bludgeoning a policeman to death with a steel pipe in Oakland. The cast of insane criminals who supported him read like a who's who of anyone's worst nightmare. There was Taylor Rippen, Rip, a Hells Angel who was only seventeen when he killed his first man as a rite of passage into the infamous motorcycle gang; Sergei Semenov, Ruskie, an enforcer for a Russian human smuggling ring and true believer in the sanctity of white purity; and Skip Fishman, Fish, a wannabe surfer from the 1970s and serial rapist who had a taste for cannibalizing his victims. Their planning was meticulous, and it went off without a hitch.

Lilith was playing both sides against the middle, a dangerously naive wager for someone who had never gamed against men with nothing to lose. There were days when she spent most of the shift on her back underneath Warden Dick and on all fours like a dog in front of Mac. Lilith told herself she was doing it for the cause, for her cause, the only one she really cared about. In typical fashion, she hadn't thought it through to the end, the final act in a tragedy no less violent or ironic than *Oedipus Rex*.

More than half the guards in the understaffed prison rushed to the yard when, as agreed with the other two gangs, a fistfight broke out between the Latin Kings and Black Guerilla Family. It was nothing outrageous, but the kind of skirmish that could escalate quickly into the carnage of the riot at Attica prison in New York State nearly fifty years ago that resulted in the death of thirty-three prisoners and ten correctional officers. Dick wasn't taking any chances when he deployed thirty guards in full riot gear to the fight, which they quelled in a matter of minutes. Unbeknownst to Dick, who had all screens on his remote surveillance system focused on the prison yard, a far greater threat crept down the hallway outside his office. His door flew open, and Mac, followed by Rip and Fish, sauntered into his office. Dick reached for the .357 magnum in his desk drawer, but Mac, with the fancy footwork that defined his boxing style, glided across the room in a heartbeat and pinned the warden's hand to the wooden desk with a corkscrew-shaped drill bit fashioned into a dagger that went straight through the soft tissue between his thumb and forefinger. Dick crumpled in pain and would have gone to his knees if the makeshift dagger had not pinned him in place like an insect stuck on a strip of flypaper.

"Boom," Mac howled. "You're crucified."

"What's the meaning of this?" Dick squealed.

"Meaning?" said Rip, mimicking the condescending tone of the prison psychiatrist. "Let's talk about your feelings."

"Shut the fuck up, Rip," Mac shouted. "Meaning is we're taking over the prison."

"Good luck," Dick said. "The National Guard will be up your ass in four hours."

"Meaning is," said Mac, grabbing the gun from Dick's drawer, cocking the trigger, and stuffing it in his mouth, "you're about to die."

"Wait!" said Dick, spitting out the front teeth Mac had knocked out with the gun barrel.

"We've waited long enough," Mac said, emptying all but one bullet from the gun and spinning the cylinder. "Time for a little Russian roulette. Ruskie would have enjoyed this."

"No need for that," Dick whined.

"Yes need," said Mac, placing the barrel back in Dick's mouth and pulling the trigger. *Click.*

"Wait!" *Click.*

"Okay, okay," Dick said. "Just tell me what you want."

"Good boy," said Mac, placing the barrel of the magnum next to Dick's right ear and pulling the trigger. BOOM! "Good decision, chief. That bullet had your name all over it. What a mess that would have made."

"All the guards in the C block cafeteria," Mac said. "Keys."

Within an hour, the prison was under AB control, all guards but one disarmed and tied up in the cafeteria, prison arsenal of shotguns and pistols in the hands of seven hardened white supremacists, and the governor on the warden's phone with Mac. As Dick had predicted, the walkways atop the prison walls were bristling with National Guard snipers five hours after the takeover. Ademar, spared due to the flight delay from the many ways in which she would have been defiled as Mac's hostage, convinced the National Guard commander to let her join his team of snipers. Muscle memory kicked in as she slid the barrel of her M24 into place on the wall and scanned the prison through the powerful scope. The yard was empty, except for the one guard who had managed to hide in a remote stairwell leading to the prison boiler room. Lilith. Bad to the bone. Playing both sides against the middle. Pushing all her chips to the center of the table. All in.

Mac knew they needed hostages, sending Fish and Ruskie to grab Georgi for insurance against any treachery from Lilith, who they thought cared for her son more than her own selfish schemes. For good measure, they snatched Amiir, Charlie, and Stone, easily more ruthless than any of the convicts when the gloves came off. He was the reincarnation of Judas Maccabeus, the mythical Jewish priest and guerilla warrior who led his people to victory against the Seleucid ruler Antiochus 160 years before the birth of Christ. They hadn't counted on the rabbi being any trouble or having a derringer on a slide under his sleeve and a commando knife strapped to his leg, standard gear any time he visited a prison. And they didn't think to look under Amiir's bed, where Ebla hid the second Fish and Ruskie burst into the cell.

"What do we have here," Mac asked when they dragged the hostages into the warden's office.

"Meat," Fish said. "Raw meat."

"Two niggers and a Jew," Rip added. "Just topping off the tank."

"Guess we don't need him," said Mac, turning casually toward Warden Dick and shooting him in the face with the .357. "Any questions?"

"Just one," said Stone. "When do we eat?"

"Eat this," said Fish slamming a forearm into Stone's head.

"Is that all you got, surfer boy?" said Stone, who had taken, and delivered, considerably harder hits on the football fields and in the boxing rings where he earned the nickname Yom Kippur Clipper.

"Easy Fish," Mac said. "We may need this one for negotiations since the warden is off duty."

"At your service," Stone said.

"Where the fuck is that bitch Lilith?" Mac said, at which Charlie's ears perked up with the memory of the incident at his apartment.

"Dunno," Rip said. "She's not with all those guards we tied up in the cafeteria."

"Best laid plans of mice and men," quipped Stone, who knew from so many battlefields that keeping your enemy off balance was one key to victory.

"Gang aft agley in the end," said Mac, finishing the line in Robert Burns's poem "To A Mouse." "I read plenty during my three decades in this joint."

"Reading ain't learning," Stone said. "Clearly, from this hair-brained scheme you've cooked up."

"Learned plenty, Jewboy," Mac replied. "Now shut your Jew mouth until I tell you to open it."

"That one over there," said Fish, pointing to Charlie Christmas, then to Amiir. "That's his father."

"Perfect," said Mac, pointing the pistol at Amiir. "Any shit from you and he's next."

"Clear," said Charlie, turning to Amiir and muttering in Somali, "*Ha walwelin, tan ayaan helney.*" *Don't worry; we've got this.*

"What's that gibberish?" Mac asked.

"Just told him to be calm," Charlie said. "It's Somali; we're from Somalia."

"TMI, asshole," Mac said. "Somali, whatever; you're just another nigger to me."

Mac smoked one of the recently deceased warden's Cubans as they waited for the phone to ring, and when it did, the governor was on the other end. Mac knew he was on a suicide mission, a shahid with a one-way ticket to his vision of paradise with his version of the seventy-two virgins, but he was determined to play it out for the others as if there was a pot of gold, or a pot of concessions on life at Stillwater, at the end of the blood-drenched rainbow. Over the course of the next twenty-four hours, he outlined their demands, from conjugal visits with partners or hookers to surf-and-turf dinners every other Sunday. The governor knew that there was only one conclusion to the talks, but he engaged in the give and take of hostage diplomacy as if Mac was wearing him down. Every hour that passed gave the National Guard, the FBI, and local law enforcement more time to hone their strategy and to position their forces in a way that would limit casualties. The negotiations seemed to stall at dawn the second day, and the governor wasn't sure whether that was a sign of progress or the trigger for an assault.

"How about a gesture of goodwill?" the governor said.

"Sure thing, Gov," Mac said. "I'm sending out one guard with a message."

"That would be progress," the governor said.

In an hour, the main door to the middle of the prison yard opened, and Ruskie emerged with a Black guard in front of him as a shield. "Here's my concession, and a message," Mac told the governor on the other end of the line as Ademar and three other snipers struggled to find a kill shot that would not risk harming the guard. "Pay attention." Ruskie reached into his back pocket and pulled out an envelope, yanking the prisoner tightly to him so there was no daylight between them. In one motion, live on every major television network in the nation, Ruskie opened the envelope, drew a shiv, and cut the man's throat from ear to ear, dropping him to the ground and scooting back inside before the guard took his last breath. "Got the message?" Mac told the governor.

"Loud and clear," he replied.

Lilith had watched it all concealed in her hidey hole on the steps leading to the boiler room behind Ruskie, and had a clear shot at his back. She was a middling shot who practiced at least twice a week at the firing range, but she didn't like the doomed guard and didn't want to squander an opportunity for redemption in what she envisioned would be a heroic gunfight against all four of the perpetrators. Besides, she thought to herself, there could be no survivors among the four leaders, or else they would surely reveal her crucial role in the prison takeover. Smugly, she stayed put, confident that Mac would repay her for the keys, for the blueprints, and for all the times she dropped her pants in the filthy mop closet and submitted to his barbarous carnal whims with her face pressed into the shelves of disinfectant and soiled rags. Mac assured her with every rendezvous, with every key or blueprint, that he would hold up his end of the deal, and the murder of Dick was the first down payment on Lilith's promotion to warden.

The governor knew the endgame to this prison catastrophe would come to define his life, would be the subject of endless investigations and media coverage, but he did not hesitate in his next order to the National Guard commander. "I'm ending this," he said. "Shoot to kill." He negotiated with Mac long enough for the sun to hang behind the snipers on the wall facing the main door, which, Ademar had explained to the commander, would give them a small advantage. She remembered Stone's words from her first deployment in Somalia—*Always fight downhill with the sun at your back*—and smiled, thinking of the havoc he was surely raising inside the prison with the leaders of the uprising. If anyone could save Charlie and Amiir, even if it meant forfeiting his own life, Ademar knew it was Stone. The governor eventually conceded to all of Mac's demands, even agreeing to a bit of macabre Kabuki theater in which the two of them would sign an agreement and shake hands.

The moment of truth, perhaps the final act in the lives of a dozen men and women, arrived when the door into the prison yard opened and out stepped Mac along with Ruskie, Fish, and Rip, sawed-off shotguns dug into the hostages' backs. Like a crowd of bloodthirsty Romans when the gladiators entered the Colosseum, more than a thousand convicts erupted into cheers and slammed tin plates or cups against the prison bars, chanting Mac's name as if he was the legendary Thracian warrior Spartacus. Mac raised his hands triumphantly, soaking in the accolades that had eluded him his entire unimpressive life. Fish bowed like an actor acknowledging an encore for an appreciative audience, with Rip and Ruskie following suit as the prisoners chanted their names. The governor, flanked by a single security agent in a dark suit, motioned them from the center of the yard, less than fifty feet from the boiler room stairwell. Lilith cocked her gun, slithering up the stairs on her belly like a serpent, coiled, tensed, ready to strike.

Stone looked to where he was certain several snipers had been stationed, figuring Ademar had talked the National Guard commander into allowing her up there, and winked. Lilith was the only wild card in Mac's plan, and he figured that she was hiding somewhere in the yard. In an effort to flush her out, he approached Georgi with a knife as the ten men met in the center of the prison yard and passed the blade slowly across her only son's cheek. Blood oozed from the teardrop the AB tattoo artist had inked there as a down payment for a murder he said Georgi would owe them for their protection. Georgi winced, but Lilith didn't move. She didn't care what Mac did to her son, and she didn't flinch when he gouged out both of Georgi's eyes with the tip of the knife. Georgi fell to the ground, Oedipus to Lilith's Jocasta in this version of Sophocles's ancient tragedy. Stone felt the universe open and stepped through it. He thrust his right arm forward, engaged the mechanical slide so the derringer whipped from his sleeve, and fired the single .41 caliber bullet between Mac's eyes. Ademar switched back and forth from her scope to her naked eye, watching the tragedy unfold in slow motion, like a series of photographs rotating through a slide carousel, then flashing on a screen. Stone, as graceful and measured as Nuryev in Swan Lake, bowed deep over his leg, paused for a second at his ankle, drew the hidden commando knife from its sheath, and ripped up into Ruskie's inner thigh, severing his femoral artery. Lilith, pistol drawn, charged like a bellowing, mad bull in a hail of gunfire that missed everyone except for the governor's bodyguard and her son. Georgi, blind but determined to protect his cellmate and only friend, somehow managed to pull Amiir under him. Charlie Christmas, without a second thought, threw himself on top of them as a shield from gunfire. Rip and Fish panicked, heads on a swivel, searching for some way off the sinking ship. Ademar took them both out with clean headshots—Fish first, then Rip. Ruskie, arterial blood spewing from his wound, wheeled the shotgun toward the primeval sound of Lilith a moment before she crashed into him. If Ruskie lived, she failed. They tumbled and fought like two feral cats, Ruskie pummeling her face, Lilith clawing at his eyes. But the Russian was too powerful, and she lost consciousness after he shattered her nose with an elbow. A hand, Georgi's hand, slithered out from under the pile and pulled her to him. Ruskie stumbled to his feet, grabbed the shotgun, and leveled the barrel at Stone's chest. "Time to die, Jewboy," he shouted. Stone smirked. If this was his fate, if he died saving Charlie and Amiir, so be it. But his death, like all death, came with a twinge of regret over those left behind.

Everyone but Amiir had forgotten about Ebla, the canine military dropout that had somehow followed them into the yard through the maze of prison hallways, and he smiled as she launched herself into Ruskie. Ademar fired a single shot, one to rival *The Shot* from the rolling ship off the coast of Somalia, within a millimeter of Ebla's chest and into Ruskie's heart. For a moment, the world froze. Charlie lay on top of Amiir, Georgi, and Lilith. Stone, with Ebla by his side, stood over the corpses of Mac, Fish, Rip, and Ruskie. The governor applied pressure to stop the flow of blood from the wound to his bodyguard's arm. Charlie slowly rolled off Amiir, both of them miraculously uninjured. Underneath Amiir, like a living reenactment of *Oedipus Rex*, lay Georgi, blinded by Mac and dead from his mother's gun. Lilith's corpse, eyes wide open in horror, staring into the abyss, was at the bottom of it all with Mac's knife deep in her chest. It was Georgi's last act, his final absolution before ascending. His proudest creation, the king he had carved in the likeness of his only real friend, Amiir—one hand coiled into a fist and the other with two fingers extended in the universal sign of peace—lay in the dirt next to his outstretched hand.

CHAPTER 15

L ife is circular, like the circle of stones the matriarch of the family that owns Rancho Seco, a few miles outside Dell City, set in the ground at the base of the Guadalupe Mountains as a spiritual monument for her children and grandchildren to the Yin and the Yang of life. Stonehenge in the high desert of West Texas. Generations of their family would skip from stone to stone, hand in hand with their revered *abuela* as they celebrated the victories of life and made peace with the defeats. And at night, when they carried torches around the magical spiral of stones, the light danced across the pistachio grove, reflecting their hope and love off the tin roof of the pavilion and into the universe.

In many ways for the Laws, the Zarkans, Stone, Charlie, and Amiir, life began and ended at Rancho Seco. Wrapped in blankets under the stars after their senior prom, Ademar and Deuce first came together at Rancho Seco, and their son was conceived in the shadows of the soaring Guadalupe Mountains. Deuce's father, Crockett Laws, shot his first deer there under the watchful eye of his *abuelo*, Jack Laws. Charlie's and Amiir's life in America began on horseback around the fringes of the ranch. And the ashes of T2 and Anil, Ademar's beloved older brother and radicalized twin, both of whom perished during a terrorist attack in Brussels, were spread at Rancho Seco.

Many a rider had crossed Rancho Seco on horseback, but none like Charlie Christmas, the least likely cowboy in West Texas. Following, in order of least likeliness, were Stone; Amiir; Amina and her son Noah; Ademar with her son, Tamerlane, on her lap; the other eight Laws and Zarkans who could still ride; and Wambleeska, White Eagle, the Lakota chieftain who led the Sun Dance that exorcised Charlie's demon. They came to Rancho Seco to celebrate Amiir's birthday, exactly one year after the prison showdown, to honor the power of hope, the power of faith, the power of one, the power of all.

All of them, except for Stone, Amina, and White Eagle, now lived in a sprawling compound on the Laws' farm outside Dell City, far from their trial by fire that passed for resettlement in Minnesota. Stone visited them often, but his duties as the rabbi of Little Mogadishu and his rising star in Minnesota politics kept him in Minneapolis.

Horseshoes clinked across the metal cattle guard at the base of the gate leading into the cluster of structures at the heart of Rancho Seco, and they rode gingerly through the fragile pistachio grove. In the still aftermath of a popup desert thunderstorm, a soaring rainbow of yellow, orange, and blue stretched like an empyrean bridge from Guadalupe Peak to the exact middle of the circular sanctuary of stones where life was celebrated and where death was mourned. The setting sun bounced off the mountains, bathing them in golden light as they dismounted and tied their horses to the Cholla Cactus and scrub brush near the spiral of rocks.

Those who have touched the divine move through life with a second sense for their place in the universe, and the group walked around the circle once, each one stopping on one of the rocks with Stone, Charlie, Ademar, White Eagle, and Amiir in the middle.

Stone went first. "*Sh'ma Yisrael Adonai Eloheinu Adonai Ehad*. Hear, O Israel; the Lord is our God, the Lord is one.

A broken heart can be stronger where it breaks, but a broken spirit never heals. All our hearts have been broken, many times, since our fates joined in Somalia. But not our spirits. We all have children, but Amiir is our child, the strong tree that grows from our roots, that bends but does not break in the storm of youth, that lives to soar over us and to provide sanctuary, solace, peace, and faith. As a soldier, I had a tradition of saving a handful of dirt from every battlefield—Iraq, Bosnia, Afghanistan, Liberia, Somalia, and, last but not least, Stillwater. This pouch holds so much more than a few grains of dirt. It carries the scars and heartbreak of war, the souls of my fallen comrades, and the spirits of the nameless men, women, children identified only as collateral damage on the tally sheets of war. I was a reluctant warrior, a peaceful man, tossed in the storms of powers greater than me. My heart, my spirit, wailed, until now.

"Justice, justice shall you pursue, that you may live, and inherit the land which the Lord your God gives you," said Stone, quoting Deuteronomy and emptying the pouch of dirt in the middle of the circle. "I am at peace."

White Eagle went next. "*Mitakuye Oyas'in.*" *All are related*, the simple, sacred prayer of the Lakota Sioux. "*Wakan Tanka*, Great Mystery, teach me how to trust my heart, my mind, my intuition, my inner knowing, the senses of my body, the blessings of my spirit. Teach me to trust these things so that I may enter my Sacred Space and love beyond my fear, and thus walk in balance with the passing of each glorious sun. We are the first people, our land stolen, our hearts broken, not our traditions or spirits. We are proud to walk with Charlie Christmas in his new land.

"These are ashes from the Sun Dance, ashes from Charlie's *other*," said White Eagle, pouring dirt from the pouch on top of Stone's. "Spirit keeper of the West, be with me. Bring healing to the people I love and to myself. Bring into balance the physical, mental and spiritual, so I am able to know my place on this earth, in life and in death. Heal my body, heal my mind, and bring light, joy, and awareness to my spirit. Black Eagle, you are our brother."

Ademar stepped to the middle of the circle, Deuce by her side with their son, Tamerlane, in his arms and Ebla the dog with a small pouch attached to her collar. *"Allahu Akbar, La Ilaha ilAllah.* I fought in the Army, *sua sponte, of their own accord,* as we say in the Rangers. Truth be known, it was not always of my own accord. Sometimes, it was under orders from someone with whom I didn't share anything, least of all my vision for this country. The true definition of fighting on my own accord didn't come to me in Somalia, Afghanistan, Bosnia, or Syria. It came on the wall of Stillwater prison—without hesitation, without remorse—when I shot straight through the dark heart of hatred. My ancestors came to this country just like Charlie and Amiir, with nothing but a few camels and faith they would find a home in this idea that we call the United States. I stand with Charlie and Amiir, *sua sponte,* of my own accord, and with any American who chooses to build bridges, not walls.

"Twice, I have spread ashes here—first for my two brothers, then for my father-in-law, Jack Laws." Deuce leaned over so Tamerlane could loosen the ties on the pouch around Ebla's collar. "These are the ashes of Buck, the best, bravest, most loyal friend any of us could ever hope to have, taken in cruel disregard for all that is good in the world." On cue, Ebla shook the ashes out of the pouch as if she had just emerged from a swim. "Truly, God is great."

Amiir went next. "I have no grand words or prayers, only gratitude to you, my friends and family. I was dead; you saved me. I was in hell; you resurrected me. I was lost; you showed me the path to hope, faith, love. I had a friend in prison, Georgi Poe, a man like me who lost hope, lost faith, lost love and embraced evil because he saw no other choice. We lived together for a year in a concrete box and discovered that there was a choice. He died for that choice and saved my life doing it.

"Georgi carved a chess set for my birthday, with this as a king," said Amiir, holding up the piece made in his likeness—black and fierce, one hand coiled into a fist and the other with two fingers extended in the universal sign of peace. Amiir placed the king, gently, on top of Buck's ashes.

"Rest in peace, my friend. You earned it."

Charlie Christmas went last. "I stand in the shadows of giants. Amiir and I would not be in this country, our country, without you. Our American journey began as a part-time job that's now a full-time avocation. I know what happens to a country that succumbs to hate, violence, and greed. Saw it happen in Somalia, and it cost me everything. I have seen it here. But I, we, won't let it happen again. That's what this journey was about. That's what Abraham Lincoln meant when he said, 'America will not be destroyed from the outside. If we falter and lose our freedom, it will be because we destroy it ourselves.'" Charlie removed his necklace, holding it up so everyone could see the amulets of his life—the ptarmigan, the letter *S*, the 7.62 mm shell, the eagle-bone whistle, the Somali flag, and the Islamic crescent—and placed it on top of the other offerings in the center of the circle. *"Allahu Akbar."*

ACKNOWLEDGMENTS

S o many people to thank for bringing this novel to life, starting with the Lynch, Schwartz, and Smith clans of West Texas, whose support, knowledge, and encouragement brought *Seventh Flag* and *Murmuration* to life. An *abrazo* to all of you, especially Roberto, who plowed through pamphlets of my literary scratching from such remote spots as Rancho Seco, La Saladita, El Paso, Denver, and Fraser. Raising a frosty Negro Modelo to all of you.

Blood and sweat falls on every page of a book, and nobody knows the frustration and elation that comes with the life of a novelist like the author's family. This book was written in large part during the Great Pandemic of 2020 under quarantine with current and future members of my immediate family. I marvel at their patience for the discussions of the nuances in my tale during all the meals at the family table. I will miss those days more than you will ever understand. My family includes two dogs, Estrella and Rue, and their joyful, loyal, brave spirits, as you have read, found their way into this book.

My experiences with Somalia and the Somali people stretch from the war in the 1990s to their brave efforts twenty-five years later combating the siren call of extremism in Minnesota. Somalis are a special people, both inside and outside East Africa,

and I stand in awe of their bravery and resiliency. Thank you
Mohamed Abdirizak; his graceful wife, Azza, and his brother
Amer; my brother Samikab Hussein; Abdi Salah; Abdi Warsame;
Amina Dable of East Village Café fame; Mohamed Farah; Deqa
Hussein; and Anis Iman. Each of you played an essential role in
the research and writing of *Murmuration*. I also must thank those
who stand by them, and all migrant Americans, in Minnesota.
First on that list is Melanie Faust, who so generously allowed me
a unique view of the food-processing industry and those who
work in it, and meticulously waded through my manuscripts
to ensure accuracy in every detail and nuance. Several others
provided indispensable guidance, including Willmar Mayor
Marv Calvin, Cardinals' football coach Jon Konold, and Natalie
Ringsmuth, the true champion of social justice in St. Cloud.

Treading lightly, without names, I want to thank those
who serve in the military, intelligence, law enforcement, and
development community who have helped me find my way
through all the dark alleys of violent extremism, and at times
saved my butt. Jim Bishop, former ambassador to Somalia,
colleague, and friend, and retired Army Colonel William Ost-
lund, former director of military instruction at West Point,
are two people I can publicly thank. Although I stand against
them, I would also note the contributions of the white supremacist and other extremist communities in America and abroad,
who, for whatever reasons, chose to open their worlds to me.
I hope you find your way back to reason; otherwise you will
inherit the wind.

Thank you to all the editors, both formal and informal,
who spent so much of their time improving *Murmuration*,
especially Elena Baenninger, Simon Elegant, Diane Dewey,
and Dana Frank. And special thanks to Stacy Meyer, climber,
architect, and artist, who shared important insights into the
ethos of my female characters; Jack Price, lifelong friend and
an alter ego in so many ways, who knows exactly how to keep

me honest; and Jonathan Wiedemann, lifelong friend and epit-
ome of the mythical *beef* who truly made "the catch" in his
edits of *Murmuration*.

Finally, thanks to all those in and around the publishing
industry who helped launch a new chapter in my life as a novelist: Marissa DeCuir and Angelle Barbazon at BooksForward,
publicists extraordinaire; Yvette Contois, a deeply talented
artist who patiently translated my idea of a book cover into a
perfect expression of the novel; and Max Martinez, Svengali
of digital and social marketing. And gratitude to all those
independent bookstores and staff who hosted me and support
independent art: Nancy Perot at Interabang Books in Dallas;
Liz Hottel and Lissa Muscatine at Politics and Prose in Washington, DC; Anne Calaway and Julia Green at Front Street
Books in Alpine, Texas; Kaitlynn Cassady at Commonplace
Books in Fort Worth; Dorothy Massey and Cecile Lipworth
at Collected Works in Santa Fe; BookPeople in Austin; Brazos
Books in Houston; and Tattered Cover in Denver. Special
thanks to Brooke Warner and Samantha Strom at SparkPress,
my publisher, who represent the best of the independent publishing world.

ABOUT THE AUTHOR

A Pulitzer-nominated national security correspondent and Writer In Residence at Sul Ross State University, Sid Balman Jr. has covered wars in the Persian Gulf, Somalia, Bosnia-Herzegovina, and Kosovo, and has traveled extensively with two American presidents and four secretaries of state on overseas diplomatic missions. With the emergence of the Web and the commoditizing of content, Balman moved into the business side of communications. In that role, over two decades, he helped found a news syndicate focused on the interests of women and girls, served as communications chief for the largest consortium of US international development organizations, led two successful progressive campaigning companies, and launched a new division at a large international development firm centered on violent radicalism and other security issues on behalf of governments and nonprofits. A fourth-generation Texan, as well as a climber, surfer, paddler, and benefactor to Smith College, Balman has three kids and two dogs.

Author photo © Nhu Nguyen, Nhu Nguyen Photography, nhuphotography.com

ABOUT SPARKPRESS

SparkPress is an independent, hybrid imprint focused on merging the best of the traditional publishing model with new and innovative stratesgies. We deliver high-quality, entertaining, and engaging content that enhances readers' lives. We are proud to bring to market a list of *New York Times* best-selling, award-winning, and debut authors who represent a wide array of genres, as well as our established, industry-wide reputation for creative, results-driven success in working with authors. SparkPress, a BookSparks imprint, is a division of SparkPoint Studio LLC.

Learn more at GoSparkPress.com

SELECTED TITLES FROM SPARKPRESS

SparkPress is an independent boutique publisher delivering high-quality, entertaining, and engaging content that enhances readers' lives, with a special focus on female-driven work. www.gosparkpress.com

Attachments: A Novel, Jeff Arch, $16.95, 9781684630813. What happens when the mistakes we make in the past don't stay in the past? When no amount of running from the things we've done can keep them from catching up to us? When everything depends on what we do next?

Goodbye, Lark Lovejoy: A Novel, Kris Clink, $16.95, 9781684630738. A spontaneous offer on her house prompts grief-stricken Lark to retreat to her hometown, smack in the middle of the Texas Hill Country Wine Trail—but it will take more than a change of address to heal her broken family.

The Takeaway Men: A Novel, Meryl Ain, $16.95, 978-1-68463-047-9. Twin sisters Bronka and JoJo Lubinski are brought to America from Germany by their Polish refugee parents after World War II—but in "idyllic" America, political, cultural, and family turmoil awaits them. As the girls grow older, they eventually begin to ask questions of and demand the truth from their parents.

Seventh Flag: A Novel, Sid Balman, Jr. $16.95, 978-1-68463-014-1. A sweeping work of historical fiction, Seventh Flag is a Micheneresque parable that traces the arc of radicalization in modern Western Civilization—reaffirming what it means to be an American in a dangerously divided nation.

Sarah's War, Eugenia Lovett West. $16.95, 978-1-943006-92-2. Sarah, a parson's young daughter and dedicated patriot, is sent to live with a rich Loyalist aunt in Philadelphia, where she is plunged into a world of intrigue and spies, her beauty attracts men, and she learns that love comes in many shapes and sizes.

Firewall: A Novel, Eugenia Lovett West. $16.95, 978-1-68463-010-3. When Emma Streat's rich, socialite godmother is threatened with blackmail, Emma becomes immersed in the dark world of cybercrime—and mounting dangers take her to exclusive places in Europe and contacts with the elite in financial and art collecting circles. Through passion and heartbreak, Emma must fight to save herself and bring a vicious criminal to justice.